My Nine Lives

Ruth Prawer Jhabvala

My Nine Lives

Chapters of a Possible Past

Illustrations by C. S. H. Jhabvala

JOHN MURRAY

Chapter 8, "Refuge in London," first appeared in *Zoetrope*

© Ruth Prawer Jhabvala 2004

First published in 2004 by John Murray (Publishers)
A division of Hodder Headline

The moral right of the author has been asserted

1 3 5 7 9 10 8 6 4 2

A CIP catalogue record for this title is available from the British Library

Hardback ISBN 0-7195-6182 5
Trade Paperback ISBN 0-7195-6197 3

Typeset in Sabon by Palimpsest Book Production Limited,
Polmont, Stirlingshire
Printed and bound in Great Britain by Clays Ltd, St Ives plc

Hodder Headline policy is to use papers that are
natural, renewable and recyclable products and made from
wood grown in sustainable forests. The logging and manufacturing
processes are expected to conform to the environmental
regulations of the country of origin.

John Murray (Publishers)
338 Euston Road
London
NW1 3BH

Contents

Apologia

T HESE CHAPTERS are potentially autobiographical: even when something didn't actually happen to me, it might have done so. Every situation was one I could have been in myself, and sometimes, to some extent, was.

The central character—the "I" of each chapter—is myself, but the parents I have claimed are not, or hardly ever quite, my own. I may not have outgrown the common childish fantasy that one's real parents are someone different, somewhere else. Or I may have been trying out alternative destinies—this time not, as usual, for fictional characters but for myself. But however many times one may set oneself up with a new set of parents—or a new country—or new circumstances—the situations in which the "I" is placed (or places itself) always seem to work themselves out in the same way: as though character really were fate.

The various countries and continents in these chapters are those I have lived in. England gave me literature—language— words in which to express my world and the ambition to do so. But instead of the Anglo-Saxon world that I thought had formed and informed me, my autobiography seems to be an amalgam of a Central European background and years of living in India.

Although I soon felt at home wherever I happened to be, at the same time I held back, almost deliberately, from being truly assimilated. It was as though I wanted to feel exiled from some other place and to be free to go back to or in search of it. But then these quests turned out not to be for a place after all but always for a person. This may have been a person I have looked up to, or been in love with, maybe even for some sort of guru or guide. Someone better, stronger, wiser, altogether other . . . Does such a person exist, and if so, does one ever find him?

I
Life

I HAVE gone back to live in India, partly for economic reasons. It's cheaper for me here than in New York, and that has been a consideration during these last years. Of course I no longer live where I used to when I came here over forty years ago—with Somnath and his family in their crammed flat in the crammed house in a maze of alleys leading off the bazaar. The house is still standing, though a part of it, cracked and crumbled during a particularly heavy monsoon, has had to be propped up. Another family is occupying Somnath's old flat, which has been divided into even smaller sections; the whole house is now a warren of subdivided living spaces let out to large families sharing sanitary facilities.

After my return, the first place I moved to was in a suburban middle-class colony. Although newly built, it was already overpopulated and not so different from the inner-city area where I used to live in Somnath's house. The streets were crowded with hawkers and pushcarts and homeless dogs and cows and an occasional pig snuffling in the gutters for discarded food. I rented a room built on the terrace roof—it was small, but enough for me and with its own toilet and shower. It also had its own staircase at the side of the house so that I was independent of the landlord's family living downstairs. At first they were very friendly to me, and once when I was sick with flu, they sent up food. I knew that they referred to me as the *"budiya"*—the old woman—up there. It is difficult for me to realize that this description fits me as it used

3

to fit Somnath's old mother: she had a hump and a chronic bad knee that she clutched all the time while groaning and calling to God for release. But I spend my days in the same feckless way I used to forty years ago—and, I must admit, with an even lighter heart. I have no responsibilities and am always alone.

Being alone is nothing new to me—from childhood I've always preferred it, except for being with my mother, and with my father, Otto. The only years when I felt my aloneness as loneliness or friendlessness—I really had no friends— was during my teenage years, from sixteen to twenty; and then it was not so much because of my own expectations and desires as those of my parents for me. My father had remarried but was in an apartment around the corner from where I lived with my mother, Nina. On Saturday nights she invariably went out whereas I invariably had nowhere to go. "Will you be all right?" she would ask me; she felt bad about leaving me and that was what made my eyes fill with tears. To hide them, I would lower my head over the book I was reading—"Oh yes," I said, "this is fascinating;" the moment she left the tears would fall on to my fascinating book and I would have to wipe them off. But by the time I had entered more deeply into my studies—I was in the oriental department at Columbia—my books really were more interesting to me than anything offered elsewhere; and my parents, though still anxious about me, could reassure one another: "Rosemary is an intellectual."

During my first visit to India, in my early twenties, I changed my name to Shanti (meaning Peace, which I was anxious to pursue and, if possible, possess). But on my return to New York I changed it back to Rosemary—which did not suit me, never had done, but was all that was left of my parents' expectations for me. Even the room that Nina had so lovingly furnished for me in her apartment—in all her apartments, whether we were in Los Angeles or in New York—had been overlaid by my own interests. Oriental texts and Sanskrit grammars filled the closet that should have held rows of pretty dresses; the vanity table with its frilly skirt had to bear my brass statues of Hindu deities; a mandala featuring the cycle from birth to death eclipsed the rosebuds on the wallpaper chosen by Nina as suitable for a young girl's bower (or "*Mädchenzimmer,*" as she and Otto called it).

All through my childhood, I tried to live up to my name Rosemary. I knew how hard it was for Nina that I was not pretty, let alone beautiful as she was. She would buy me frocks that would have looked lovely on some other little girl and I put them on eagerly. But it was Nina herself who said, "Take it off, darling," and she would turn away—in tears, I imagined, so that I ran after her and clung to her. Then she would say, "Never mind, darling, what's it matter?" But that only made me more miserable because I knew how much it mattered to her.

Nina herself had been a spectacular beauty. In Germany in the 1930s, before they were forced to emigrate, she had begun a career as a film actress that might have led to stardom. Nina left because she was married to a Jew—my father, Otto Levy; she herself came from a Catholic family of modest means (petit-bourgeois, she said, but only just). The Levy family had sufficient influence to arrange for visas to America; also sufficient funds to start a New York branch of their prosperous business in fine leather goods, with Otto as the managing director. Nina and I did not stay with him for long. By this time they fought a lot, and I believe Susie too had already attached herself to them. But mainly it was because Nina felt that her place was in Hollywood, and following up some leads and promises, she boldly packed us up and left.

Her stunning looks, her courage, her perseverance, and maybe to some extent Otto's money with which he was always generous to us even after their divorce, all these helped us through. She did have some success in Hollywood, though never on the scale she might have expected in her native Germany. She always played foreigners, for though her English was fluent and even racy, her accent remained heavily German; and with this accent, and her sultry, pouting looks, she was inevitably cast as the bad woman—during the war years even as a Nazi—in contrast to the wholesome American heroine. They were not good parts, nor were they good films, and she spoke of them disparagingly, pretending to shrug them off as merely her, and my, bread and butter. But in fact she worked hard at her roles, however small and unworthy they were, analyzing them, researching the background, extracting possibilities of depth that may have been in her but were not in the characters she was called on to play. And after a while, when she got older and heavier—she always had a weight problem—the parts that came her way were smaller and fewer, until finally she decided that it was not worth staying in Hollywood but that she might as well go back to New York, to allow Otto a share in my upbringing.

It was Otto who found the Upper East Side apartment in which Nina and I lived for so many years. He and Susie, whom he had since married, were just around the block, so we became one fairly harmonious family. He and Nina no longer fought the way they used to; they had far too many interests in common and were eager for each other's company. Susie did whatever they did, but since she had less stamina, they preferred to leave her at home for their more strenuous activities, such as their "antiquing" expeditions. Both loved buying objects and both had the same taste. Nina had a flair for picking up bargains, and they always returned flushed with victory and loaded with vases and clocks and tapestries for Nina's and my apartment. Susie didn't care to have too many things in her and Otto's place—they only collected dust, she complained, and that was a problem for her who could never keep household help for more than a few weeks. But she joined them on their visits to museums and private openings at galleries; on Sundays they attended chamber music concerts, on Wednesdays they had subscription seats at the Metropolitan Opera; and of course there was always the theatre, classical theatre, where Nina sat far forward in her seat with clasped hands and bright eyes, imagining herself as Hedda Gabler or Madame Arkadina. Otto loved to arrive at these events with a woman in furs and jewels on each arm, himself impeccable with his white silk evening scarf and his Clark Gable mustache.

Otto was very correct, very German, in the tradition of his family who had, until told otherwise, considered themselves entirely, patriotically German, reveling in every German triumph, which they regarded as their own. But there was one strain in their ancestry at odds with these characteristics. Of course as Levys they were of the priestly tribe—which they treated as a joke, worldly uncles bantering about it over their pork cassoulet and their lobster mayonnaise. But there was one item of family memorabilia, dating from the seventeenth century, that filled them with pride, even as they joked about it. This was a letter—a farsighted uncle donated it to the Hebrew University in 1936 (before himself emigrating to Argentina where he too did well in the leather business)— written by a Rabbi Mordechai Levy who had been sent by his Frankfurt community to Smyrna to inquire into the authenticity of a self-proclaimed Messiah. The letter he sent back home to Frankfurt confirmed every claim—yes yes yes, it is He, the Messiah sent to redeem us; and we must do His bidding immediately and sell all our goods and properties and go to Jerusalem to await our redemption. But my ancestors were too hardheaded and cautious for that, and anyway the Messiah later turned out to be false. Otto always kept a copy of the letter from Smyrna, in its German translation—the original was in Hebrew, which he could not read—and later he had an English translation made. That was the one I read and I suppose somehow its expectations entered into me; that cry of yes it is He! He has come! though I never seriously expected a real Messiah to enter my life.

As a small child, I asked the usual questions that children like me ask about God and Death and Time, and Nina did her best to answer them. Even when she was on the point of going out, looking over her shoulder to check if the seams of her stockings were straight, she would pause to find some suitable reply for me. But later, when I reached my teens and should have been asking other kinds of questions, she became impatient. I know she and Otto discussed me—"Why doesn't she have any friends—any boy friends?" Nina would ask. "My goodness, at *her* age—" She rolled her eyes heavenward at the thought of herself at my age.

Finally, she had to resort to giving me the answers to questions I hadn't thought to ask. She made a solemn occasion of it: we went for tea at the Plaza—I loved that, because I knew she often met friends there and they talked about Life, which was such an overwhelmingly important subject for her. And now she was here with me, in the crowded, scented, opulent room, among banks of hothouse flowers and the string orchestra playing and the waiters with their trolleys of giant pastries oozing chocolate and cream. It was with me that she was discussing the human condition in its weightiest aspects. She talked the way I had seen her do with others—with men, all of them artists and intellectuals—her elbows propped on the table, her sleeves pushed up from her creamy, rounded arms with bracelets tumbling down them. Her eyes vague and dreamy through the smoke of her cigarette, she informed me what it was that men and women did together. This information, though entirely new to me, did not engage my interest; and the only question I asked was why they did it. She opened her eyes wide in surprise (her eyes were green but looked dark because of her lashes, black as patent leather). Then she laughed: "But darling—because they love each other." "The way I love you?" I asked—sometimes, I have to admit, I was deliberately childish with her, to amuse her, but that time I was serious. However, I *had* succeeded in amusing her and she responded in the way I loved most: with a burst of laughter, her lips parting to reveal her still perfect teeth, her healthy tongue, and she leaned forward to kiss me, enfolding me in the warmth of her breath, her perfume, the smell and taste of the good strong coffee she drank all day long, even at tea-time.

Although in the years ahead she and I often talked about Love, she hardly ever again brought sex into it. When she did, she was dismissive: "What is it, after all? Just technical." And whenever she broke up with a lover, her invariable verdict against him was: "All he cares about is sex. Men are swine." Only Otto was exempt. They had long ago ceased any sexual relation but were bound by other, stronger ties: myself, their past, their conception of the importance of experience, the course of life, of Life—*das Leben*. But what was for her the highest, finest part of it she shared not with Otto but with me: it was with me that she discussed Love as she understood it, as something entirely, overwhelmingly other, breaking into a different dimension altogether. And that's how I understood it too—perhaps influenced by her, certainly by my feeling for her, which was my first indication of what love could be.

I was sent to very expensive private schools, gladly paid for by Otto, where I was miserable because all the other girls were so much smarter, in the fashionable as well as the intellectual sense, than I could ever hope to be. I worked hard but the results were far from encouraging, and it was doubtful whether they could ever be good enough to get me into college. Fortunately, during my last two years in High School, my interests became focused on oriental studies, where I discovered the same questions I had been asking since I could remember and even some approximate answers to them. It was when I entered the oriental department at Columbia that Otto and Nina began to say—with pride, for they had a tremendous respect for intellectuals—"The child is intellectual." Neither of them had had a college education. Otto had gone straight from school into the family business, while Nina hadn't even finished school but at fourteen, to her everlasting regret, had begun to model, act, flirt, and generally have a good time. For the rest of her life she tried to make up for this by reading books. She read avidly, indiscriminately, with passion. She adored the classics—Tolstoy, Chekhov, Thomas Mann—but also the latest bestsellers, swallowing everything with the same ravenous appetite, her eyes racing down the page as though devouring the print.

And she adored intellectuals, male ones, that is—she hated "bluestockings," turning down the corners of her mouth in pronouncing the word. Her lovers were all writers, musicians, philosophers, philologists, even a theologian—sometimes several of them together, so that she would quote from the works of one to the other. Most of them, in Los Angeles and later in New York, were European refugees. She didn't care for Anglo-Saxon men, whom she characterized as sexually puerile and stingy with money ("Can you imagine! He wanted to go Dutch treat! Dutch indeed—it's a purely American invention"). Whatever their line of intellectual pursuit, all her refugees were of the same type: suave, cynical men who gave the impression of a difficult past stoically borne. Some were handsome, others extremely ugly, but whatever they were, Otto was always jealous. Even when Nina and I were in Hollywood and were communicating with him only by telegram and trunk call (daily, and often several times a day), he could sense the appearance of a new lover across the entire continent. Not that she ever kept him guessing long—he was always, apart from myself, her first and most intimate confidant: a role that, however much it made him suffer, he could not have lived without. But none of these affairs lasted long, and when they ended, Otto and I would have whispered conversations over the phone. He instructed me to hide her sleeping and blood pressure pills, for she had twice tried to take an overdose.

In spite of their respect for my studies, my parents regarded me as very naive. "The child knows nothing about Life," they would tell each other. It was true that life at first hand only began for me with my visits to India, and this would not have qualified as Life for Otto and Nina. In the earlier years, I usually stayed with my friend Somnath's family, sleeping on a mat in a corner of their verandah, which was also a general passage. Somnath was a sales clerk in an old established firm of drapers and outfitters in Connaught Place, at that time a fashionable shopping center. I don't think he could ever have been a forceful salesman, he was much too reticent for that; but he was courteous and obliging and spoke nice English, so that customers sought him out. He had a large family to support and from time to time was forced to ask his bosses for a raise. This was always an embarrassing task for him, for he respected his bosses and could not bear to see the disappointed look that came over their kindly faces while he stated his request. Finally his wife, a more forceful character and also responsible for balancing the family budget, would put on her good sari and shoes and come to the shop to clinch the matter.

Somnath and I had met in the park in the center of Connaught Place where clerks from surrounding shops and businesses came for their lunch break. It was not a beauty spot—the grass was worn away, the benches broken—but it was somewhere to sit in the shade of trees. Most people were in groups and were quite jolly, but he was alone and so was I. Neither of us was good at striking up conversation with strangers, but he overcame his shyness when he saw that I was reading a Sanskrit text. I gladly showed it to him—he could read it but admitted he couldn't understand it: he had forgotten the lessons in Sanskrit he had had at school, long ago. He smiled when he said it, showing a row of splendid teeth rather too large for his face. His smile did not enter his eyes but seemed to make them even more melancholy. He smiled often, with a sudden flash of those large white teeth, but it was always as if he were apologizing—for what? Later I thought that perhaps it was for a lack he felt in himself, for not being more than he was. Or—and this too came to me during the years I got to know him—it may have been for a lack he felt not only in his own life but in life in general, that it could be better for everyone. He loved poetry and wrote some himself. He took me to symposia held in the courtyards and small rooms where his friends lived, all of them poor and all of them intoxicated with poetry. When a particularly poignant line was sounded, a cry of ecstasy rose from all their throats.

My excuse for my prolonged and frequent visits to India was the research I was doing for my PhD thesis. My subject was a woman poet—I guess she could be called a poet-saint—whom I had found through one of Somnath's friends. He was her grandson and himself a poet, though earning his living as a clerk in the Income Tax Office. He hadn't even known that she had written poetry till after her death when he rescued a batch of what everyone else thought was useless scribblings. Before that he, like the rest of the family, had thought her almost a madwoman because she kept running away and had to be brought back from distant temple sites and caves and even mosques and graves of Sufi saints. Her subject was the same as that of earlier poet-saints—the search for the Lover, the Friend—so I really don't know why my PhD advisers were so sceptical about her except that she had been dead only ten and not five hundred years. But that was what attracted me to her—that I felt I could put out my hand and almost touch her.

I was taken to the house where she had lived with her family—they were still there, at the end of an alley, across a courtyard, in a tenement not so different from Somnath's. I was shown the corner where she used to sit, singing and combing her white hair—which was long, for though a widow she refused to let it be cut off, wanting to be beautiful for when the Friend at last would come. I saw a photograph of her taken at a granddaughter's wedding, where she didn't look very different from other widowed grandmothers, skinny and wizened and already a ghost in the shroud of her white cotton sari. I also traveled to the places she had run away to: these were never well-known pilgrim spots but deserted, inaccessible sites outside anonymous villages, ruined piles of brick hidden in overgrown thickets of shrubs or exposed on barren land under a burning sky of white heat. Since my long vacations came in the summer, my visits always coincided with the hottest time of the year; but heat never really bothered me, maybe because I had ancestors who had wandered forty years in the desert. At noon I would cool my head under a wet handkerchief knotted at the corners, which probably made me look as mad as everyone thought she had been.

My parents considered India an unsuitable, dangerous place. Otto even had firsthand reports from relatives who in the 1930s had emigrated to Bombay, that being the only place where they could get an entrance permit. Although they had done well there, establishing a successful confectionery business, they never got used to the alien atmosphere. In long letters to their relatives—all the family wrote long letters to each other, it was a characteristic of the Diaspora, going right back to the Levy who had been sent to Smyrna to check up on the Messiah—they reported on conditions of squalor and ignorance that made the country completely impossible for cultured Europeans like themselves (after the war, they sold the confectionery business and returned to Germany). I could never convince my parents of my own, very different experience. Anyway, almost every time I was in India, there was an emergency that made it necessary for me to return home. Once it was because of Otto's heart attack, which Susie declared was brought on by worry about me; another time Nina took pills that Susie said I should have been there to hide from her. Even when the emergency was over, I couldn't return to India because they needed me in New York, their nerves having been shattered by the crisis and my absence. Susie's nerves were shattered the most—she was psychologically frailer than Otto and Nina; and physically too, she appeared frailer, for unlike Nina, who was dark and heavy,

Susie was pale, sandy, and so slight that it seemed any breeze might blow her away.

Then one year Nina said she wanted to go with me to India, to see for herself what it was all about. Otto opposed the idea—he said it was absolutely impossible and that he would definitely put his foot down. In their confrontations, he was always putting his foot down, and when he said it, he looked stern and strong, though perfectly aware that Nina would always do what she wanted. But this time, for her trip to India, she needed Otto's cooperation, in the form of financial assistance. My own visits to India didn't cost much, but she could not be expected to travel or live there the way I did. She sent me off to explain this to Otto—"Be nice to him," she told me, as always when something had to be wheedled out of him. I knew from experience that he found it hard to refuse her anything, especially money, with which he was so generous to her that Susie often warned we would all end up in the gutter. But he was genuinely worried about Nina. What if she fell sick in India with one of those diseases people got there? "Yes, and if she does something silly again?" Susie said. "You can hardly expect Otto to go running after her, not with his—" and she tapped her chest to indicate his heart condition. I myself was ambivalent about her proposed trip. I did want her to see the place that meant so much to me, but what if she didn't like it, found it abhorrent as others had? Nevertheless, I persuaded Otto with promises to take good care of her until finally he wrote out a check—"with a heavy heart," he said as he did so, while shielding the figure from Susie, who was craning forward anxiously to see it.

I realized that this time my stay in India would be very different. Instead of living with Somnath's family, I joined

Nina in her suite in an enormous Moghul-style hotel. It was built of sandstone like the Red Fort, though in salmon pink and with great domes stuck on at every available corner. Inside, it had marble walls and crystal chandeliers and bearers tall as maharajas in turbans and scarlet cummerbunds. Reproductions of Persian and Moghul miniatures lined the corridors, with the same scenes of princes hunting tigers woven into the carpets that lay thick as moss in the suites and staterooms and were beginning to smell from the damp that had seeped in during the rainy season. Nina only left her airconditioned rooms to go shopping—until she discovered that it was not necessary to go out at all, because the hotel had its own shops of precious merchandise. Moreover, the bearers were always ready to introduce salesmen into her suite; they came like magicians with humble cloth bundles out of which they poured torrents of silk and jewels on to her carpets.

My Indian family—I thought of Somnath and his family as my own—were very excited to hear that this time I had come with my mother, and of course I had to bring her to see them. This was not a success, though everyone pretended it was. To reach their house, it was necessary to turn off the main thoroughfare and, leaving the car behind, to walk through a series of intertwining alleys. I had been here so often that everyone had gotten used to me; but Europeans and Americans were rare enough to attract attention, and of course someone like Nina was a sensation. Everyone stared and commented; children came running from all directions, and the more daring touched her clothes (she was in a black and white moiré outfit) and related to the others what they had felt. So even before we had made our way up the narrow staircase that it was no one's particular business to keep clean, Nina had set her face in a fixed smile; and this never relaxed throughout her visit. Somnath's wife and old mother and sisters and sisters-in-law and a few neighbors were all in their best saris, which were the same colors as the sweets they had set out. They also brought platters of fritters fried in mustard oil and milky tea in crockery cups they had borrowed to supplement their own meager stock. Nina, fortified with her fixed smile and super-gracious manner, accepted everything like a ceremonial offering and merely touched it with her fingertips. Afterward she said what fun it had been and so colorful, but from then on she stayed exclusively in the hotel; and Somnath's family thanked me for bringing her and praised her beauty and graciousness but neither she nor they suggested a second visit.

When her funds were exhausted, Nina returned to New York, and I moved back to Somnath's for a few days before setting off on one of my long bus and train journeys across India, this time to Vinaynagar. It was there that Otto's telegram reached me and I set off immediately for New York where he met me at the airport and took me home to where Nina was dying. I didn't reproach him for not calling me earlier: my presence would probably have made no difference, although I might have suspected what doctors in New York, familiar only with the more advanced diseases, no longer knew how to diagnose. I had seen cases of typhoid fever in India, in the tenement where Somnath lived, in one of the little whitewashed rooms with niches for gods, where first a cadaverous old widow and then her granddaughter lay moaning on a string cot. Everyone there knew what it was, and the granddaughter was saved with modern medicines though the old woman died. But now to see this fever ravaging the pampered body of my film-star mother, tossing in her satin-backed, gold-crenellated bed, was too incongruous to be accepted.

We moved her to a hospital, to a private room where I could stay with her day and night. The right medicines were by now being injected into her, but already the fever had taken on a life and rage of its own. Not that she didn't struggle hard; she wanted to live, there was too much she was required to give up. But she was no longer on the same level of consciousness as Otto and myself who sat by her bed, or as Susie, who sat silent and frightened in a corner. Nina was calling out names I had never heard—though Otto knew them—and recalling places she didn't want to leave (again it was only Otto who had known them). Once, at night when she and I were alone together within the vast stillness of the hospital where not clocks but life-supporting machines clicked out the seconds, she suddenly opened her beautiful eyes and asked, "But where did I catch this?" It was a question I had already asked myself, and one I had had to answer for Otto too: when I had assured him that she had not eaten outside the hotel—unlike myself, who freely ate at wayside stalls whatever was cheap and available. Then Nina said, "It was that green sweet," and I recalled the bright green pistachio sweetmeat—more expensive than anything the family could have afforded for themselves—that had been offered to her at Somnath's. But she hadn't eaten it; she had only touched it with her fingertips in symbolic acceptance—I tried to remind her of that, calling out to her urgently but unable to reach her where she had already returned to times and places I didn't know.

The question of the green sweet remained unsettled. Nina died—even now, after all these years, I write the words in disbelief, unable to fit the subject to the predicate. Her funeral too had nothing to do with her—as always at funerals, there was a dull, depressing drizzle—and it was only the cluster of her women friends in their furs and designer hats who could be connected with Nina. But afterward, when I had to clear out our apartment which the landlords were waiting to repossess, she sometimes came alive for me again among her possessions: so that when I ran a scintillating necklace through my fingers, it seemed to be she herself who came sparkling back to life. Susie often stood watching me, and her eyes too lit up—"Oh isn't that pretty!" She took the necklace and ran it through *her* fingers. But then it became just a piece of jewelry again; and since Susie liked it so much, I said, "Why don't you take it." "No really? *No*, Rosemary, I couldn't!" so that I had to insist. Then she let me help her fasten it while she stood before the mirror, her eyes and the jewels both glittering, and she kissed me and said thank you like a sweet little girl.

Otto shrank into a querulous, quarrelsome old man. It was Susie he quarreled with now—not the way he used to fight with Nina, but in niggling, spiteful arguments. They often made separate appointments with me, so that each could complain about the other. After I had cleared out Nina's apartment and Otto had given up the lease, he had wanted me to move in with himself and Susie; but she said it would be difficult because she had turned one of the bedrooms into her studio—she had begun to paint watercolors, mainly as therapy—and the other was needed for guests (though, so far as I knew, she never had any). So I rented a room in some old lady's apartment—on a temporary basis, I thought, because soon I would be going back to India. However, week by week, month by month, I had to postpone this return because of the situation between Susie and Otto; and in the end I had to move into their apartment because Susie moved out of it. She checked herself into a hotel; staying with Otto, she said, had ruined her nerves and she was heading straight for a nervous breakdown.

After he died—he did not survive a second heart attack— she moved back to the Madison Avenue apartment. By this time I had a tutoring job at Columbia, so she thought it would be more convenient for me to live uptown, nearer my work. She phoned me every day and often I had to go visit her, if she had a cold or the pain in her back was bad. But she appeared to thrive on her own in the apartment with the fine furniture that Otto had inherited from his family. Some of it came from hers, for she was from the same sort of prosperous German-Jewish family as Otto's. Susie used to refer to Nina as "from the wrong side of the tracks" (she liked using these phrases—of my unmarried state she would say, for instance, "You've missed the boat, Rosemary"). Susie was always very tense about Nina, which I suppose was only natural, especially as Nina had never really bothered to hide her opinion of Susie. "That mouse," she called her—she even nicknamed her "Mousie." It was true that, in comparison with Nina, Susie was quite insignificant, in looks and person- ality. But later, when she was alone and in sole possession of Otto's apartment, she came into her own. From being sandy, mousy, she became as pastel as the watercolors she painted. Wearing a pale blue-and-pink smock, she sat in her studio, which was also pastel-colored, and grew serene. All her nervousness dropped away; she painted not for therapy now but for fulfillment.

I was around thirty at this time and Susie in her fifties, but we were like sisters and I the elder. We were also united by our financial interests, Otto having left half his estate to each of us. Although he had not, as she had predicted, ended in the gutter, he had in his last years lost all interest in his business and had finally sold it for much less than expected.

There was enough left for Susie and me to live on, but every now and again it struck her that our money might be running out. Then I had to reassure her and also make some financial adjustments. As she rightly pointed out, I didn't need much whereas she had all those expenses. These worries, as well as her constant difficulties with domestic help, so wore her out that the doctor had often to prescribe a cruise or a vacation in Europe. And it was true that, when she returned, she was serene again and very affectionate and charming to me. One year she came back with her face smooth as glass, and when I congratulated her on the beneficial effect of her holiday, she smiled, though painfully as though afraid something might crack.

As the years passed—and not just two or three years, for she survived my parents by over twenty—Susie became more and more opposed to my going to India. I had already given up my winter trips because, as she said, I could hardly expect her to be alone for Christmas. Then she began to fret when the summer vacations came around; and if she didn't fall ill before I left, then it happened more than once that I had to be recalled for some medical or other emergency of hers.

Even when I did manage to get away, I could never recapture the complete ease, the freedom, the irresponsibility of my earlier Indian years. In Delhi, I still stayed with Somnath's family, but here too circumstances had changed in the course of the years. There had been a number of deaths—I was there for his mother's funeral, which was treated as a joyful occasion since it was an old person who had died, rich in years and offspring. I saw Somnath dance in that procession, laughing and spinning around, though with tears of grief rolling down his cheeks. And there were other deaths—that of a brother-in-law who died suddenly after a hernia operation, leaving his widow and three young children with no one to provide for them except Somnath. His own children were growing up—especially his eldest daughter, Priti, of whom he was very proud because she had won a scholarship to go to college. There she met girls from very advanced homes and became scornful of her own family's oldfashioned ways. She cut off her hair and also brought home some very modern ideas, which made Somnath smile with pride in her, whom he loved most deeply. But the women shook their heads, taking her advanced opinions as a sign of worse to come. And worse did come, when she was discovered in secret meetings with a college boy who was not only not of their caste, he wasn't even a Hindu but from a family of Christian converts who ate beef and pig.

With the widowed sister and her family moved in, the house was too crowded now for me to stay there. Anyway, I no longer spent much time in Delhi, but following the subject of my thesis, I traveled all over the country, to the places where she had escaped till brought back by her family. All she had wanted was to be in the company of some holy person, usually a dead one, in a tomb or in a sacred spot marked by a little whitewashed temple. And all I wanted was to be in her company; but, like her, I too was brought back—always by a telegram or trunk call from Susie. Once I was in what I thought must be the remotest part of a remote province, trying to decipher the inscription on a Sufi poet's grave, when a horde of excited children descended on me, shouting, "Mem! Mem! Telephone!" They led me back in triumph to the telephone in the post office, which was only another village hut; and everyone, adults and children, stood around smiling and commenting while Susie called down the line to me to come soon, to come quickly because her bathroom ceiling had sprung a leak and she was too ill with nerves to deal with it. I laughed, was exasperated, yet I had to go back.

Susie never revealed her age, but by this time she must have been in her eighties. Physically she was marvelously well—of course she was very careful, taking regular massage and salads with no dressing—but her mind was more fragile. When it was no longer possible for her to live on her own, I had to move back in with her. It became impossible for me to leave New York. Besides the nursing arrangements for Susie, I had to make financial ones for both of us. There was still my tutoring job but since I had not yet managed to complete my PhD thesis, I couldn't apply or hope for more. I sold some good pieces of furniture and silver, and in view of the sliding market, I had to learn about stocks and have meetings with our accountant and stockbroker. I discovered we owed back taxes as well as estate duties, and to pay them I had to sell more stock, more silver, and also some of Nina's jewelry— this last with great caution, but Susie never noticed. She remained completely serene. Even when I could no longer afford the maintenance on our apartment and had to move us to a cheaper place, she maintained her daily routine of eating and napping, often humming to herself happily in a way she never had in younger days.

I had letters from India. Somnath wrote about his family, always beginning with the regular salutation, "We are all well and happy." Occasionally I had no time to read further, so that I may have missed certain items of not so good news. I did read how his daughter Priti had gone away to marry her Christian boy friend—his feelings on the subject were confined to this simple statement of fact, followed by other facts such as the high price of staples and vegetables. I don't remember any mention of his own illness. When I was too busy to read his letter to the end, I stuffed it in my pocket for later and then forgot about it and put it through the washing machine; so he may have somewhere mentioned the mysterious illness and the tests and the hospitals and the expense, the expense.

By now I knew for myself what it was to be consumed by worries, eaten up by Life not in the radiant Nina-sense but as something insidious as a worm. Finally his eldest son wrote. The letter was dignified, calm, weary with acceptance the way Somnath himself had been. It might have been a fitting elegy if it hadn't lacked that other element I knew to be his: that sudden leap of recognition—as when listening to poetry or music—that this is how life could be and maybe, somewhere else, really was.

Susie also died—or passed away, she would have said—as serene in her pastel nightie as she had been for the past two decades. By that time our money was gone, mostly on round-the-clock nursing for her. Fortunately I myself was an old woman by then and could draw my social security. It was not enough to live on in New York but would see me through a modest existence in India. I bought a one-way ticket to New Delhi where I have been ever since, first in the upstairs flat in the new colony with the landlords living downstairs. I've stopped traveling—I'm not planning to finish my thesis, for even if it were to be awarded the PhD degree, I'm too old to get a teaching appointment. But it's all right, I don't have to travel far now to be where my subject had been. Every Thursday evening I take a bus to Nizamuddin, to listen to the singers in the courtyard of the mausoleum compound. There is a wash of pink-tinted light over the white marble until the sun finally sets; then the sky, stretched between tombs and mosque, is a soft silk cloth with stars sewn into it—such a beautiful setting for the words of praise and longing so lustily sung for rupees by the muscular performers in shirt-sleeves. One of them smiles and sways to the sounds he is squeezing out of the harmonium, and peace flows from the night and the music, soothing the madmen in their chains who have been brought here to benefit from the influence of the live music and the dead saint. Other evenings I take another bus, which deposits me near the river. Here I join a little group of women—most of them widows, all of them old—and they too are singing, in the same strain though to a different god or, in their case, gods. I sing along with them, while they laugh at my pronunciation and try to teach me better. They have no difficulty accepting my alien presence, for though my face is white, it is as wrinkled as theirs; I have taken to wearing a cotton sari, which is more convenient, especially to draw over one's head as a protection against the hot sun. We are all singing the same songs and all enjoying the river when it is in spate or, when it is not, the liquid luminous sky flowing above the bed of dry mud.

I notice I've been using the present tense—as though all the above were the present. But it is not. If it were, I might have been able to end my days as serenely singing as Susie did hers. One day, while returning from an excursion to the river, maybe still singing and smiling to myself, I heard someone behind me in the bus line calling my name. "Is it you? Really you?" She embraced me as no one had done in a long time. It was Priti, Somnath's daughter, though it took me some time to recognize her. I had last seen her when she was a student, in love, with a defiant short haircut and ideas to match. Now it was many years since her romantic elopement and she was almost middleaged. My bus arrived, and when that happens, there is no time to waste (more than once, unable to move fast enough, I've been knocked down in the rush to get on). I just managed to shout my address to her, and she came to see me the very next day. It was a holiday and she didn't have to work. Yes, she had a job—not a good one, underpaid, in a travel agency run by a greedy and tyrannical woman; but the hours were good, so that she only needed part-time help at home. Fortunately, her children were bigger now—sixteen and seventeen—and her husband, thank heavens, no longer lived with her but was drinking himself to death in Bombay.

She came often; she said she loved to be with me and talk about the past. But it was mostly the present we talked of, *her* stressful present, which included a bad relationship with her brothers and sisters, all of whom had made conventional arranged marriages and felt themselves entitled to look down on her. (At that she proudly tossed her hair, still short, the way she used to.) She also loved, she said, to be with me in my cozy, comfortable little place—here her eyes roved around, in the slightly calculating way of women who have for years had to look out for themselves. I was surprised: "cozy and comfortable" were not words truly applicable to my little whitewashed room, at least not for anyone but me. I had a string bed with a mat beside it on which I slept more often than on the bed. The room was on the roof, so there was a lot of light—also heat, but I possessed a big black table fan that I had bought from my landlords when they installed their airconditioner. Priti said she felt more peaceful here than anywhere else. At home, the children brought back friends and played loud music, which was disturbing to her when she returned from work, often with a headache brought on by the stressful situation with her employer. How she would love to come and relax in a place like mine—although of course she didn't want to disturb me in any way. I suggested that, if I gave her my key, she could just come and rest here for an hour or two when I was out. Well, I was always out at dusk when I went down to the river or, on Thursdays, to Nizamuddin. This worked out perfectly because those were the same hours that Priti was finished for the day, and it was a great relief to her to have my quiet place to come to.

I began to suspect that she did not come there alone, but I didn't mind. I even liked the idea of Priti bringing a friend. I knew she had had a bad marriage—she told me details that I didn't want to hear—and I also knew that she was, like my mother, a person who thirsted for love. This too she often told me, and in any case, didn't I remember her as a young girl defying her whole family and all her caste and traditions, for the sake of love? I began to stay out later than usual so as not to disturb her time together with her friend. By the time I arrived home she had gone, with everything as I had left it, except sometimes for a lingering smell of liquor and tobacco smoke.

But one night she was still there. She had locked up my place and was on the stairs, and so was my landlady. Their voices could be heard down the street, and some neighbors had also come out to listen. Fights were not uncommon in the neighborhood—if they were between men, they could turn violent and not long before there had been a murder, a brother mortally stabbing his sister's alleged seducer. But women tended to confine themselves to deadly invective shouted out loud for everyone to hear. By the time I was walking up the stairs toward them, I had already understood what the fight was about. I realized that my landlady had misinterpreted the situation, and I tried to calm her by explaining that Priti was only using my room to entertain a personal friend. "*One* friend!" screamed my landlady. Then she turned on me—how I had fooled everyone, with my white hair and simple ways, insinuating myself into a respectable home to carry on my nefarious business. Of course I was not allowed to stay another minute but had to pack up there and then; Priti came back up with me and helped me. The only difficult part was to carry down my trunk—not that it had much in it, but it was one of those metal trunks they have in India as a precaution against rodents and destructive insects.

Priti very quickly found another place for me. This one is further out—since I first came here, Delhi has proliferated into widespread new suburbs and colonies—so that after work Priti has to hire a motorcycle rickshaw to bring her here. But she seems to think this expense worth her while. Her mood is altogether much better nowadays than when I first met her again. Her circumstances appear to have improved from that time; she often wears new clothes and her face too is smoother, brighter with more make-up. Far from borrowing money from me as she sometimes had to, she leaves little gifts for me, such as a picture framed from a calendar. Altogether she has tried to make my room more attractive and comfortable. I have a solid wooden double bed now instead of the narrow string cot I had in the other place; the new bed is really too big for the room and also for me, so I sleep on the mat, which has been changed and is very colorful. I don't often meet Priti, for I try to stay out beyond the time that she is entertaining her friends. But sometimes she waits for me to come home, and then she is very nice to me and asks me whether I'm comfortable in this new place and not disturbed by the people living in the downstairs part of the house.

It is true that these tenants, who are all women, are noisy, especially at night when they entertain clients with music and dancing, and probably drinking too, for their voices and laughter become very loud. Sometimes there are fights, and once or twice the police have been called. I would have liked to make friends with my new neighbors, but I don't often see them, for after their lively nights they like to sleep late into the day. However, we live together very amicably, and I'm glad to help them out with little household items, such as sugar for their tea. They like to sip it hot and sweet, while sitting on the steps leading up to my room—large, plump, youngish women in shiny satin saris and with cascades of jewelry.

I'm now too far from Nizamuddin and from the river to visit there as regularly as before. But there are always nice peaceful places to be found in India, even in the middle of a crowded city. On the outskirts of the new colony where I now live is a cluster of crumbling little pavilions; there are tombs inside them with inscriptions that have become indecipherable so that I have no idea who is buried here. I sit inside one of the pavilions by the tombs—there are three of them, side by side—waiting until I can go home without disturbing Priti. Although there is a hole in the roof, it is cool in here—anyway, cooler than outside where the sun beats down on the flat earth with only dry shrubs growing out of it and no trees. When the sun has set, the bats come out and cut into the soft skin of the darkened sky. When I first came here, I was completely alone and would squat on the stone floor, leaning against a tomb with a book, or with my unfinished thesis and the poetry quoted in it. Now other people have begun to join me. First there was an old man, a retired accountant, whose eyes were failing so that he asked me to read to him. Then more have come—mostly old people, but also one or two young clerks who love to hear or recite poetry in the way Somnath and his friends used to. One old lady has a very sweet voice and she knows all the songs of Mirabai, which she sings to us and encourages us to join in. When we are not singing or reciting, we talk together, often about the hardships in our lives: some suffer from their kidneys, others from bad daughters-in-law. I suppose it is a relief to be able to talk of these matters with others. But sooner or later we are back singing again. Not that these songs are free from suffering; on the contrary, sometimes they sound like a cry of anguish—of desperate love for the Friend who will not come, who will not come, not even now at the end of our lives of unrequited longing.

2

Ménage

LEONORA WAS my mother, Kitty my aunt. Kitty had no children, she never married because Yakuv didn't believe in marriage, and once she met him, she never looked at anyone else. "He treats her like dirt," my mother used to say, the corners of her mouth turned down—an expression I knew well, for it was often how she regarded me while telling me, "You'll end up like Kitty: a neurasthenic." Physically, it would have been impossible for me to become either like my mother or my aunt. They were both tall, statuesque, whereas I have taken after my father who was a lot shorter than my mother. It's odd that both these sisters chose men who were short—though this was all that Yakuv and my father Rudy had in common.

Leonora dominated Rudy and he liked it. She was a wonderful manager of all practical details, but at that time I resented and perhaps rather despised her orderly bourgeois ways. I often took refuge with Kitty, who lived in three tiny rooms in a subdivided old brownstone. My parents had a large apartment in an expensive building on Central Park West, filled with some very fine furniture and pictures that had belonged to Rudy's family of prosperous Berlin publishers. Unlike Rudy and Leonora, who had funneled out his family money through Switzerland, Kitty had arrived here in 1937 with nothing—except of course my parents, who were a constant support to her.

Kitty's apartment was always in a mess, which for me

was part of its charm. I associated disorder with artistic creation, and there was usually some piece of work lying around. She had begun with etchings and woodcuts but later became a photographer; there were prints tacked up of her charming portraits of little girls picking flowers in a meadow. Kitty herself sat on the floor, her arms wrapping her knees and her long reddish hair trailing around her. If my mother was there—and Leonora often came to check up on her sister—she would be tidying panties off the floor, washing the dishes piled in the sink, while clicking her tongue in distress and disapproval. But that didn't bother Kitty at all, she continued sitting there talking to me about some artistic matter, even when Leonora found a broom and began to sweep around her.

My parents adored New York, were completely at home here, and continued to live the way they might have done if they had been allowed to stay in Berlin. They spoke only in English, though their heavy accents made it sound not unlike their native German. They had many social and cultural activities, mostly with other prosperous émigrés from various Central European countries. It was at one of these cultural events that Kitty first met Yakuv, who had been engaged to give a piano recital after a buffet supper at some rich person's house. The house was pointed out to me later, a rococo mansion at 90th and 5th, since pulled down. At this concert Kitty had behaved in a crazy way that was not uncharacteristic of her: the moment Yakuv had finished playing, she dashed up to the piano and, kneeling down, she kissed his hand. Leonora said she nearly died of shame, but Rudy was more tolerant of his sister-in-law's behavior, which he said was a tribute not to a person but to his art. As for Yakuv himself—I don't know how he took her gesture, but probably it was in his usual sardonic way.

On account of his art, my mother was prepared to forgive Yakuv for many things: among them, his background. He came from Eastern Europe, from what she assumed to be a tribe of pedlars and hawkers; the language they spoke was to her a debasement of the High German with which she had grown up. But this had nothing to do with Yakuv's art: "Even if his father peddled toilet brushes," she explained, "an artist is born with his talent. It's a gift from the gods and comes from above." His real background might have disturbed her more. His forefathers had been rabbinic scholars, but more recent generations had abandoned these studies in favor of Marx and Engels, Bakunin and Kropotkin. Some of them had rotted for years in jail as political prisoners, and at the beginning of the last century an aunt had been executed for her part in an unsuccessful assassination attempt. The glowering intensity that pervaded Yakuv's music, and our lives, must have been inherited from these revolutionaries. His looks were as fiery as his playing. He was very short but with broad shoulders and an exceptionally large head, which looked even larger because of his shock of black curly hair.

A year or two after his first meeting with her, Yakuv moved into the brownstone where Kitty lived. His rooms on the top floor were even smaller than hers on the second and just as untidy. But I have seen Yakuv get much angrier than my mother at the mess in Kitty's rooms, kicking things around the floor in a fury and sweeping crockery off her table. Then she would fly at him, and a dreadful quarrel break out. These were the first passionate fights I ever witnessed, for between my parents there was only a slight tightening of the lips to indicate one of their rare differences of opinion. Kitty's fights with Yakuv frightened and thrilled me by their violence. They always ended the same way, with Yakuv going upstairs to his own den as though nothing had happened—he might even

35

have been smiling—while she was left quivering, prostrate on the floor. But soon she would get up and rush to the door to scream up the stairs—uselessly, for by that time he was back at the piano and she could not be heard above his playing.

At the time we first knew him, in the early 1940s, there was a surfeit of talented refugee pianists, so Yakuv had to struggle to make ends meet. He played for a ballet class and gave piano lessons to untalented students, of whom I became one. At six, my eager parents had sent me for piano lessons to a little old Russian lady, who spent most of her time with me writing appeals for visas to consular officials. But when I was twelve, my parents decided that I should take lessons from Yakuv. I was very reluctant, for I had often seen his pupils coming down from their lessons in tears. I knew this would be my fate too—and deservedly, for he was a great musician and I had very little talent. He made no attempt to disguise his despair, putting his hands over his ears and imploring to be struck deaf. He begged me never to come back again, never to think of the piano again, and of course I would have liked nothing better; but however much we swore an eternal farewell when I left, I always returned on time for my next lesson. I knew—we all knew, including himself—that he needed the money, and since he had driven most other pupils away, it seemed up to me to stick it out, however painful this might be for both of us.

And actually, apart from my playing, I liked being with him. He had three little rooms, and the one in which he gave lessons was only just big enough to hold his piano. The window faced the back yard which was wild and overgrown since the first-floor tenant had no money to keep it up. At that time the mammoth apartment buildings had not yet been built, so the house was surrounded by other brownstones with similarly untended gardens and trees growing tall enough to fill his window. Yakuv, in a shabby jacket and rimless glasses, filled the room with smoke from his little black cigars. A cup of coffee stood on the piano, and since I never saw him make a new one, it must have been stone cold; but he kept sipping at it, and dipping a doughnut into it. Although coffee, doughnuts, and cigars appeared to be all he lived on, he was full of energy. He roared, stamped, heaped me with his sarcasms. Sometimes I got so mad, I banged down the piano lid, and that always seemed to amuse him: "I see you have inherited your aunt's sweet temper." But then he pinched my cheek, almost with affection, and walked me out the door with his arm around my shoulders.

I was not the only one in the family to take lessons from him. I don't know whether my father did this because he really wanted to learn or to contribute to Yakuv's income. He came not to play the piano but to sing Lieder; he loved music but was unfortunately as unmusical as I am. I have heard Yakuv tell Kitty that the entire neighborhood was trilling *Die Schöne Müllerin* while my father was still struggling with the first bars. Poor Rudy—he must have endured the same sarcasms as I did, but all he would say was that Yakuv had the typical artistic temperament. Then Kitty said: "So artistic temperament gives one the right to be a swine?" She spoke bitterly because he fought with her, wouldn't marry her, wouldn't let her have a child with him. This last always came up in their quarrels: "All right, so don't marry, leave it, forget it—but a child, why not a child!" He wouldn't hear of it; and it really was impossible to think of him as a father, a gentle comforting presence like Rudy.

Yet he and Kitty had their tender moments together. Sometimes on my visits to her I found them in bed together. They were not at all shy but invited me to sit on the side of the bed. We played games of scissors, paper, stone, with the two of them quickly changing to scissors if they saw the other being paper; or he would teach us card games and didn't contradict when she told me that he could have made a living as a card sharper. "Better than the piano," he said cheerfully. Without his glasses, he looked almost gentle, probably because he was so nearsighted; and it was always a surprise to see that his eyes were not dark but light grey.

Then there were the times when he was a guest at one of my parents' dinner parties. On those evenings Leonora sparkled in a low-cut evening gown and the sapphire and ruby necklace she had inherited from her mother-in-law. Her successful dinners were her personal triumph, so that she was entitled to the little glow that made two red patches of excitement appear on her cheeks. But at that time, when I was about fifteen or sixteen, I was embarrassed by what I thought of as her smug materialism. It seemed to me that she cared only for appearances, for her silver, her crystal and china, and for nice behavior (she even tried to make me curtsey when I greeted her guests). She was in her middle thirties, in wonderful shape, radiant with health and the exercise and massage she regularly took: but I thought of her as sunk in hopeless middle age with no ideals left, if ever she had any, which I doubted.

Except for me, everyone appreciated her dinner parties, including Yakuv whenever he was invited. In his crumpled, rumpled evening suit, he ate and drank like a person who is really hungry: which he probably was, and certainly Leonora's exquisite dishes must have been a wonderful change from his stale coffee and doughnuts. After dinner he was persuaded to sit down at the piano, and this my parents made out to be a special favor to them, though before he left Rudy's check had been tactfully slipped into his pocket. He played the way he ate—voraciously, flinging himself all over the keys, swaying, even singing under his breath and sometimes cursing in Polish. All this made him perspire profusely, so that afterward he could hardly respond to the applause because he was so busy wiping his face and the back of his neck. The enthusiasm was genuine—even unmusical people realized that they were in the presence of a true artist; and I could well imagine how Kitty had been so carried away the first time she heard him that she knelt at his feet.

Kitty resented the fact that Yakuv performed for my parents' guests, that he had to do so in order to earn money; and also that he himself didn't resent it enough. He never complained, as she did constantly, about his lack of reputation and success. He probably didn't think it worth complaining about. A bitter sardonic person by nature, he expected nothing better from fate, which he accepted as being terrible for everyone. When Kitty tried to make him say that he only went to Leonora's parties because of Rudy's check, he said, "Oh no, I go for the food—where else would I get veal in a cream sauce like Leonora's?" And never losing an opportunity to provoke her, he added, "If only you learned to cook—just a few little dishes, one isn't even expecting miracles—"

"Oh yes, now you want me to be your cook-housekeeper! How you would hate it, hate it!"

He laughed and said that on the contrary, a cook-housekeeper was just what he needed; but we both knew that he didn't mean it because the three of us were on the same side—what I thought of as the artistic, the anti-bourgeois side.

This was the way things stood with us when I went away to college and then, two years later, on my own quest—which

I won't go into now except to say that I may have been in-fluenced by Yakuv's view of life. I mean by his pessimism, his assumption that no hopes were ever fulfilled in this life; and while he left it at that, it may have been the reason why I, and others like myself, Jewish and secular, turned to Buddhism. For a while I wanted to be a Buddhist nun—it seemed a practical way out of the impasse of human life. But then I dropped the idea and got married instead.

With all this happening, I became detached from my family in New York. I skimmed through their letters only to satisfy myself that everything was as it always had been with them. It was difficult to tell my parents' letters apart: they had the same handwriting with traces of the spiky Germanic script in which they had first learned to write. The facts they presented were also the same—the concerts and plays they had liked or disliked, an additional maid to help Lina who had got old and suffered with her knees. Kitty in her scrawl did not report facts: only excitement at a painting or a flow-ering tree, anguished longing for a child, Yakuv's impossible behavior. He of course did not write to me. I don't suppose he wrote any letters; to whom would he write? Apart from our family, he seemed to have no personal connection with anyone.

The only change they reported was that the brownstone in which Kitty and Yakuv had been renting was torn down. That whole midtown area was being built up with apartment blocks where only people with substantial incomes could afford to live. Kitty gave me a new address, downtown and in a part of the city that had once been commercial but had been moribund for years. When I went to see her on my return to New York, I found the warehouses and workshops still boarded up; the streets were deserted except for a few bundled-up figures hurrying along close to the walls. This made them look like conspirators, though they may only have been sheltering against the wind, which was blowing shreds of paper and other rubbish out of neglected trash cans. But some of the disused warehouses were in process of being revived, one floor at a time. In Kitty's building there were two such conversions, and to get to hers I had to operate the pulleys of an elevator designed for crates and other large objects. Kitty's loft, as she called it, seemed too large for domestic living though it had a makeshift kitchen with a sink and an old gas stove. Kitty's own few pieces of furniture looked forlorn in all this space; even Yakuv's piano—for his furniture too had come adrift here—seemed to be bobbing around as on an empty sea. He himself wasn't there; he was on tour, things were better for him now and he was getting engagements around the country. And Kitty's career also seemed to have taken off: she had rigged up a dark room in one corner of her space, and in the middle of the floor was a platform with two tree-stumps on it, surrounded by arc-lights and a camera on a tripod.

Instead of going to my parents, I had come straight to her from the airport. I felt it would be easier to tell her about what I saw as the dead end of my youthful life—I had abandoned both my Buddhist studies and my marriage—and it was a relief to unburden myself to her. She listened to me in silence, which was really quite uncharacteristic of her. There were other changes: the floor had been swept, there were no dishes in the sink. After I had finished telling her whatever I had to tell, she murmured to me and stroked my hair. How right I had been to come to her first, I felt; I knew I could not expect the same understanding from my parents, whose lives had been so calm, stable, and fulfilled.

My parents' building and all its neighbors stood the way they had through all the past decades, as stately as the mansions that they had themselves displaced. The doormen were the same I had known throughout my childhood; so was the elevator man who took me up to where Leonora was waiting for me in the doorway. She held me to her bosom where I remembered to avoid the sharp edges of her diamond brooch. "But now it's my turn!" Rudy clamored, caring nothing about having his good suit crumpled as I pressed myself against him, inhaling his after-shave and breath-freshener.

But "No not here, darling," Leonora said when I started to go into my room. My father cleared his throat—always a sign of embarrassment with him. But Leonora exuded a triumphant confidence: "Because of the piano," she said, ushering me into the guest bedroom, which was considerably smaller than mine. I didn't understand her: the piano had always been in the drawing room and was still there. "The other piano," she said. "*His.*" She spoke as if we had already had a long conversation on the subject. But we had not, and it took me some time to realize that this other piano was Yakuv's new one that Rudy had bought for him.

Again skipping intermediate explanations—"It's so noisy at Kitty's," Leonora said. "Could someone tell me why she has to live in a warehouse? He needs peace and quiet; naturally—an artist."

So there *had* been changes, and principally, I noticed, in Leonora. Her coiled hair was newly touched with blonde; her cheeks had those two spots of excitement I knew from her dinner parties. She kept taking deep breaths as if to contain some elation inside her.

Rudy took me for a walk in Central Park. As usual on his walks, my father wore a three-piece herringbone suit, a Homburg hat, and carried a rolled umbrella like an Englishman. From time to time he pointed this umbrella in the direction of a tree, an ornamental bridge, ducks on a pond: "Beautiful," he breathed, loving Nature in its formal aspect. Around us towered the hotels and apartment blocks of Central Park South and West, which he also loved—for the same decorative solidity that had formed the background of his Berlin youth and his courtship of my mother.

"It's a privilege for us to give him what he has never had. A quiet orderly home, meals on time—yes yes, this sounds very—what do you call it? Stuffy? *Square?* But even artists," he smiled, "have to eat and sleep."

"What about Kitty?" I said.

"Kitty. Exactly. They're too much alike, you see; artistic temperaments. Sometimes he needs—they both need—a rest from the storm and stress. Nothing has changed. Leonora and I are what we have always been."

"Mother looks wonderful."

"You know how she has always adored music above everything." Then he exclaimed: "Dear heaven, who says we're not sensible grown-up people! We've learned how to behave. You're still a child, lambkin." He squeezed my arm, in token of my misery and failure. "One day you too will learn that everything turns out the way it has to, for good; for our good." He pointed his umbrella—at the sky this time, inviting me to look upward with him toward the immense perfection that was always with us, encompassing our small mismanaged lives.

A week or two after my arrival, Yakuv returned from his tour. *He* had not changed. He at once went into what used to be my bedroom—without apology, probably he didn't realize that it had been mine, or simply took it for granted that it was now his. He greeted me with a comradely clap on the shoulder, not as if I had been away for several years but as if I had showed up as usual for my weekly lesson. Leonora followed him into the room; she had to unpack his bag, she said, because if she didn't it would stand there for weeks. But this was said with a smile, not in the reproachful way she used for Kitty's and my untidiness. After a while, during which Rudy went for another of his walks, she emerged with an armful of Yakuv's laundry. Soon came the sound of his piano, and every day after that it seemed to fill, to appropriate the apartment. If I moved around or shut a door a little too loudly, she or Rudy, or both, laid a finger on their lips.

Leonora did everything possible to create the best conditions for his work. She arranged his schedule with his agent, whom he often fired so that she had to find a new one; and since it infuriated him to have anyone disarrange his music sheets, she cleaned his room herself. Otherwise he was calm, immersed in his work. He rarely asked for anything and good-naturedly accepted even what he didn't want—Leonora once gave him a dark blue velvet smoking jacket, and though he mildly protested ("So now I must look like a monkey"), he let her coax him into it. He also smoked the better brand of cigars she bought him to replace the little black ones he was used to. He had personal habits but was not entrenched in them, and if it made no difference to him, he gladly obliged her in everything.

That was during the day. But during the evening meal, he would push his plate back and without waiting for the rest of us to finish—he still ate in the same rapid, ravenous way— he went out, banging the front door behind him. He never said that he was going, or where; he was not expected to, and anyway, we knew. But there were times when he did not return for several days, and while I had no idea what transpired between him and Kitty during those days, I was very much aware of the effect his absence had on Leonora. She behaved like a sick person. She stayed in her bedroom with the curtains drawn, and "Leave me alone," was all she ever said to Rudy's and my efforts to rally her. It was not until Yakuv returned that she got up, bathed and dressed and tried to return to her normal self. But this was not possible for her; she appeared to have suffered a collapse—even physically she had lost weight and her splendid breasts sagged within her large bra. I don't think Yakuv noticed any of this; anyway, it did not affect him since in his presence she made a brave attempt to pull herself together and go about her household duties as usual, especially her duties to him. She would not have known how to stage the sort of confrontations that he was used to with Kitty; and since these were lacking, he probably assumed that everything was fine with Leonora—that is, insofar as he thought of her at all.

Rudy wanted to take her on a Mediterranean cruise. A few years earlier they had enjoyed sailing around the Greek Islands, but now Leonora was reluctant to leave. She said she couldn't; Lina was too old and cranky to look after the house properly, everything would be topsy-turvy. I could hear my parents arguing in their bedroom at night, Rudy as usual calm and reasonable, but she not at all her usual self. In the mornings Rudy would emerge alone from their bedroom, and he and I would discuss ways of persuading her. We laid stress on her health—"Look at you," I said, making her stand before her bedroom mirror.

She drew her hand down her cheek: "You think I look terrible?"

"You'll see how well you'll look after a change—young all over again. Young and beautiful."

"Really?" She continued dubiously to regard herself in the mirror.

It was only when I promised to take over all her responsibilities that she began to accept the idea of Rudy's cruise. But first she had to train me in the arts that she herself had learned from her mother and grandmother; and it was only when she was satisfied that I knew how to take care of all Yakuv's needs that she finally agreed to leave. Rudy was overjoyed; he whispered promises of another honeymoon. He packed their suitcases in his expert way but humbly unpacked them again when she, who also prided herself on her packing, pointed out how much better it could be done.

It was only when he saw these suitcases standing in the hall on the day before departure that Yakuv realized what was going on. His reaction was unexpected: he took the cigar out of his mouth and said, "Why didn't anyone tell me?" When Leonora began to speak, he waved his hands and stalked off into his room. We waited for the piano to start up but nothing happened; only silence, disapproval seeped from that room and filled the apartment and Leonora's heart so that she whispered, "We can't go."

I had never seen my father so angry. "But this is too much! Now we have reached the limit!" Leonora and I gazed in astonishment, but he went on, "Who is this man, what does he think?" Then—"Tomorrow he leaves! No today! Now! Hop!" He made straight for Yakuv's door, and had already seized the handle when Leonora grasped his arm. They tussled—yes, my parents physically tussled with each other, a sight I never thought to see. She pleaded, he insisted, she used little endearments (in German) until he turned from the door. His thinning grey hair was ruffled, another unprecedented sight in my serene and serenely elegant father. In response to Leonora's imploring looks, I joined in her pleas to postpone this expulsion, at least until they returned from their trip. "Our second honeymoon," Leonora pleaded, until at last, still red and ruffled, he agreed.

But later that night he came to my room. He told me that by the time they returned from their cruise, Yakuv would have to be out, pronto, bag and baggage, and it was up to me to see that this was done. His mouth thin and determined—"Bag and baggage," he repeated, and then, in another splutter of anger: "Ridiculous. Unheard of."

They were to be away for six weeks and during that time I had to get Yakuv to pack up and leave. But he gave me no opportunity to talk to him. He stayed in his room, and all day the apartment resounded with music of storm and stress. Only sometimes he rushed out to walk in the Park; once I followed him, but there too it was impossible to talk to him. Hunched in an old black coat that was too long for him, he appeared sunk in his thoughts. His hands were in his pockets and he only took them out to gesticulate in furious argument with whatever was going on under his broad-brimmed hat.

I had to turn to Kitty for help. The change in Kitty was as marked as it was in Leonora, but in the opposite direction. It was Kitty who looked calm, and though no longer young, she now appeared younger than before. Instead of her long skirts and dangling loops of jewelry, she wore a flowered artist's smock that made her look as wholesome as a kindergarten teacher. Her eyes had lost their inward brooding look and were clear and intent on the proof-sheets she was holding up to the light. She made me admire them with her—they were all of pretty little girls posed on her tree-stumps—and she only put them down when I told her of the task my father had imposed on me.

She laughed in surprise: "I thought Rudy was so proud of keeping his own little Paderewski."

"He thinks Leonora is getting too nervous."

Now she really laughed out loud: Leonora nervous! It was the word—together with neurasthenic, or later, neurotic—that had always been applied to Kitty herself.

"And Yakuv too," I ventured.

She put down her proof-sheets: "Oh yes. He's in one of his moods. The other night I was busy in my dark room and that made him so mad he stamped and roared and tore down the pictures I'd pinned up. He said he couldn't stand the way I live. Well, nothing new—I've heard it a thousand times before . . . But Leonora? Are you telling me he misses Leonora?"

It was then that she offered to tell Yakuv to get out of our apartment. I was glad to be relieved of this task and to have time to go about my own business. After all, I still had a divorce to take care of, as well as deciding whether to go back to college or to find a job. And what about all those existential questions that had so troubled me? I needed to become involved again with my own concerns rather than those of my parents and my aunt. I decided that, as soon as Rudy and Leonora returned, I would look for a place of my own. Picking up some old connections and making new ones, I was out and about a lot and continued to see nothing of Yakuv. I'm afraid I neglected most of what Leonora had left me to do for him, but he didn't complain and perhaps didn't notice. Whenever I was home I heard him playing a lot of loud music. I assumed he was preparing for his next tour and hoped that he would have left on it before my parents returned. He showed no intention of moving out but presumably he would as soon as Kitty had talked to him. Meanwhile he continued to thump away behind his closed door; he seemed to be there all the time now, even at night.

Then late one evening Kitty herself showed up. It was

pouring with rain, but it turned out she had walked all the way from downtown. When I tried to make her take off her wet clothes, she waved me away—her attention was only on the sounds from Yakuv's room. "So he's still here," she said, partly in anger, partly in relief.

It may have been because she was so drenched, with her hair wild and dangling as it used to be (though dyed a more violent shade of red), that she had reverted to the Kitty I used to know. And her mood too was charged in the old way. She told me how she had tried to call Yakuv all day and every day, though she knew he hardly used the telephone and certainly never answered it. The last time she had seen him was when she had told him of Rudy's ultimatum. Without a word and waving his hands in the air, he had rushed out of her loft and had not returned. She had begun to fear that he had packed up and left our apartment in offended pride, abandoning not only my parents but Kitty too. Tormented by this thought—that he had taken himself out of our lives for ever—she had come running through the dark and the rain: only to hear his piano as usual in the room he had been told to vacate.

Suddenly she rushed in there. I was surprised and apprehensive: even when they had still been living together in the brownstone, Kitty had rarely dared to enter his room while he was playing. If she did, there would be a fearful explosion, with objects flying down the stairs until Kitty herself came running down them, declaring, "He's a madman, just a crazy, crazy person;" and Yakuv would appear at the top of the stairs, shouting the same thing about her. But now there was no explosion. The playing stopped abruptly. All I heard was her voice and nothing from him at all. I went to bed, expecting them to do the same. And why not? Two people who had been living together, on and off, for over twenty years.

Later that night they woke me up. They sat on either side
of my bed; they appeared exhausted, not as after a fight but
after long futile talk. It was almost dawn and it may have
been the frail light that made them look drained.

"He claims he can't live without her . . . He used to laugh
at her!" She turned on him: "Now what's happened? Because
it's you she cooks for now, all her potato dishes, is that what
you can't do without?"

He shook his head, helplessly. He didn't have his glasses
on and looked as I remembered seeing him in bed with Kitty:
mild, melancholy, his grey eyes dim as the dawn light.

"My aunts always told me, 'The way to a man's heart is
through his stomach.' I thought they only meant people like
my fat uncles. I didn't know artists were included. If that's
what you are!" she cried. "You thump your piano loud
enough: what's all that about? Passion for food or for the
housewife who cooks it?"

He remained silent—he who was always so flip, so quick
with his sarcastic replies. He stretched across me to touch
her: "Kitty," he said, his voice as sad as his eyes.

"Let me be!" she cried, but obviously this was the last
thing she wanted.

My parents returned two weeks earlier than expected.
Their second honeymoon had not been a success. They had
sailed through the classical world, and for him it had been
an enchanted return to civilization: *his* civilization, of order,
calm, and balance. But she, who had upheld this rule of life
with him, had seen it crumble away. She wept, she suffered.
He held her in his arms, which he couldn't get entirely around
her, she was so much larger than he. While promising
nothing, he began to consider means of adjusting to their
new situation.

It was amazing how well he managed to restore the

harmony of our household. His relief at finding Yakuv still installed in the apartment was almost as great as hers. Her husband's forbearance evoked Leonora's gratitude—and maybe Yakuv's too, though he probably took his own rights for granted. Soon Leonora was herself again. She sang as she moved around her furniture with the feather duster that was her scepter. Practical, punctual, perfect, her figure restored to full bloom, she dispensed food and comfort in return for the love of men.

Yakuv continued to practice behind his closed door, emerging only for meals. His music no longer stormed in rage but was as calm as could be expected of him. My father too was calm—that was *his* nature—but now with some hidden sorrow that made me postpone my plan of finding my own place. Sometimes I joined him on his walks, or we played chess, a game he loved though he always lost. That didn't matter to him; he was a bad player but an excellent loser.

Kitty changed—or rather, changed back again. Instead of the simple flowered smock, she reverted to her flamboyant dresses, looped with large, noisy pieces of costume jewelry. Several times she came storming into the apartment, probably after walking all the way from downtown, as she had done on that rainy night, and as on that night, ready to burst into the room from where the piano rang out. But each time she was prevented by Leonora who stood in front of the door, her arms spread across it. Then Rudy intervened; he took his sister-in-law's hand and spoke to her soothingly. Kitty let herself be led away meekly, saying only, "Do you know how long he hasn't come to me?" Then I realized that Yakuv had been spending not only all his days but many of his nights in our apartment.

It might be thought that their rivalry would turn the sisters into enemies, but this was not at all what happened. Instead they drew closer together in an intimacy that excluded even Rudy and me. They met several times a week, not in our apartment where they could not be alone, nor in Kitty's loft—Leonora refusing to venture into that part of town, which seemed wild, dark, and suspect to her. Their favorite rendezvous was the Palm Court of a large hotel, probably similar to the sort of place they had frequented in their youth, with gilt-framed mirrors, a string orchestra, and ladies and gentlemen (some of them lovers) seated on plush sofas enjoying their afternoon coffee and cake. Here Leonora and Kitty exchanged their intimate secrets, just as they had done when they were young. At that time Leonora had confided the tender ins and outs of Rudy's courtship, Kitty had analyzed the characters of her lovers whom it had amused her to keep dangling on a string. Now the confidences they shared were about the same man. They would also have spoken—this was their style—of Life in general, of Love. Sometimes they may have glanced at their reflections in the hotel mirror, pleased at what they saw: though older now, they were still the same handsome sisters, Leonora in her elegant two-piece with the diamond brooch in the lapel, Kitty still bohemian under a pile of bright red hair.

A decade passed in this way within my family. Meanwhile, I came and went; I saw that the situation was not going to change in a hurry nor was there anything I could do about it. Rudy encouraged me to leave, even though I was the only one to whom he occasionally showed something of his own feelings instead of pretending he didn't have any. I went back to college to finish my degree, I read a lot, I began to write. I had one or two stories published in little magazines, and these made my father so proud that he bought up copies to give to everyone he knew.

Yakuv also came and went. He was often on tour, for his reputation was now established and he had engagements all over the country. It did not improve his temper—on the contrary, he became more difficult. He was still firing his agents so that Leonora had to find new ones and also secretaries to attend him on his tours. Usually these secretaries returned without him; either he had fired them or they couldn't stand him another day. He would cable urgently for a replacement, but by then everyone had heard about him and no one was willing to go. He blamed us for this failure— what could he do, he said, if we sent him nothing but block-heads and idiots, and meanwhile how was he to manage, again he had missed a plane and left the suitcase with his tails in a hotel? Twice Leonora went herself to take care of him, but when they came back, they were not on speaking terms and Rudy had to make peace between them. Leonora refused to undertake another tour with him; and after a barrage of urgent messages from Kansas City, Kitty was dispatched to him—with misgivings that turned out to be justified, for he sent her back within a week.

Sometimes I suspected that his tantrums were not entirely genuine. I have seen him turn away, suppressing a smile— exactly as he had done in earlier years after some wild fight with Kitty. The music we heard him play after one of these upheavals was invariably tranquil, romantic, filling everyone with good feelings. With me, too, his manner had never changed from the time I was a child and he my teacher. He gave me books he thought I ought to read, and when he wanted to relax, he called me to play some game with him— dominoes usually, to my relief, never chess at which I suspected him to be a master. When he wanted to be

53

affectionate, he still pinched my cheek; and when he was angry with me, it was not as with the others but as with a child, wagging his finger in my face. This made me laugh, and then he laughed too. Eventually it happened that when he was in one of his moods, Leonora and Kitty would send me to calm him down. It was as though I were free of the web that entangled them—by this I suppose I mean their intense sexual involvement with him. I felt nothing like that; how could I? For me he was just an elderly little man, almost a dwarf with a huge head and a mass of grey hair. His teeth were reduced to little stumps stained brown with tobacco.

When another crisis arose with another secretary fired in mid-tour, it was natural for someone—was it Leonora, was it Kitty?—to suggest that I should take my turn with the job at which they had already failed. It was my father who objected; he said he had higher expectations for me, and hoped I had for myself too, than to be handmaid and servant to Yakuv on his travels. Leonora and Kitty reared up as one person—it was strange how united they were nowadays; they said it would be a rich experience for me as well as a privilege to be in close contact with an artist like Yakuv. Rudy made a face as though saying—perhaps he actually did say—hadn't we had enough of this privilege over the past ten years? But he gave me money for the trip and told me to wire for more when I needed it, especially if I needed it for my ticket home.

Almost the first thing Yakuv said to me was, "You'll need some money." This was in a cab on our way from the airport—unexpectedly, he had been standing there waiting for me. He put his hand in his pocket and drew out a fistful of notes: "Is this enough?" He put his hand in his other pocket and drew out some more. From then on it was the way we carried out all our financial transactions: he didn't pay me a salary but just offered me everything in his pockets to pick out as much as I needed. This was not very much, since my hotel room and plane tickets and cab rides were all included in his, paid for by the sponsors. I lasted longer than anyone else had done, traveling with him from one city to another. We always checked into the same kind of hotel, I in a small single room and he in a suite that had often to be changed, due to his complaints about noise and other inconveniences. During the day, if I didn't go to his rehearsals, I stayed in the hotel by myself; I wasn't interested in the cities we were in— they were all the same, with the same sort of museums built in the early 1900s by local millionaires to house their art collections. At night I attended his performances in a concert hall donated by a later set of millionaires; I was very proud of him, his playing and the effect it had on his audience. He was not only a superb pianist, he looked the part too as he lunged up and down the keyboard, his coat-tails hanging over the piano stool, a wild-haired artist, profoundly foreign, an East European import from an earlier era. Afterward there was always a reception and dinner for him; surrounded by rich and wrinkled women, his eyes would rove around the room, and when he found me, he shrugged and grimaced from behind their jeweled backs.

Leonora had given me careful instructions about his routine, what to do with his clothes, when he would need the first cup of black coffee that he drank throughout the day. Of course, like everyone else, I got things wrong and he flew into a rage but always one that was tempered to me— that is, to the child I was for him. And with me he got over it more quickly than with the others, and also pitched in to help, so that somehow we muddled through together. Whenever there were a couple of hours to spare in the afternoons, we would go to a local cinema; he liked only gangster or cowboy movies, and since the same program was always playing in the different cities we visited, we saw each one several times. At night I sat up with him in his suite, waiting for the pills without which he couldn't sleep to take effect. He read aloud to me—Pushkin in Russian, Miłosz in Polish; I didn't understand but liked to listen to him in these languages that seemed more natural to him than the English he spoke in his sharp Slavic accent. During the time I spent alone in the hotel, I continued with my own writing; it was the first time that I attempted poetry, maybe because he liked it better than prose. He encouraged me to read it to him, listening carefully, asking questions, sometimes making a suggestion that often turned out to be right.

He asked about the years I had spent on my own travels. He was particularly interested in my Buddhist period. He himself was of course a complete agnostic, that was the way he had grown up among those whose mission it had been to overthrow everything. I said that had been my mission too, to overthrow the nihilism they had left us with. "But a nun," he said, smiling. Although I had long ago given up that ambition, I defended myself. I said that having started on a path, I wanted to follow it as far as it would take me—I had more to say but stopped when I saw the way he was looking at me. His lips were twitching. I didn't really expect him to take me seriously; it wasn't only that I was so many years younger than he, I suspected that he took none of us seriously. He even seemed to have the right to be amused by us, as though he were a much wiser person. I don't know whether this impression derived from the fact that he was a great artist, or from the mixture of the Talmud and Marxist idealism that I thought of as his background.

Since it seemed to take longer and longer for his sleeping pills to have effect, our conversations became more protracted. He wanted to know about my marriage, a subject that I disliked talking about except to say that it had been a mistake. He drew me out about the nineteen-year-old boy who had been the mistake. I admitted that what had attracted me to him was his frailty, which I had interpreted as vulnerability (later he turned out to be hard as nails). It had started when we had bathed together in the Ganges and I saw his frail shoulder blades—it was the first time I had seen him without his robe. "His robe?" Yakuv asked; so then I had to admit that he too had been in the religious life and had been planning to become a monk. I glanced at Yakuv, and yes, his lips were now twitching so much that he could not prevent himself from laughing out loud. I laughed too, maybe ruefully, and he pinched my cheek in his usual way. Only it wasn't as usual, and that was the first time I stayed with him all night. Although for the rest of the tour we still took separate rooms, we usually stayed in his, except when he was very tired after a concert and then he said I had better sleep in my own little nun's bed. But mostly he wasn't tired at all but with plenty of energy left in his short and muscular body. His chest and back and shoulders were covered in grey fur; only his pubic hair had remained pitch black.

He gave me no indication of what to tell or not to tell at home, but it turned out to be easier than expected. Leonora and Kitty were astonished at the way I had stuck it out with him. All their questions were to do with the practical side of my duties—how I had managed to make him catch planes on time and tidy him up for his performances. I gladly supplied them with answers, adding an amusing anecdote or two which made them clap their hands in joyful recognition. They had been there before me. Soon everything settled down. Yakuv and I continued to play dominoes, Leonora fulfilled his daily needs, and he had another home in Kitty's loft where he kept his furniture and his other piano. Kitty visited us often and she and Leonora met to exchange confidences in their favorite Palm Court rendezvous. They still did not invite me to join them, considering me too young and immature to understand.

However, I understood more than I had done. For instance, I realized that when Yakuv was shut away in his room and there was only the sound of his piano, he was not as oblivious of us as I had always thought. Somehow he was tied to us as we were to him. My mother and aunt never realized that I too was now part of the web that bound them. They took it for granted—and it was a relief to them—that I would accompany him on all his tours. In New York, there was no sign of what went on between us on these tours. Only occasionally, during meals, he slipped off one of the velvet slippers my mother had bought for him and placed his feet on mine under the table. While he was doing this, he kept on eating as usual with his head lowered over the plate, shoveling food into his mouth with tremendous speed.

I was never sure—I'm still not sure—about my father. It was impossible to tell if he suspected anything: he was so disciplined, so used to accommodating himself to difficult situations and handling them not for his own satisfaction but for those he loved. Every time I packed my suitcase to go on tour with Yakuv, Rudy came into my room. I said, "It's all right: I *like* it." He continued to watch me in silence while I happily flung clothes into my suitcase. At last he said, "And your writing?" He sounded so disappointed that I tried to think of something to make him feel better. I said I was continuing my attempts at writing, and in fact, inspired by Yakuv's performances, I had begun to write poetry. I knew that for my father poetry and music were the pinnacle of human

58

achievement, so perhaps he really was consoled and not only pretending to be so.

Yakuv outlived Rudy by many years; he also outlived Leonora and Kitty. He became a wizened little old man, more temperamental than ever, his hair, now completely white, standing up as he ran his hands through it in fury. He continued his tours till the end and became more and more famous, people lining up not only to hear but also to see him leaping around like a little devil on his piano stool. He made many recordings and was particularly admired for his blend of intellectual rigor and sensual passion. When he died, he left his royalties to me, as well as quite a lot of other business to take care of. Of course I have all his recordings and often listen to them, so he is always with me. I no longer write poetry but have returned to prose and have published several novels and collections of stories. These are mostly about the relations between men and women, which appears to have been the subject that has impressed itself most deeply on my heart and mind. I keep coming back to it, trying again and again to render my mother's and my aunt's experience, as I observed it, and my own. This account is one more such attempt.

3
Gopis

M<small>Y</small> FATHER had been a successful publicist, and during his last illness, I took over his business. I have been very lucky; I know that the girls who work for me would like nothing better than to become as I am now. Besides his office, I have inherited my father's apartment in a doorman building on the Upper East Side. My social life is mostly confined to my clients, though occasionally I have dinner in a neighborhood restaurant with a friend at which we exchange confidences. I used to have a lot to confide, but in recent years I have been listening more than talking. That is one indication of how things have changed for me. Looking back at the past, I'm astonished by my former self; though this would be nothing to the way my former self would be astonished by my present one.

When I first met her, Lucia was twenty years old. She didn't have a job or an apartment of her own, nor any ambition for either; all she seemed to want—as I did at her age, twenty years earlier—was to go to India. But it was far from there that I met her: at one of those public relations charity dinners that I have to attend as part of my job. It was the usual sort of affair where tables for $50,000 each had been bought by some corporation with the careless generosity of a tax write-off. The only reason Lucia was there was to fill up one of the places at my client's table. She had been brought by my secretary, a former room-mate of Lucia's, who had since moved far ahead and seemed inclined to patronize her.

Only this was difficult because Lucia did not appreciate the occasion, what appeared to her friend to be its glamor. To lend star value to the event, a famous Hollywood actor had been invited as the guest of honor. His presence was like an electric charge. Everything scintillated—he himself of course, in his fame; and the room, which was a ballroom in a hotel with walls mirrored and silvered and a ceiling that hung down in a swath of silver clouds. The women glittered with their jewels and their newly blonde hair, and the men glittered too, with polished bald heads and velvet lapels. Faces were turned toward the top table where the actor radiated glorious sun. There were speeches, jokes generating obedient laughter, references in respectfully lowered voices to the good cause of the charity, and then at last panegyrics (some respectfully humorous) for the actor met by cheers and a thunder of applause.

Lucia stood out in not even pretending to listen to the speeches or focus her desire on the star. Instead she pushed the food around on her plate—food that to me is always symbolic of these occasions, as dead as the speeches and the laughter. By contrast, the waiters serving it are very much alive—young men, most of them out of work actors, greatly in need of the evening's wages and therefore as alert as for a performance on stage. I noticed that Lucia sometimes looked up to exchange glances with the handsome young waiter serving her, and these seemed to me the only true flashes of human intercourse taking place that evening.

She was wearing a flimsy little flowered dress, which may have had the label of a famous designer or have come off a rack in the street. She had long hair, some strands chopped off and others dyed in a mixture of colors. She was probably the only woman there who had not been to a beauty parlor that day—apart from myself, that is, for it is my policy not to dress up too much. It isn't my job to be noticed but to have others noticed, photographed and publicized. It may have been this fact that drew Lucia's glance toward me occasionally; after some whispered questions to her friend, she suddenly leaned across the table, her attention and her eyes at last alight, and called: "Diane, have you been to India?" It was the beginning of our friendship.

She was learning Indian dance from a woman teacher who had recently returned to India to be with *her* teacher. She wanted Lucia to follow her, and of course Lucia was dying to go. But she had to reckon with her parents—not so much her mother, who was too engrossed in yet another relationship to have time to worry about Lucia, but her father. It was he who had to finance the trip, and Lucia, he said, was not responsible enough to take it. "*He* can talk," Lucia told me— this was over a little dinner in a neighborhood restaurant to which I was treating her. She leaned across the table, her multi-colored hair dangling over it, along with her chains of oversized colored stones. "Every time I turn around there's a new girl friend, and all of them younger than I." She laughed with a dry ironic sound which was at once swallowed up in her usual fervor: "Talk to him, Diane."

This was the role she had assigned to me: to talk to her father and convince him that, despite exposure to India, it was possible to remain perfectly sane and make money in business. "If he meets you just once, he'll know that it'll be all right, that I'll be all right." It made me laugh—her assumption as well as my own feeling of ambiguity about it. She told me that I would be an antidote to her dance teacher whom she had introduced to her father. It had been a mistake. The teacher, middleaged but painted and dressed in flamboyant colors, talked with a dancer's passion and incessant movements, her hands fluttering in strange gestures, her eyebrows—dyed pitch-black like her hair—emphasizing her eyes, which had a double existence through being encircled by kohl. While she spoke, she kept touching the father's face and hands to convey the philosophy and beauty of Indian dance. She failed—"Daddy is such a *stick*"—but, not realizing it, kept phoning him. "Get that bitch off my back!" he had yelled at Lucia who recalled this with the comment: "Of course it would have been different if she had been a nineteen-year-old blonde . . . Or you, Diane. He'll listen to you."

She continued to call me and visit me at home with little gifts of pretty rings and bracelets she had picked up at street fairs. She fitted them on me, then stood back and admired me so much that she had to kiss me—not only because of what she wanted from me, though that too, but because I was her friend. Finally, there was no way I could not meet her father; except that now something happened that made us both change course. This was the unexpected, unexplained appearance at my door of my Indian past: Vijay, whom I had known, and more than known, all those years ago. He came with the huge suitcases that Indians bring abroad to fill up with shopping for the return journey; and he wore the sort of shiny suit with wide flapping legs that he had always worn, and new shoes that he took off as soon as possible. It appeared he had no money for a hotel, so naturally he stayed with me. We hadn't seen each other for longer than either of us cared to say—but "You haven't changed at all, Diane, no, not one bit. I'm not telling you a lie," he said, looking at me with the innocent eyes he made when telling a particularly outrageous lie.

So the next time Lucia came to claim my help and friendship, she found him ensconced in the center of my largest and most comfortable sofa, helping himself to the contents of my liquor cabinet. He was completely relaxed and at home, in a muslin kurta and his knees apart under his cotton lungi.

These flimsy garments showed off his huge bulk; he had kept the studs of his kurta open to an expanse of chest with a forest of hair that I remembered as black but was now mixed with grey. Less adept than he at telling lies, I could not say that he had not changed: he had become bloated with drink and age; and yet—and yet—I could see that he impressed Lucia as he had impressed me at her age. Of course there was the fact that he was Indian—tremendously, overwhelmingly Indian—to enchant her now as it had me then. He was different from the men one had known; *more*, somehow, and not only in bulk. And there was his easy familiarity, which made him greet Lucia as though he had expected her, was glad to see her, and felt privileged to be her host. He poured a glass freely for her from the vodka bottle he had already half finished; and laughed uproariously when he heard she was a teetotaller, *and* a vegetarian—"Like you," he said, turning to me, with difficulty, for his trunk was too heavy for easy turning. "Like I used to be," I corrected him, having long since abandoned my program of inner purification. But Lucia was still intent on this ideal, for which, like me, she hoped to find fulfillment in India; and maybe also in Vijay in whom she saw some sort of physical embodiment of India. And besides, he was regarding her with an appreciation to which any woman could thrill and respond; she may not have noticed that he was showing the same toward me. It was a trick he had of making one feel unique and uniquely desired. Or it may not even have been a trick but something he truly felt: the love of women, all women, indiscriminately bestowed by Krishna, by the god of love himself.

I had first met him in his shop in New Delhi. It may be odd to think of the god of love as a shopkeeper, but that was what he was, what his ancestors had been; it was his caste—shopkeepers, moneylenders. He had a crockery shop, a large, well-stocked establishment taken over from his grandfather and his father. He was very much the proprietor in charge, far more knowledgeable about every item in stock and its current price than the assistants whom he sent scurrying around. Yet although he gave the impression of belonging to the place, and it belonging to him, there was also a sense that he extended into other, wider regions. It was not clear to me, and never became so, what these might be. He certainly seemed to have more money than one would expect to be generated from his shop—he only had to put his hand in his pocket to draw out bundles of notes, some held by rubber bands, others loose so that they dropped to the ground. He also appeared to have many connections, which made it easy for him to fix anything I asked for: a ticket to the Republic Day Parade, a seat on an overbooked train. It was thrilling to think of a secret life stretching into the recesses of New Delhi politics, or even into a criminal underworld. And maybe there were several secret lives, a whole tangle of them, of which I too constituted one strand.

He certainly kept me secret; he could hardly do otherwise, for he was not only a respected businessman, a member of the chamber of commerce, but also of a large extended family, with a wife and many children. I never met any of them but I did see them—this was when I had become so infatuated with him that I lurked around places he might be, not to spy but simply to get a glimpse of him. He lived in a large pastel-pink house he had built for his family, with little balconies inspired by Indian miniatures and a large concrete porch copied from some architectural magazine. Several imported cars stood outside and I saw him shoo his family into them—a horde of little boys and girls shining with satin and oil, and stout women slow-moving in their heavy brocades and weighty jewels. They often drove to one of the big hotels; and here too I peered in at them, in the dining room done up like the Ajanta caves where they sat among dishes overflowing with pilaos and tandoori chickens, surrounded by a posse of waiters whom he tipped out of the cornucopia of bank notes bulging in his pockets.

He never took me into any such place, or anywhere at all where we might be seen. I had rented a room in a guesthouse known to young Europeans and Americans traveling on very little funds. It was not far from his shop—in fact, around the corner in the service lane on to which several restaurants backed with their refuse and their waiters squatting to smoke or urinate. I had wandered into his shop to buy a water mug, and it amused him that I couldn't afford its price. He said something to his assistant who protested, so he said it again and I realized he was saying, "Give it to her." He wrapped it himself and soon we were in conversation. He seemed familiar with the guest-house where I was staying—how? Had he visited other girls there, pale wanderers like myself? He came to see me that same evening when he had shut up his shop, and after that it was the place where we mostly met.

It is easy to see how I came to love him so much: my age, my aloneness, my openness to travel, to adventure, to India. And he: handsome, easy, experienced, some twenty years older than I. He would never admit his age outright but—"Guess," and then he would laugh and say, "Wrong." He was still saying it to Lucia now: "Guess," and out of politeness she would guess many years less than he could possibly be; and then he would laugh as before and say: "Right." He must have been in his late fifties by now and he looked it. Grossly overweight, he would breathe heavily and groan when he had to get up out of a chair. But his face remained more or less as it had been, his expression open as a boy's, receptive as a lover's. He drank too much; he had always needed alcohol, he used to come to my room with a bottle of whisky that he tried to make me drink with him out of the mug he had given me. But I remained at that time staunchly non-alcoholic, though I did everything else he wanted.

I knew how much he hated to be alone, so in a way I was glad that Lucia was keeping him company. In India he had always had somewhere to go, people to be with. Besides his large extended family, there was his shop, and his buyers and suppliers, and every morning a group of cronies in a coffee-house; and his errands in maybe high or low places, all of them kept secret. And there was I in my room, never knowing when he would show up but happy to see him whenever he did; and there may have been other girls—how would I know?—waiting for him somewhere else in the city around which he roamed so freely. But here in New York he was alone, a stranger with nowhere to go; and he was old now and alcoholic and so big that I had to give up my room to him, which was the only one with a double bed. At night I often had to help him into it, and out of his clothes, for he had drunk a lot by that time and each movement caused him to call on his god (*"Are Ram, Ram"*). When I left him, he appeared sunk in the heaviest sleep, but then the phone rang and he would snatch it up at once and I could hear his voice through the wall—low, monosyllabic, the way I used to hear him talk on the phone, but now with a new note in it, of fear.

Lucia told me that there were phone calls during the day too, some he received from and others he made to India (this was confirmed by my phone bill). She described how he put his hand around the mouthpiece and spoke in a muffled voice—unnecessarily, since it was all in a language she didn't understand. And after he put down the receiver, his hand shook while he poured himself another drink, and then another and another, and still his hand was shaking. It took some time before he was calm enough to resume his conversation with her. What did they talk about? Probably she did most of it, as I used to in my time with him in my hotel room when I had so much to confide, such an unspecified pressure on my heart.

"Today I danced for him," Lucia told me one day, still flushed from the experience. She modestly lowered her eyes, kohl-rimmed like her teacher's, and said, "He liked me. He said I have a real talent for *Bharat Natyam.*"

Bharat Natyam! I used to love to go to all-night sessions of Indian dance and music. I went with other young travelers, all of us dressed up in our Indian clothes—sort of cotton rags—some of us spiritualized on drugs, others only on the music and the dance. When I tried to tell Vijay about these experiences, he seemed to think they were mainly for foreigners. He himself liked only film music and the sort of dances that shook the stout hips of Indian film heroines. He sang those songs for me and imitated the heroine dancing— this big manly man turning himself into a simpering maiden smiling coyly from behind her veil. And as he sang and danced for me, using my pillows for breasts, he went into the same kind of swoon as we did at our concerts, overwhelmed with passion—but also in his case with laughter at his own performance, so that he fell backward on my bed and pulled me down on top of him.

He couldn't dance for Lucia—he could hardly stir from his armchair—but he did sometimes sing for her. These were the same lyrics he used to sing for me, for it was only old films that he knew and loved, he hadn't kept up with the new ones.

"No time," he told Lucia—he was so taken up with all his business, and then he resumed sighing, remembering his business. "Does he mean his shop?" Lucia asked me, as perplexed as I had been to think of him as a shopkeeper. But he told us that his eldest son was now in charge of it—all his children were grown up and married, he had grandchildren and he often drew out their photographs, chuckling over them and retailing some cute things they had said or done.

Once, during my time with him, he had spent several days locked up in my hotel room. I never knew why but realized that he was lying low—from what, from whom? My room was one of several leading out on to the roof, and when it wasn't too hot, I went out there to look over the city that was already at that time half-smothered in the smog and smudge of its pollution. The other residents—impecunious foreigners like myself—would also come here to hang up their washing, meditate, smoke whatever it was they were smoking, and exchange travelers' information. But when Vijay stayed there, he never came out and he made me shut the door. There was a pay phone down by the front desk where the Armenian proprietor sat, but Vijay didn't want me to use it for the messages he gave me to pass on. These were always cryptic and in Hindi, which he coached me to pronounce correctly. This was difficult for me and my attempts made him laugh, even though the messages I had to convey on his behalf were very serious.

During these days he communicated with no one except me, or through me; except once a skeletal and tattered man came to our door with a suitcase, which Vijay took from him. They haggled for a while and then Vijay drew out a handful of notes, and after counting them, the man went away satisfied. Vijay opened the suitcase and it was stuffed with so many bundles of notes that I gasped and he patted my cheek, pleased at my being so impressed. Next day he sent me on a very impressive errand with the suitcase—I had to go to the house of an Official who was so important that he had an armed guard standing outside. I was amazed by the easy passage I had past this guard right into the room where the Official sat alone. When I handed over the suitcase, he opened it just a crack to peer into it; and then he gave the same sign of satisfaction—a quick sway of the head—that the tattered man had given at the amount he had received. Then he put the suitcase under his chair and asked me a few perfunctory questions—the sort one is always asked by people one meets in India: what country are you from, are you married, do you like our food? Shortly afterward whatever problem had kept Vijay lying low in my room seemed to have been resolved, for he left without explanation and went about his usual business.

But the days he spent in New York dragged on into weeks and nothing appeared to be resolved. He rarely left my apartment, and often incapacitated with drink, he became careless, forgetting to turn off the shower, or the gas. It was a busy season for me, so I was dependent on Lucia to look after him during the day. At the same time I felt uneasy at asking her to do this—of letting her get involved in a way I recognized from my own experience. Vijay himself, with all his troubles, was concerned about her, and he often asked me, "What will become of her?" It was the same question that he used to ask me, when I was young and so terribly in love with him.

There had been a tragic incident in my New Delhi guest-house: a French girl had killed herself in her room leading off our roof terrace. Just a few days before she had come to borrow some scissors—I pretended I didn't have any, she was always borrowing things and never returning them. I have to admit that she was not an attractive girl; she was dirty, sullen, and quarrelsome, and we all avoided her. Shocked and guilty, we stood outside the door where she was hanging from a hook in the ceiling. We didn't know what to do: we were all young and had come to India to deal not with worldly matters but to improve our inner lives. The proprietor, terrified of scandal—it was the second suicide in his hotel—ran around helplessly, wringing his hands. At some point the police arrived, followed by a doctor, who cut the girl down and declared her dead. All was chaos, the terrace roped off, we were asked questions and gave confused answers. Then Vijay arrived and everything was sorted out. The girl's embassy was called—the girl removed—the police persuaded to ask no more questions. But all of us were shaken out of the carefree lives we had been leading, and it was then that Vijay first asked me, "What will happen to you?"

"Don't worry," I said, "I won't hang myself."

He cried out and clicked his fingers to keep evil spirits away. Then, "Diane," he said, "it's not right: to be alone, no family, no one, nothing."

"But there's you."

He shook his head, sadly: sad for me, because he couldn't do more for me. How could he? He was a family man, he had many responsibilities, at this very time he was arranging a marriage for his eldest daughter (one year younger than I). Yet he liked having me there. Although I'm sure he had many women, I was a new experience for him—a young foreigner with no husband or father or any ties at all, alone and free to be visited or not whenever he pleased. Yes, he had enjoyed it but now his concern was for me: my welfare, my future.

From this time on he urged me to go home, finish my education, get married; whatever I liked but it had to be something. I tried to tell him that there was nothing I wanted except to be with him, but he didn't like to hear that—not for fear of being burdened but for my sake. He even tried to visit me less often, but that made me desperate and I kept telephoning him—in his shop, in his home; I hung around wherever I could see him, so that he too became desperate. But he never blamed me, only himself, for making me miserable and, God forbid, ruining my young life. And he was so truly unhappy about what he said he had done to me, so guilty, that now it was I who tried to comfort him. This went on for a few weeks during which slowly I began to change, and to listen to him when he talked about my future, and even to envisage one which did not include him.

In later years, I twice revisited India, both times staying in a luxury New Delhi hotel where he visited me and where we had sex together. Once he came to New York, but he had his wife and two of his daughters with him so our meetings were limited to those times when they didn't need him to carry their shopping. He came to my apartment, but he was no longer keen on sex; he was drinking a lot and had become huge. He also visited my office where he looked around and said, "Diane, I'm proud of you," and he really did shine with a sort of paternal pride in me.

My early circumstances had been the same as Lucia's: divorced parents, a couple of sets of step-parents, two Christmas dinners every year erupting into the same kind of fights . . . India had been for me, as it now was for Lucia, a higher world, an escape from this lower world in which I had grown up. But for her it also represented those refinements of love and religion that her study of Indian dance had opened up for her: the love of the milkmaids, or *gopis*, for their Krishna, their emotional turmoil as he now played with them, now disappeared only to reappear with other women's nail marks on his chest. Lucia's dance teacher had known all about those emotions, had suffered them herself, so that when she showed Lucia the traditional gestures and facial expressions for hope, love, and despair, she had infused them with her own experience, leaving her panting like a deer or a discarded mistress.

Vijay was a shopkeeper, and maybe also a middleman in murky politics; he wore a big shiny suit and too many rings on his hairy, handsome hands. But in retrospect I see that it had not been difficult for me to identify him with the god celebrated in Indian dance and poetry. But what about Lucia? He was now nearly sixty years old, alcoholic, fat, and frightened. Sometimes he had to be helped to the toilet where he sat astride like a pregnant woman, groaning while he relieved himself. But Lucia accepted all this: for her, as for the *gopis* she wished to emulate, the transcendence of sex— of the lover's person—was the essence of love itself.

The secret phone calls continued, and there were also letters for him containing newspaper cuttings, which he quickly destroyed. His only refuge was a constant supply of drink, but by now he was so frightened to go out—frightened of whom? of what?—that he sent Lucia to the liquor store. Once she phoned me—as intense and secret as he was when he spoke on the phone: "I don't have any money . . . For him; for his vodka," she said, impatient at my lack of immediate understanding. I told my staff that I had a family crisis, and on my way home, I stopped at a money machine to take out several hundred dollars. Lucia took some from me at once and hurried to the liquor store. When I reproached Vijay for not telling me that he had run out of money, he said, "I'm taking too much from you. Staying here, so long, your guest . . ." His head was bowed to his chest. I held his hand in both of mine; I wanted so much for him to share whatever it was that was troubling him. I think he was tempted to speak—he began, "What did I do? Only what everyone else does," and then tears choked him; they rolled down his face and I kissed his wet cheek and it was at that moment that Lucia returned from the liquor store. She looked at us both, then opened the bottle and filled his glass and gave it to him, and while he drank, sighing in relief and pleasure, she looked across at me with hostility. I showed her where I put the money I had brought in a drawer: "This is for him," I told her, and "All right," she said, her tone expressing indifference to this mundane transaction.

Now she had a new plan, and one morning she came to my office to propose it. My office is in a huge commercial mid-town building, and all day the elevators go up and down crowded with employees and messengers and maintenance men, and the whole place, including the inner room where I sit, is frenzied with activity of a kind that would be distasteful to anyone with unworldly or other-worldly inclinations. But Lucia had only come here—as I used to visit my father—to ask for money to go to India. She explained that she needed it to release Vijay from imprisonment in my apartment and to take him home. I began to say that Vijay was staying—in fact, hiding—in my apartment because he *couldn't* go home, but she interrupted me impatiently: he himself had told her that it was all a plot, that there was nothing against him, that he had done nothing. The best plan now was for him to go back and expose the enemies who were intriguing against him and for her to go with him; all they needed was money, which I could easily give them, if I wanted to. When I was silent, she accused me of plotting to keep him here dependent on me, making him helpless, destroying him with drink. I propped my elbows on my desk and held my head; it was in sorrow for Vijay, for this description of what he had become. Lucia too began to cry, though she tried to comfort me, saying it would be all right, she would take him home and he would become himself again, what he had been. I wept with regret for the past, and she in longing for the future; and of course if money was all that was needed to dry our diverse tears, then I was more than willing to give it.

It turned out to be unnecessary, even superfluous. Vijay's passage home was paid for by the Government of India, who were bringing him back under an extradition order. Then Vijay did become himself again, as I remembered him—calm, resolute in the face of a crisis. It was the way he had been when the girl in my New Delhi hotel had killed herself, and he had dealt not only with all the practical arrangements but also with me, with my double anguish. I had been devastated by my sense of what her last hours must have been, and my own guilt at having refused so much as to lend her a pair of scissors. Vijay absolved me of both: by his acceptance not of her fate alone but of fate in general, which awaited us all.

It was the way he met his own fate when it came. He refused to take legal aid against the order but submitted to it at once. At the same time he tried to calm Lucia who wanted to call everyone she could think of—Interpol, the Attorney General, the President—any president, India, America, who cares! she cried when Vijay smilingly asked her which one.

He packed his bags and I helped him, while she hovered around us, pleading: "All you need is a good lawyer, Daddy'll get you one, it's just the sort of thing he knows about."

He was trying to zip up his bag and she was trying to stop him. "Lucia, let me go home," he said. "I'll get a good lawyer."

"Promise! Promise me!"

"Everything will be done, God willing," he said.

Two Indian police officers sent from New Delhi came to fetch him. He received them like a courteous host, commiserating with them for the fatigue of their long journey and the necessity of repeating it almost at once. He offered them vodka which they had to refuse, since they were on duty, but they encouraged him to go ahead. He finished the bottle, while conversing with his captors, joking with them in Hindi; all laughed and liked one another. When it was time to go, he wouldn't allow Lucia or me to help carry his large suitcases. His only regret was that he hadn't been able to fill them with shopping to take home to his family, all the trinkets and gadgets they loved so much. I promised to send them on, but he said, "No, no, the customs! They'll charge two hundred percent!" "Three hundred percent!" said his captors and they hit one another's palms in appreciation of the joke.

Lucia and I followed their cab to the airport where they were ushered inside by the airline staff. We followed as far as we could, and he turned back to us once and waved. He was wearing one of his shiny suits from Delhi, with a broad necktie, and his rings flashed as he waved to us. He had not been handcuffed, maybe because they were all friends by now, or maybe for fear the metal would set off the alarm at the security gate.

*

The rest of this story belongs to Lucia. I went back to running my business, but she followed him to India. I sent her money whenever she needed it, and she faxed me newspaper reports. In these Vijay figured only marginally, as a middleman in the case against a cabinet minister and several top bureaucrats accused of taking large-scale bribes. Vijay was arrested with them, and some of the newspaper photographs showed him being taken into custody with the others, all of them shackled. There were reports of how they were let out on bail, then more reports of their re-arrest. In India it takes not weeks or months but years for a case to come to trial, and in the meantime there are constant alternations of arrests, court appearances, bail, and further arrests.

Lucia remained there waiting for over three years, and I had very little news of her and no address other than the American Express office in New Delhi. She continued to send newspaper photographs of Vijay being taken from jail to court—each time he looked more worn, more tattered, unshaven and unkempt, until he was indistinguishable from any long-time prisoner. The last but one clipping that Lucia sent was just a few lines from some back page to say that Vijay had died from kidney failure while in custody. The last clipping announced a change of government, the reinstatement of the minister to his cabinet post, and the annulment of the case against him and his co-accused.

When she returned to New York, Lucia looked as harrowed as if she too had served a long sentence. During all her time in India she had been able to see Vijay only very rarely. She had visited him in jail as soon as she arrived and had found him cheerful; he had made friends with his jailers and was in a position to pay for all sorts of perks. He assured her that his confinement would soon be over and asked her not to visit him again. She realized that he was embarrassed by her presence and the amusement it caused to both jailers and fellow prisoners. However, when he was not released as quickly as expected, she attempted to see him again: only to be refused admittance to him while other prisoners whistled and made sweet sounds to invite her into their cells. By this time she had run out of money and had to vacate the lodging she had taken in a transit hotel. While waiting for me to send her more money, she slept under the arcade outside the American Express office, along with other foreigners waiting for their checks from home. She was still refused admission to see Vijay in jail, and there was no news of his next court date; so when her money came, she took the train to the little town where her dance teacher had gone to stay near *her* teacher, her revered guru, her transference god.

Here another disappointment awaited Lucia, for her teacher had in the meantime had a falling-out with her guru and was attempting to set up a rival school of her own. She welcomed Lucia with her usual fervent kisses, smearing her with her melting lipstick and mascara, but instead of teaching her about disinterested love, she drew her into the feud. With one shabby little school intriguing against the other, all the students were involved, and the affair had become a local scandal. In this atmosphere it was difficult for Lucia to keep her own ideals intact, and abandoning the dance, she got the train back to Delhi. On the way she was diverted by the sort of adventures young girls alone in India always have, and she went with various people who invited her to their homes, some out of a spirit of pure hospitality, others with more mixed motives. She felt she was getting to know the country of her heart on another level—a deeper level—and continued to make her way toward her original destination.

Although she arrived at a time when Vijay was out on bail, she had no opportunity to meet him. She did what I used to do—lingered at a corner of his street to watch him from a distance shepherding his family of stout ladies. Once she went into his shop, but he pretended not to see her, so she took a cup and saucer and carried them where he sat by his cash desk. He took her money, and when he gave her the change, said, "Lucia, go away; go home." Before she could speak, another customer came up to pay, so she left with her purchase unwrapped. She stood outside his shop, blinded by tears, not knowing what to do; finally she smashed the cup and saucer on the sidewalk, watched by two hawkers—one selling pens and watch-straps, the other demonstrating mechanical toys— both of them shaking their heads and laughing at yet another crazy foreign girl.

After several weeks out on bail, Vijay had to appear for his next court date. It was easy for Lucia to slip into the chamber, dense and sweaty with relatives, reporters, scribes and a crowd of onlookers. She was too far back to hear the exchanges between judge and lawyers, but she had a good view of Vijay among the other accused. He looked rested after his stay at home, freshly shaven, in his shiny suit and broad tie; he was completely sober, in a way she had never seen him in New York, facing the judge with an expression simultaneously proud and submissive to fate's decree. At this hearing, bail was revoked for most of the accused; and amid the ensuing pandemonium—relatives wailing, lawyers protesting—Lucia managed to fight her way to the front of the crowd watching the prisoners being led to the vans outside. When Vijay was led past her, she managed to touch his sleeve. She hardly felt the angry push by the policeman to whom he was chained: for at that moment Vijay turned his face to her, and he smiled at her the way he used to—with affection, grateful for her love and puzzled by it, and also in apology for himself, his own condition. It was only a second before he was dragged on, with a passage being cleared for him among the clamoring, pushing crowd. The next time she tried to see him in prison, she was again refused admission, and the time after that she was told that he had been taken to hospital.

Since this was not the prison hospital but a general one, it was easier for her to see him. She was used to Indian hospitals, having had to go for a series of rabies injections after a stray dog had bitten her. The crowds and smells, the mutilations, the red stains that may have been blood or betel juice were not so different from what she had witnessed in other places, such as the railway stations where she had sometimes spent the night. Vijay was behind a screen put up around his bed, and she had to walk the length of the ward, stepping around patients on the floor for whom beds had not been found. It was very crowded, not only with patients but with their families surrounding them. Again it was not so different from the railway station, each family picnicking on food brought in little pots.

When Lucia reached the screen at the end, she found a policeman sitting outside it on a stool; he had a rifle but was asleep, so she slipped quickly around the screen and was alone with Vijay. He was lying under a blanket on a bed as narrow as a plank; probably it was a plank. He was hooked up to some sort of machine, which took up almost the entire space and appeared to be very old, for it both wheezed and pounded noisily. Vijay himself made no sound at all, he didn't even seem to be breathing; maybe the machine was doing it for him—Lucia felt that she and the machine were alone together. It occurred to her that Vijay might already have gone, have died, without anyone knowing; she put out her hand to touch his face but at that moment the policeman erupted behind the screen, shouted loud abuse and pushed her out. She walked away without protest, feeling she had seen and accomplished nothing; some of the patients or their family members called out to her, but she couldn't understand what they were saying. During all this time in India, she had never managed to understand a word of any language, only signs and gestures, which she may have misinterpreted.

The one thing she had kept in the course of all her wandering was the key to my apartment, and she went straight there on arrival in New York. When I returned from the office, I found her asleep on the sofa, still in the thin cotton rags in which she had traveled around India. All the color had faded from her hair and from her face, with only her eyes ringed with kohl; the soles of her feet were black with the mire and dust of the continent she had traversed. She slept for a long time, and when she got up, she was still exhausted. She stayed with me for two weeks, and I thought she had no plan for anything further, but it turned out that she had.

She was going to stay with her mother in Connecticut— she made a face to show how distasteful this prospect was to her, but "*Some*body has to," she said. It seemed her mother had been through a bad time while parting company with her latest boy friend, or was it another husband? Lucia wasn't sure, and her father wasn't sure either, and anyway he had completely washed his hands of his ex-wife and pronounced her to be a mental case who should be committed. She had tried to kill herself again, and again unsuccessfully—which showed, Lucia said, that she really didn't mean it and only wanted someone to take care of her. So Lucia was going down there to try and do that, though they had never got on together. Her mother used to dress her up in clothes, like pink tutus and matching tights, that even at the age of four Lucia had despised; and later, when she was a teenager, her mother taunted her with her lack of boy friends. She had scorned and ridiculed Lucia's commitment to Indian dance, so that Lucia had refused to see or speak to her for months. She hadn't even said goodbye to her mother before leaving for India, but since her return, they were constantly on the phone to each other. "She's calmed down," Lucia said, "and I guess I have too." Anyway, the subject of Indian dance was no longer an issue between them, since Lucia had decided that it was not for her. "I thought I could do it," she said, "love in spite of, love as absence—all that Krishna and *gopi* stuff;" but now she was giving everything up, dance and love, and was going to stay with her mother. Well, she was not looking forward to it—as anyone would understand who knew her mother! But now, in her sixties, who else was there for her except Lucia? No one.

4

Springlake

WHEN WE decided to sell the house, my brother George kept saying, "It's *The Cherry Orchard*, American style." But this was far from being a close parallel. For one thing, we aren't all that American—not in the way that Madame Ranevsky and her brother were Russian. I suppose this is one of the differences between America and pre-revolutionary Russia: nobody here goes back as far as they did, where generations of landowners handed down their estates, their houses, their serfs from father to son. There are a few hereditary estates left in our area—rambling houses on the Hudson River, with the descendants of the original owners still in them though without the means of keeping them up, so that the roofs are leaking, the curtains hanging in tatters.

Our house, Springlake—the one we were trying to sell—was bought by our father about thirty years ago, perhaps as a way of establishing himself as an American instead of the European immigrant he was. Or it may have been that he wanted to rival the landowners—in Silesia, Galicia, or wherever—whom he had perhaps heard or read about or admired from a distance in his youth. He had always wanted to be a rich man, and when he became one, he knew how to spend money like someone used to having it. But by the time he had bought Springlake and repaired and restored it with all its period detail intact, it was too late for George and me to accumulate childhood memories in it. We were already well into our adult lives; and when I pointed out to George how our house really didn't fit into a *Cherry Orchard* context, he replied that our lives did—his, mine, and Teddy's, our personalities.

George liked to think of himself as a futile character. It suited him and was an excuse for not doing anything very much. It also suited our mother, who had made him into the companion Father was too restless and energetic ever to have been. George lived with her in her New York apartment till she died, and then continued there by himself, without ever changing anything; he even retained her ancient housekeeper. But he also began to spend weekends at Springlake, which we had jointly inherited. Here he made friends with the owners of other large houses who were mostly, like ourselves, newcomers to the area. They had made money in New York and had come to settle down as country gentlemen. They all became expert chefs and interior decorators—several of them had been professional decorators of other people's houses before making enough money to buy and do up their own. They gave each other exquisite dinner parties, sometimes inviting the old ladies who still lived in the moldering mansions of their ancestors. These old ladies were good value at the dinner parties, for they had many stories to tell of their family past—of Cousin Hamilton who had accidentally shot off a foot while hunting in Africa with Cousin Billy—giving the new owners the sensation of being part of and maybe taking over from a genuine American aristocracy.

While cheerfully admitting his own likeness to the futile brother in *The Cherry Orchard*, George also compared me to the sister, Madame Ranevsky. In denying it, I conceded some parallel to another Chekhov character—Madame Arkadina in *The Seagull*; and George agreed that yes maybe, if only because she was, like myself, an actress. And here George said no more, for he did not want to point out that

Madame Arkadina had been a successful actress. George felt as badly about my career as I did myself. We had both had such high hopes of me! Since childhood, we had decided that I was going to be an actress and George a writer; and while he never published, I did get some parts after drama school and even had an agent, Paul, who has since lost interest in me. I don't want to talk about this, or think about it. Success or failure don't appear to be dependent on talent, as is clear to me when I compare my career to that of others who have become famous. My first husband Teddy used to say that I wasn't hungry enough; and I have to admit that going to auditions and waiting to be called back after being snubbed and humiliated—all that was too degrading to me, a violation of the art to which I had dedicated myself. I never thought about money—of course Father saw to it that I didn't have to—nor much about fame: for me all that mattered was the thrill of performance, the giving of myself on stage as in life.

George says that my first husband, Teddy, represents Trofimov, the tutor in *The Cherry Orchard*. Trofimov is idealistic, ardently hopeful, very poor—all characteristics of Teddy, both then and now. Trofimov was in love with Madame Ranevsky's daughter Anya—but of course this parallel would not hold, since Teddy is the father of my daughter Lisa; and Lisa is not like Anya but more like her sister Varya, with whom no one is in love. Lisa has been on anti-depressants since she was a teenager; these keep her in a more or less even mood, for though she has no highs, she does tend to go very low and then she becomes bitter and hostile to all of us, especially to me.

One main character from *The Cherry Orchard* is missing in our little group. This is Lopakhin who has made a fortune and finally buys up the estate, the cherry orchard, on which

his father and grandfather had been serfs. Or it may be that
our father, George's and mine, represents Lopakhin, at least
in his ambition to own this house and with it a recognized,
recognizable place in American society. Although as urban a
character as the rest of us, he really enjoyed Springlake as a
possession. At first he knew nothing about period furniture
and wallpapers, but he soon made himself an expert on the
subject, and while employing professional designers, he guided
and did not succumb to their taste. But when it was all done,
he didn't spend much time here. All summer he preferred to
be in Europe, so there were usually only weekends in the rest
of the year. Our mother never cared to be here or to leave
her Fifth Avenue apartment. So Father usually brought one
of his girl friends, and since he liked company, he filled the
house with guests who drove up from the city on Saturday
afternoon and left again on Sunday night. George and I rarely
joined him on these weekends. We had our own interests in
New York, and anyway never cared either for his girl friends
or his guests, all of them more socially ambitious and more
money-orientated than my brother and I.

Nevertheless, we kept the house for more than ten years
after Father died. George would come for weekends, and
sometimes he managed to persuade our mother to accompany him, wrapping her knees in the fur lap-robe she always
kept in her car. While at Springlake, she never walked around
the grounds but sat in the smaller sitting room, laying out
her cards the way she did in New York, or talking on the
phone to friends, telling them how bored she was here. Lisa
too was bored whenever she came and could be seen
wandering around the orchard—it was an apple not a cherry
orchard but had been neglected so that only very few and
very sour apples grew there. If George and I invited her to
join us on our rambles around the estate, she always refused

and continued to walk disconsolately by herself, chewing on a blade of grass before spitting it out.

This left George and me free to discuss our problems and secrets with each other. In earlier years, these mostly concerned my career—a part I had tried or hoped for. I would explain my interpretation of it to George, and would act it out for him—and really nowhere, and with no one else, did I have the sense of fulfillment that I felt when performing for George. And it was the same when I spoke to him about my love affairs, of which I had many in those years, most of them finally as disappointing as my hopes as an actress. The disappointment was somehow of the same quality. And while my failure to get a certain part appeared inexplicable to both of us, that with a man was explained to me by George as due to my weakness for the weak, and for the needy in need of my money. This was where he compared me with Madame Ranevsky, who foolishly threw away quantities of money neither she nor her family could afford and allowed herself to be exploited by those who always betrayed her and left her (and even then she took them back!). Well, there have been stories like that in my life, but they are different from the one I'm telling now.

It was not only my foolishness with money that made us decide to sell the house. After Father died, we tried to keep it up and to make our weekends there enjoyable for ourselves and our friends. But more and more often something turned up that made us unable to leave the city—a concert, the opening of a friend's exhibition, the beginning of what might turn out to be an interesting relationship. And while George and I never really thought much about money, we were discovering that the house was swallowing up a lot of it. One year we had to replace the entire electrical wiring, then dry rot got into the woodwork—all problems that left us dependent on local workers, who often abandoned us in the middle of a job because of personal troubles, with drugs or girl friends. So there was always a lot of unfinished work— one whole summer the floorboards in the drawing room were up, and for several weekends all the bathrooms were out of operation. The house was really draining away too much of our resources—that is, the money left to us by Father, which we had always thought of as inexhaustible; and probably it would have been, if either of us had had any sense of how to do anything with it except spend it.

There was also my ex-husband Teddy. While most of my lovers have turned out to be exploitive, this could not be said of Teddy. It is true that he was always asking for money, but it was usually for some grand idealistic scheme he had become involved in. His own needs were very small; when I first met him, he was living in an abandoned shed on someone's property, with no electricity or sanitation. Probably this was what attracted me—the romance of strolling through the woods, leaving behind Father's mansion, and then to encounter this youth in his simple hut among the trees. The very first time I saw him he was naked to the waist and chopping wood, or trying to (he wasn't good at it). We became friendly, and then more than friendly, and then I was pregnant with Lisa, so Father thought it best for us to get married. Everyone agreed that this was a good idea—even our mother, who was a terrible snob and might not have been expected to welcome a down and out son-in-law living in a hut. But Teddy was charming and goodlooking—fair and slight and full of romantic ideals. These qualities might not have appealed to Father, but what did appeal to him was the fact that, like Springlake and the furniture bought to go with it, Teddy was genuinely American. His family didn't go back as far as it was possible to go back in America—but still, they had been here since at least the eighteenth century, mostly in the South where they were ruined by the Civil War. His mother was from Louisiana, partly French and completely mad; when I first met Teddy, she was still alive but in a state asylum so that she couldn't attend our wedding. He didn't seem to have any other relatives, which to me was part of his attraction—the way he was so unencumbered, truly free to live for his ideals.

These ideals have taken him far out into the world and far away from our marriage. He has lived on the beach in Goa, entered a Tibetan monastery in Dharamsala, has exported second-hand clothing to poor people in Mexico. Off and on we lost sight of him—sometimes for years at a time when he was in far-off places. But when I needed a divorce to marry again, we managed to contact him and he was amenable and friendly about it, and very supportive when on his return he found me suicidal among the wreck of that second marriage.

Teddy showed up again at the time when George and I were deciding to sell the house. While sympathizing with our difficulties, Teddy tried to discourage us from taking this step. He had always liked the house, not so much for its comforts as for the opportunities it offered. And for Teddy this always meant opportunity to do good. Even when Father was alive and spending his weekends here, Teddy had proposed all sorts of plans. Once, at a difficult period of East European history, he had tried to persuade Father to throw the house open for some of the refugees who had sought asylum in the States. Father refused point blank: lighting one of his cigars, he said he was a refugee himself, came indeed from a long line of refugees, some of them kicked out from the very place that was now having its own troubles. Teddy perfectly understood—it was in his nature to see other people's point of view—but shortly afterward he came up with another proposal, this time to convert the house into a Performing Arts Center. Father waved that away too—he said he liked his performing arts at the Metropolitan Opera or at Carnegie Hall—but then Teddy urged my case: how it would give me the opportunity to practice my art in complete independence. Father still didn't like it; he came here to relax, not to have the place swarming with actors and other bohemians. But still, for my sake, he didn't want to say no outright, and sensing his hesitation, Teddy at once laid all sorts of plans to start us off.

I'm sorry to say that this scheme foundered before it had begun, and the reason was that Father simply couldn't stand Madame Voronska. Yet George and I admired her from the moment she swept into the house—and she really did sweep, her long gown trailing over Father's Persian rug, so that he had to lift her hem slightly with his walking stick. She took it as an act of gallantry on his part and thanked him profusely. I might add here that she never did anything other than profusely—whether thanking or greeting or, especially, complimenting people. This was her style, and I assumed it was Russian, though it turned out that she was originally from Kansas. It wasn't even clear that her name came from a marriage; she didn't mention a husband any more than other details of her past. Most of it she passed over with a sigh that alerted one to ask no questions. Yes, there was this sense of having suffered about her, though she was in those years a blooming youngish woman, with pink cheeks, golden hair, and big breasts. If she had dressed differently—that is, not in those flowing skirts and oversized jewelry—she might have been taken for a healthy farm girl. Although her professional name was Voronska, she liked her friends to call her Maggie.

Teddy had met her in New York where she had set up as a drama teacher and speech therapist. He told us that she had a reputation for discovering talent and developing it. When he first brought her to Springlake and introduced her to us, she held my hand in hers, which felt warm and plump like a little cushion. She pushed up my sleeve a bit as though she wanted to hold more of me: and she breathed a long "*Yes*" of recognition—which I took to be recognition of my talent and was thrilled. She greeted George in the same way and and was about to do so to Father except that he withheld his hand. Smiling, she turned from him and looked instead around the house; she seemed to be measuring the size of the rooms and the height of the ceilings, and again she breathed "*Yes,*" which made Teddy glow since it confirmed his promise that the place, along with my talent, held every potential for development.

After that first visit she came to see us often, and when there was some difficulty with the studio space she used in New York, she began to stay for a longer, indeed an indefinite period. She took over the upstairs front bedroom, which was usually occupied by Father's more important guests. When he brought them on occasional weekends, we informed her a day or two before he was expected, in order to give her time to pack. But he always sniffed the air, loudly demanding, "Who's been holed up in here?" and then pushed up the sash windows as high as they would go. He made no secret of his dislike of her, but she very sweetly continued to speak of him with great admiration for his qualities. She looked up to him—literally, for she was very short—and seemed not to notice his intense irritation. But we, who knew how choleric he could be, tried to keep her out of his way. Our weekends tended to bifurcate, with Father and his guests engaged in social and sporting activities, and the three of us—

George, myself and Teddy—clustered around Maggie, discussing our artistic plans. Only little Lisa—three years old at the time—ran freely between both groups, first to Father, to be lifted up and kissed by him and absorb his smell of cigars, liqueurs, and strong coffee; and then to Maggie who also kissed her, bending down to envelop her in her pungent perfume and smeary lipstick.

As soon as Father and his guests departed, Maggie moved back into the front bedroom and continued to fill our days with excitement. In recollection, these were our best years: Teddy and I were still together, we adored little Lisa, and George too was with us; and there was Maggie, still so blooming and yet also experienced and deeply intuitive. In the winter we sat around a big log fire, in the spring we walked among the daffodils spreading lakes of yellow in the grass. Blossoms flew through the air, there were fresh buds on the trees and nests of fledgling birds inside them. Little Lisa skipped in and out among us, crowned with a daisy chain that Maggie had knotted for her. I felt confident of my talent—of what I loved to do more than anything in the world. And Maggie reassured me—reassured all of us—that it was right to dedicate ourselves to expressing our deepest emotions through an art that she was there to foster. The house was in its pristine glory at the time and so were the grounds—even the apple trees had been sprayed and revived enough to put out blossoms for a shimmering two weeks— and Father was still there to keep everything in order and pay all the bills.

But one day Father arrived in the middle of the week. Looking grim, he called Maggie into his study and shut the door behind them. She went in smiling and she came out smiling; with unperturbed good humor, she packed her bag and got into the cab that Father had called to take her to the station. He left the same day without explaining anything to us; but just as he got into his car, he looked back at us and shook his head under the checked cap he wore for motoring in the country: "What's going to happen to you three when I'm no longer here? And what's going to happen to my sweetheart?" he said, including little Lisa in his despairing glance.

I suppose it could be said that his premonition turned out to be correct. Even before he died, our personal lives had begun to slide downhill. Teddy and I went our separate ways. He left for India to pursue a new path, and I continued to be sent to a few auditions until I became emotionally too distracted to show up for them. George had the same distractions, in his case even more turbulent since they were mostly with feckless boys who specialized in making men like him unhappy. Then the trouble with Lisa started in her adolescence and she had to undergo various treatments. But actually, with the help of her anti-depressants, she alone emerged intact from those years. She managed to complete her studies and to get a job with an investment firm where she proved to have been the only one to inherit Father's talent for business. George retreated into the smothering atmosphere of our mother's apartment, while I continued to live in the one Father had bought for me, though I had to resort to my lawyer's help to get my last lover out. Strangely, George had the same experience at Springlake—with a local boy whom he had moved into the house and then had to engage legal help to get him moved out. This was an additional reason for our decision to sell the house, though an unspoken one; for while I told George every detail of my unhappy affairs, he preferred to keep his to himself, and I respected his privacy.

So this was our situation when Teddy resurfaced and said we were crazy: "You want to sell *this* place? What about our plans for it, our Performing Arts Center?"

George smiled tolerantly: "Teddy dear, that was twenty-five years ago and we've moved on."

"Moved on? How can anyone move on from an immutable ideal?"

This was the sort of thing he was still saying, and meaning it. Teddy, though his adventures had been so much more far-flung than ours, was the one who had changed the least. George, now past fifty, had taken on the appearance and maybe some of the cautious character of a banker; he wore excellently tailored suits to disguise his too wide hips. Teddy had remained as thin as he had been when I had first seen him chopping wood outside his hut; in fact, he looked as though he might cheerfully go back to that hut, if there was no other place for him. True, in repose he could sometimes look sad, as sad as George did for all his appearance of good living. But Teddy rarely was in repose—his expression was very mobile and he never sat still for long.

He spoke of the Performing Arts Center as though no time had passed and no disappointment had come to him or to any of us. "And Maggie's come back," he urged. "She'll help us, she's wild to get going on something."

"Maggie!"

George and I hadn't thought of her in years; even the question of why Father had turned her out, though still un-answered, no longer interested us. "But where's she been?" Unlike Teddy, who had turned up every time he changed direc-tion in his various careers, she had disappeared from view.

Teddy couldn't tell us much, for he too had lost sight of her. She no longer went by her Russian name but was now called "Princess," having married an Arab with connections to some royal family. She had met him in Bombay—"How on earth did she get to Bombay?"

Teddy grinned in the sweet lopsided way he had when he

didn't want to admit something he had done. "Well yes, all right," he finally replied to a question we had not yet asked, "she went with me. But our paths soon diverged—my Lord, *how* they diverged!" For by the time he went up to his monastery, she had met and presumably married her Arab prince and was living with him in a double suite in the Taj Mahal Hotel.

"But now she's broke again, same as I am."

We were used to Teddy being broke—he was broke every time we met up with him, and every time we were glad to help out, with money and a place to live. It now appeared that Maggie also had no place to live, and while George and I were still silently communing with each other, wondering whether to ask her to come visit us in the house, Teddy turned over George's wrist to consult his Rolex: "Oh my—that late! I have to meet the train, Maggie's on it, she took the 10.45 from Penn Station."

Like Teddy, she had not really changed. She took my hand in hers in exactly the same way as she had done before, pushing up my sleeve a bit, and breathing, "*Yes.*" She was much stouter than she had been, which made her look even shorter, but her hair was still golden—*more* golden—her cheeks pink, her eyes a child's porcelain blue. And these eyes again took in our rooms, and when she walked around them, she seemed as before to be measuring them. There was something slow and solemn in her tread, with her small feet turned slightly outward; and also something compelling that drew one behind her, as though afraid of missing what she might do or say. She was in a long gown—was it the same one, twenty-five years later? I remembered how Father had lifted the hem of it to save his carpet. "God only knows what sort of filth she's been dragging around in," he had said.

Well, wherever it had been, she was now very tired, and for a few days she slept a lot. It turned out that not only was she tired she was also hungry, and she ate voraciously, greatly appreciating the gourmet dishes George prepared for her. Although George and I had not thought of the Performing Arts Center for years, now we seemed to be waiting for her to speak of it. Teddy warned us to let her rest first: "If only you knew how she needs it." He also warned us to say nothing of our intention to sell the house, because she would be so horribly disappointed: "And, poor soul, she's had enough of that in her life."

"Who hasn't?" George said. But he followed Teddy's advice and kept quiet, waiting for her to recover sufficiently to inform us of whatever plans she had for us.

On the following weekend, and before Maggie had quite finished resting, Lisa arrived, and far from keeping quiet about the sale of the house, she had come with the intention of discussing it. "Discussing" is the wrong word: like Father, Lisa was in the habit of letting us know her decisions after she had made them. She never called us by anything except our first names, Teddy and Helen; I suppose it was impossible for her to think of us as responsible enough to be anyone's parents, let alone hers. In some ways, her attitude to us, as well as to her Uncle George, was the same as Father's had been. But whereas Father had regarded our lack of practical sense with affectionate amusement, for Lisa it was a source of constant irritation. Whenever she came to see us, she had a frown—a frown of suspicion as to what we might have done or left undone. We, on the other hand, the three of us, greeted her with cries of joy and fussed around her in an attempt, usually futile, to make her pleased with us.

Maggie was overjoyed to see Lisa again, now grown up; and she fondled not just one hand but both of them in hers, while stepping back to study her. She retained her smile, but no doubt she was surprised by the way Lisa had turned out. It had been a surprise to all of us: as a child, Lisa had been, like Teddy, pale and delicate; and also like me who had grown up looking not unlike the American girls with whom Father had sent me to school. Father even had a theory that, if you were successful in America, your money would endow your daughter with the thin ankles and silky fair hair typical of an American girl of Anglo-Saxon origin. But he had to revise this theory later, when his granddaughter reverted to his own origins: Lisa was heavy, with very dark eyebrows that she refused to pluck and sturdy legs that she would not shave. The frown of displeasure with which she usually regarded us did not lighten her appearance: and under Maggie's scrutiny, it grew more intense and angry. She didn't withdraw but actually snatched her hands out of Maggie's warm and loving grasp.

Afterward, alone with us, Maggie said how thrilling it was that the child she had known so well and had crowned with daisy chains was now a serious career woman, in a business suit, wearing stockings and medium-heeled pumps. We eagerly supplied more details of Lisa's successes—how she had overcome the depression and eating disorder of her sophomore year to complete her course with honors; and while her entrance into the Wall Street firm may have been due to Father's influence, she owed her rise in it entirely to her own ability. Maggie kept nodding—yes yes yes, it was all very wonderful, and how even more wonderful that such a strong-minded, practical person should be there for the four of us; and here she smiled, looking from face to face and laying her hand on her embroidered blouse to include herself—all of us unworldly scatterbrains, bohemians, artists.

"Who the hell is she?" Lisa asked, as soon as she had come down from her room where she had changed into jeans and sweatshirt.

"Lisa! You remember Maggie! You loved her so! How you carried on when she left!"

Lisa had cried so much that Maggie had had to climb out of the taxi that had been called for her to kiss her once more. But now Lisa asked, "Why did she leave in such a hurry? . . . Did she have to leave? Did Grandpa make her leave?"

We had to admit that this was so, but when Lisa probed further, we dealt with her questions in the same way we had done for ourselves: "Oh you know how Father was—so suspicious, always putting detectives on people's trail. Probably when you're in business, dealing with huge amounts of money and whatnot, that's how you have to be."

"Yes," Lisa confirmed, "that's how you have to be . . . What did he find out?"

"Oh Lisa! Once you start digging up things about people, there's no end to it!"

Whenever Teddy came to the house, it was taken for granted that he slept with me in my bed. There was plenty of room in it; we were both small, and after a long absence Teddy was usually skinny. When he undressed, which he did very naturally with me, as I did with him, his ribs could be seen sticking out. That night I ran my hands over them and over his chest—as soft and smooth and hairless as it had been when I first saw him chopping wood. I said, "You've been starving again."

"A bit," he admitted.

Our hips and legs touched companionably under the sheet: "Teddy, how come you went to India with Maggie?"

He laughed: "It's a long story."

"Tell it. We have all night with nothing else to do." There was no sex left between us, only friendship, affection, maybe love of a fraternal sort.

The story wasn't all that long, or surprising. In those years many people went to India, for various reasons, most of them on some quest for a different mode of living, insight: whatever. "And she?" I asked about Maggie. "Was she on a spiritual quest too? Hard to imagine," I said, for Maggie was so very much of this world, of this earth, as could be seen in the way she trod it with her firm little feet.

"Quests, all quests," Teddy explained, "start with dissatisfaction, and Maggie was dissatisfied. Nothing had turned out the way she wanted; you know the feeling, Helly, we've all been there. Maybe everyone gets that way, once they reach a certain age, or stage in their pilgrimage. That's where we were, Maggie and I, when we caught up with each other again. I had already decided to go to India—I was doing a tremendous amount of reading, the Upanishads and so on: it's terrific stuff, Helly, one day I'll read them with you."

"You read them with Maggie?"

"No, I was having sex with Maggie. It was inevitable, Helly honey—you can understand that: I mean, *Maggie*. Even now."

"You mean now that she's so fat and sweaty?"

"Yes, isn't she?"

We both laughed but only briefly. He went on to tell me about their joint passage to India. They landed in Bombay where Maggie soon entered a circle of art-lovers and theater enthusiasts. Teddy too felt at home with them for a while; everyone was so sincere, and even the people with tremendously well-paid jobs in advertising or tobacco companies had these sort of deep Indian eyes that showed how they yearned for some other mode of being. They were also very hospitable, and Maggie and he enjoyed staying in their grand houses and flats overlooking the Arabian Sea. Maggie started theater workshops and elocution classes—all were eager to change their accents for the Tennessee Williams and Harold Pinter plays they staged. But Teddy decided that his journey lay beyond Bombay; he longed to go up into the Himalayas to breathe the pure air that suffused the ancient texts he loved. Maggie gave him money—"She's very generous when she has it, or has friends who have it"—though after a time his needs were fully met in the monastery he had entered. He missed out on Maggie's period with the Arab husband or lover, and by the time he came down from the mountains, she had gone from Bombay, no one knew where. He didn't catch up with her till just before he brought her to Springlake, having found her in New York, once more poor and on her own, though now a Princess.

George, who was a romantic, loved her title. He asked her about its derivation—the age and origin of the dynasty and so on—but she was as evasive about this as she was about other aspects of her past. We didn't hear much about the Prince either—just the sad smile she had for all lost souls, or all those who had treated her badly. "He needed a lot of help," was as far as she went. She and George became close and had long conversations together. I watched them walk up and down by the lake. It was George who did most of the talking, though sometimes they stood still and she talked to him, while he listened with lowered head like someone being told something for his own good.

On her first visit here twenty-five years ago, George had admired her as we all did (except Father), but they had had no particular relationship. Of course at that time our mother was still alive. Father used to say that Mother smothered George—and the word "smothered" suited the way they lived together among her outsize cushions and the arum lilies delivered every second day from her florist. There were times when George escaped: once, he took a house in Mexico for six months, to live with a friend. Our mother telephoned all the time, and then implored him to return home, if only for one evening to take her to the opera; and he did, because he loved the opera and to be seen with her, still at that time a platinum blonde and wearing her silver furs. But when he returned to Mexico, the friend had moved another friend into the house and there were dreadful scenes before George managed to evict them both and abandon the place and return to Mother in New York.

Maggie explained—in the same words she had used about her husband—that George needed help. She said this to me, to apologize for spending more time with him than with me. "But now you and I are going to have a real talk," she told me. She was sitting on a sofa, with her long skirt spread around her, leaving little space, so I sat at her feet, which did not quite reach the ground. When she smiled down at me, an attractive dimple appeared in her cheek; she looked both sexy and maternal, and I did want to talk to her, unburden myself in the way George had presumably done. Only of what? When my silence became too long, she laid her hand on my head as though to awaken something in me. Nothing happened, and I felt sad, remembering how we used to talk about the Performing Arts Center. Now none of us spoke of that any more, and there seemed to be no more plans.

After dinner on the day of her arrival, Lisa informed George and me that she had something to tell us. Although we weren't yet through with our dessert and coffee, we got up when she did. Maggie, with her immense tact, pretended not to notice her exclusion, modestly lowering her eyes to where she swirled the sugar around in her coffee cup. But Teddy followed us into Father's study where Lisa had led us. She stopped in the middle of the sentence she had already begun and looked at him with her bushy eyebrows raised. "I'm your father," he said and sat down with us, apologetically but as by right. Lisa could do nothing about it—nothing about him: he *was* her father, surprising as that fact never ceased to be.

With Father gone, it was Lisa who had assumed his authority. At first George had liked to think of himself as the head of the family responsible for all decisions. But after he had made such a mess (I'm sorry to say) of our financial affairs, Lisa took them away from him—just in time, before we lost more than we could have afforded. "George is an idiot," was her comment. Yet she continued if not to trust at least to respect him more than she did Teddy and me. It was easy to see why. Teddy and I have remained physically as slight as we always have been—and Lisa would say not only physically; but George's added weight has given him an air of authority that waiters and even cab drivers respond to. He has become a person of substance, who can't be ignored the way it is easy to pass over Teddy and me. So it was to her uncle George that Lisa unfolded her plan, turning to him as the only sensible person in the room.

It was about Springlake. Instead of selling the place, Lisa had decided to lease it to her own firm, as a retreat for its senior officers. She pointed out that it was ideal for this purpose, within easy reach of the city and of course fully and splendidly furnished the way Father had left it, with its closets crammed with linen, its sideboards with dinner services and silver. She would negotiate an excellent price, making it a source of income instead of a constant drain for the three of us. "For Uncle George and me, and Helen," she said—unnecessarily, for Teddy knew himself excluded. Father had made no arrangements in his will for Teddy—which of course was perfectly natural since our marriage had long since been dissolved. But it always made me feel guilty, so that, whenever Teddy needed money badly, it was a relief for me to give it to him. Now too I pressed his hand to assure him that, whatever might come to me from the lease, he would be entitled to a share of it. He returned my pressure; but I knew that it was not only about the money that we were in agreement. He was as distressed as I was by the decision Lisa was handing down to us; and I could see that George too was not happy about it, shifting uneasily in his chair from one big buttock to the other. Yet none of us made any protest—how could we? It was obviously the best possible solution for the place; and besides, Lisa always knew best and it was not for us to contradict her. So she said, "Good," into our silence, which she was entitled to take for assent. Then she too was silent for a moment, maybe waiting for us to thank her for the clever arrangement she had made. When we expressed no gratitude, she shrugged—the way she often shrugged at what we did or failed to do. "Typical," was all she said.

It was only when we were alone and in bed together that Teddy and I whispered our dissent. We decided to consult with George and made our way along the upstairs passage to his bedroom, tiptoeing past Lisa's and past Maggie's. But we found Maggie with George—in his stately four-poster in which one would never have thought to discover any woman. Maybe that was why neither of them was embarrassed; they were just two people, two friends, talking over a shared problem.

Maggie tried to console us: "George says you were going to sell the house anyway."

"That was before you came."

"*I!*" Maggie laughed—she had a surprisingly gruff laugh, also loud, which made us nervous that Lisa might hear. Maggie didn't lower her voice: "But I'm just one of your guests. *And,*" she pointed out, laughing again in the same way, "one whom your father personally turned out of the house."

"Maggie, really." Teddy was as annoyed as he could ever be. "That was years and years ago when we were all—when we all did such stupid things. Look at Helly," he said, smiling to lighten our mood. "She even married me."

We remained gloomy. George said, "The sort of people Lisa is bringing into the house never did a stupid thing in their lives."

"Businessmen. Stockbrokers. Rich people. What's wrong with that?" said Maggie. "Your father was a businessman. *And* rich."

"Oh, but Father wanted us to be different! He was so proud whenever I was in a play, he'd travel miles to see me; and George's poetry . . ." I trailed off and George waved it aside. "And he wanted us to start the Arts Center in the house, he would have given us any amount of money if we'd kept it up. If you'd stayed to keep it up for us." This was our first reference in years to that old idea.

And at once it sprang up again, alive: "Why shouldn't we?" We looked at one another, George, Teddy and I: "And now you're back," we said to Maggie.

But Maggie said, "Lisa doesn't like me."

"If she got to know you," George said slowly and weightily, "she'd realize that you were—what you are. A very sensible person. A very warm dear sensible person who would do wonders for all of us."

Teddy and I shared George's trust in her, though it was

difficult to say on what we based it. Seen objectively, Maggie was as much a failure as the rest of us. After having done so many things in her life in so many places and been both a Russian and a Princess, here she was dependent on us for a place to live—and for money too, though she was very tactful about asking for it. She never approached me directly but always through Teddy, who was not embarrassed about borrowing, either for himself or for others in need. And George probably didn't have to be asked, he was so used to giving it to people he liked and wanted to keep near him.

That same weekend we saw Maggie walking up and down along the lake with Lisa, in the intimate way she had done with George. She was talking, explaining—we assumed it was about the house and our plans for it. However, shortly afterward Lisa came storming into the drawing room where we were watching the sunset, as we did most evenings. "Have you been giving money to that woman?" she demanded. Maybe George and I looked as if we were about to deny it, so she continued, "She told me herself. Yes and how much, and I think you're both crazy and so is she. Would you believe it, she wanted it from me too, an outrageous sum, who the hell does she take me for!"

George and I exchanged looks of surprise but then he began to explain, "Well of course for the house—our plans for it—"

"Nonsense. It was for herself. She even told me in what name to make out the check—she calls herself Princess now."

"She *is* a Princess," George said.

"Yes and all sorts of other things too." Lisa bit in her lips as though too outraged to say anything further. But then she did: she told us everything that Maggie had told her. We were amazed because it was much more than she had ever told us. She had worked her way backward with Lisa—starting from the Arab prince, she told her about his Russian predecessor who had *pretended* to be a prince but had only been a small-time actor she had met on a film-set where she had been an extra, trying to make a little money to survive. Yes, she told Lisa, she had always had to struggle and so had her mother who had had to work at every kind of miserable job after Maggie's father had run off; and then Maggie herself had run away because of her stepfather's behavior with her while her mother was on night shift. She was only sixteen at the time, completely alone and helpless, so that just in order to eat and have somewhere to stay she had been led into doing things she should not have done, stupid things that sometimes got her in trouble.

"So now you know what Grandpa found out about her," Lisa said. "All he had to do was look up her police record." And she went on and on, telling us what Maggie had told her—her progress from the streets of America to those of the world. George and I listened, enthralled by what seemed to us a thrilling tale of adventure and daring; and while listening, we watched the sun sinking behind the trees and a flock of birds flying in the orange flood of its setting. But Lisa had her back to the window, and she told Maggie's tale not as the romance that we saw but as something sordid and shameful.

Lisa left for her office early next morning. She said she was returning the following weekend with some members of the board to view the house; and by that time, she threatened us, Maggie had better be gone. George and I were bewildered: why had Maggie done what she had, and instead of explaining to Lisa about our plans, had asked for money for herself? Maggie seemed under no suspicion that there was anything wrong or that she was again being turned out of the house, this time by Lisa. She had come to see Lisa off and had kissed her goodbye—"in the Russian way," she announced as she planted her lips on Lisa's. She had turned away before the car drove off, so she missed seeing Lisa wipe her mouth. Maggie was in a good mood, humming to herself, and she stayed in it day after day. She was very much at home by now, mostly lying on a sofa with her feet up, doing her nails, sipping a drink—comfortable little things of that sort. It would have been a pity to disturb her with our questions.

Instead we turned to Teddy. It was not the first time that George and I had brought our difficulties to him. Teddy was a very simple person, and he hadn't had much education either, unlike George and myself who had been sent to the best schools. But there was a sort of wisdom in Teddy—even Father had called him "a wise fool"—which had nothing to do with education or reading books, nor even with his experience of knocking around from place to place and living on nothing. It was more something inborn, maybe even part of his simplicity, which was a kind of selflessness in him. He had a lack of self-regard that made him as tolerant of others as most of us are of ourselves. It also gave him understanding—anyway, he understood Maggie: "She wanted Lisa to really know her, know what sort of a life she has had."

"Did she tell you any of that?" we asked Teddy.

"Some of it," Teddy said.

"About why Father had turned her out?"

"Not exactly, but I guessed. You see, that's what's so great about Maggie: that she's been right down in the dirt and then she's come up like some beautiful flower. Lotus, is it—that flower growing out of mud? And that's what she wanted Lisa to know, where she's been; you can't really appreciate what she's grown into if you're ignorant of that."

Certainly, George and I regarded her with new eyes. In comparison with her, how innocent, how blank were the two of us who had started off and continued with every material advantage; and how easy it had been, under these circumstances, to keep ourselves immaculate—well, at least socially. But even while respecting her more, I couldn't help thinking about the dirt Teddy had mentioned and to notice anew that the hem of Maggie's long gown was soiled from trailing on the ground; also—something I struggled to hide from myself— that she perspired heavily and did not, it seemed, bathe every day. I wondered whether George shared these unworthy thoughts; I was sure that Teddy did not, for he never thought ill of anyone.

Meanwhile the week went on, with Maggie as happy at the end of it as she had been at the beginning, and even more comfortable as though sinking deeper into our sofas. But George and I became more uncomfortable at the approach of the weekend, and with it Lisa's arrival. Of course there was no question of Maggie leaving, but we wished we had some explanation for Lisa as to why it was essential for her to stay. In any case, we longed to hear and talk more about our plans—about her plans for us, for our Center. The days passed and Maggie said nothing but continued to lie on her favorite sofa. She was now reading a great deal, turning the pages very quickly—as quickly as she ate her meals, which she always finished long before we did, especially George who masticated very thoroughly. We circled around her, waiting for the right moment to raise our subject, but she remained entirely engrossed in her book.

At last, the day before Lisa's expected arrival, in desperation almost, we stood before her. I cleared my throat nervously; George, just behind me, cleared his: "Maggie, we must talk."

She looked up, took off the glasses she wore for reading, and gazed at us in kind inquiry.

"The house," I said.

"Our Center," George said.

"Oh yes," she agreed, "we must have a chat about it all. There's plenty of time—Art is short but Life is long—no the other way around, I always get mixed up." She gave her gruff laugh and put on her glasses to continue reading, only looking up briefly to tell us, "This is such marvelous stuff—in translation unfortunately but still—" She turned another page.

"Lisa is arriving tomorrow."

"I know it," she said. "I'm well aware of the fact." This time she didn't bother to look up; what she was reading at that moment was so astonishing that she made an exclamation point in the margin with the little gold pencil she had borrowed from me.

But next morning she was transformed, and so was the house. She rallied our staff—a local widow and her teenage daughter—and hired extra help to scour and polish everything in sight. She herself whirled around the kitchen, where all the pots and pans had been taken out, and she stirred in one after another and added and tasted and added some more. When everything was ready—the house gleamed and the staff were exhausted—she went up to change and did not come down until Lisa and her board members drove up. It was only when they were already in the entrance hall that she began to descend the stairs, and before she had quite reached the end of them, she stood still and called down, "Welcome!" Everyone looked up to where she stood—in a brand-new lilac gown, hung about with jeweled chains and an aigrette in her gilded hair. "George," she murmured, so that he stepped forward and held out his hand to help her down the remaining steps: "The Princess," he introduced her. Smiling, she stretched out her hand to the guests—four burly American stockbrokers, who might have kissed it, had they known how.

She had laid the table in the dining room for what she called luncheon, with every refinement that Father had purchased and that we ourselves had never put to use. She had also selected the wine from Father's cellar and knew how to discuss its merits with Lisa's guests, who had all made enough money to be connoisseurs (one of them had a little diary in which to check up on the vintage). It was only after serving coffee and liqueurs that she started her tour of the house, flinging open doors and explaining all its beauties. We followed in her wake, astonished by her expertise. During her stay here, she must have studied every ornament on every mantelpiece and estimated the worth of all the pictures and lamps and carpets and hangings that Father had bought. And after the house, she led them around the grounds—the apple orchard and the fishpond and the stone fountain with benches around it; and if there had been time, she would have taken them for a row on the lake where two majestic swans were floating as if specially placed there. The guests—and they seemed to be hers now—had to get back to the city, though she made them promise to return the following weekend and bring their wives; and before they left, she insisted on giving them tea, which she served the way she had drunk it in her days as a Russian, with lemon and a spoonful of raspberry jam.

Later, when they had gone, Lisa thanked her. "My pleasure," Maggie said—and she kissed Lisa, again in the Russian way and this time Lisa did not wipe her mouth. For the rest of the weekend, they spent most of their time with each other. It appeared they had a great deal to talk about, and when Lisa left on Sunday evening, she hardly nodded to us but told Maggie that she would be back with all the details.

What details? We could only ask this question of each other, for the moment Lisa left, Maggie again became engrossed in her reading.

Teddy was hopeful: "Don't you see? They're planning for our Center."

"Then why don't they tell us?" George said. "Why don't they talk to us? Why doesn't she?" His large face sagged, the way it did when he was disappointed in love. I saw him wandering by the lake where he had walked arm and arm and deep in conversation with Maggie. He was always alone now—at night too, for she no longer came to his bedroom, he admitted, and when he tried to go to hers, he found the door locked.

Teddy attempted to keep up our spirits; he was absolutely sure that all Maggie's plans were for us. She was bringing Lisa around too, he promised, that was why she had been so nice to Lisa's colleagues; and maybe even—maybe, he smiled at this possibility on his rosy horizon—she was working to collect funds from Lisa's firm to make the structural additions and alterations that would be necessary to turn the house into our Center. "It's going to cost," he warned us. He led us from room to room, pointing out their potential, and in the process made us as excited as himself. We longed for Maggie to join in our tour and unfold her plans, which were sure to be even grander than ours. But she continued to lie on the sofa, rapidly turning the pages of some great work of literature.

Lisa didn't wait till the weekend—she came in the middle of the week, and now it was she and Maggie who walked around the house discussing alterations. At the weekend more board members arrived, and some of them brought their wives; they swarmed all over the place, each one with a different suggestion for changing it. No one seemed to know who we were, and Lisa and Maggie were too busy to introduce us. It was late at night when the visitors left, and by then the two of them were exhausted and went straight to bed. George said we must wake them at once and demand an explanation. There was this about George—his usual self was mild and amenable, but when roused he took on some of Father's imperious personality. Teddy and I had to pull him away from Maggie's locked door and persuade him to postpone his confrontation till next morning. At last he went off to his room, stamping his feet the way he had done as a small boy to show displeasure.

Teddy and I sat up in bed discussing the situation. It was nice to have him with me, comforting me, but I was sorry to think of George brooding alone, so we went in to him. We found him sitting up in bed, with the tufts of hair that still ringed his head standing up on end in anger. "It's outrageous," he said the moment we entered. But he seemed glad to have us there to share our troubles. He was cynical, bitter. "Are you still trying to tell us that she's arranging for the Center? For us?" he asked Teddy.

"Well," said Teddy cautiously, "she's arranging for something."

"Yes, for herself. No doubt she's had a lot of practice at that."

Teddy had to agree but couldn't suppress a smile, probably thinking of all Maggie's shifts and arrangements, or at least those he himself had witnessed when they had traveled together.

"Tomorrow she packs her bags," George said.

Teddy and I cried out in protest—as we had done when Father had issued the same order, more or less in the same words. "But Lisa is so fond of her!" we had protested to Father, reminding him how Maggie let little Lisa play with her lipstick and try on her high-heeled shoes. Now too Teddy and I said, "What about Lisa?"

"I don't know why we have to be so scared of Lisa," George grumbled.

But he knew as well as we did that it was *for* her that we were scared. He had lived through her teen years with us and had tried to help her. We had all had psychological problems ourselves, but Lisa's took a different turn from any of ours. I always thought of mine as part of the creative life: for how can one hope to recreate emotional and psychological turmoil unless one has lived through it, every bit of the way? So I regarded my sessions with my various analysts—I changed them in the course of my various phases—as not so very different from the theater workshops I attended. But Lisa's relationships with her analysts were more clinical, requiring medication and a spell in a sanatorium. Teddy had assured us that it was nothing terribly serious—"Not, oh my Lord no, like my poor Mama who was completely—oh my Lord yes," he concluded in sad remembrance of his mother. And it was true—when Lisa grew older and gained confidence through her competence in business, and with the help of her anti-depressants, she became calmer, steadier. But we remained nervous about her condition, handling her with care and avoiding any kind of confrontation that might upset her.

We didn't hesitate to confront Maggie, though we waited until Lisa had gone back to New York. Maggie took us on with a sort of sweet candor, denying nothing. She confirmed that she had undertaken to help Lisa convert the house into a retreat for businessmen, for their conferences, their stag parties, and for family holidays taken in rotation. She explained to us the structural changes that would have to be made—she had it all at her fingertips. Of course it would take a lot of organization; and Lisa had asked her to stay on and oversee that stage as well as afterward to be a resident manager, a permanent hostess responsible for the smooth running of the retreat and the entertainment of the guests.

"And you've agreed?" George said. He had listened to her in deadly calm, rocking backward slightly on his heels and with his arms folded.

"I could hardly refuse dear Lisa," Maggie smiled.

"No. But what a pity that you won't be here. What a pity that you're going up this minute to pack your bags and get out of here. This minute! Pronto!" he cried—up to then he sounded as calm as Father had done but on this last he became more the George we knew.

"Goodness. How excitable you are," Maggie said with a kindly smile. "But that's you—the three of you. It's your artistic temperaments, of course; your charm . . . Don't be silly, George. I can't go."

"Oh you can't?" George said. "Then let me show you how you can."

"Yes—and what about Lisa when she comes back on Saturday? With her Big Boss—the one who has to take the final decision. Lisa is trembling in her shoes. She tells me he's a hard nut to crack and will need some very delicate handling."

"Oh yes: handling. That's your specialty," George said, bitter now more than angry.

"So you think that's what I've done? Handled you?" And she looked around the three of us before continuing: "Don't forget I've been turned out of this house and yet I came back. Why, why do you think I did that, swallowed my pride—oh yes, I have some, but I swallowed it and came back. Why? Why did I do that? For whose sake, George?"

My poor sweet brother: he was shuffling his feet, he was embarrassed, he was shy. Yet he wanted to speak, to answer her, have a scene with her the way he used to with our mother. Teddy and I wandered away to leave them alone, and when we all met up again, a reconciliation had taken place. It was how his scenes with our mother had also regularly ended.

That night George came into our bedroom and said, "She's right, you know."

He began to explain to us whatever it was she had explained to him. He appeared so convinced that we pretended to be so, too. Yet I was sad and wanted to ask, "What about everything she promised us?" Although I didn't say it out loud, George answered as if I had. He assured us—as she had assured him, and she had had all day to do it—that what was being planned was more important than our ambitions. It was—"*Real*, Helen. Real life . . . Life is long and Art is short."

"No, George. It's the other way around: *Ars longa, vita brevis est.*"

"Thank you, Helen. I was made to learn Latin too, and much good it did either one of us . . . Don't you see that what she's made of herself is much greater than anything we could do? Art is imitation but she's real. The real thing. Everything she's done."

"Everything?"

"If Father were alive today, he would be grateful for what she's doing—for Lisa, for the house, and for us."

I said, "All right, George." I didn't want him to say any more, and I think he was glad not to have to.

Next day he and Maggie were both on the phone a lot with Lisa, discussing the work to be done for the weekend. Some tasks were allotted to Teddy and me: George had unlocked the silver, which hadn't been used for a long time, and Teddy took pride and pleasure in making it shine. He tried to dispel my misgivings for the coming weekend—"You'll see: it'll all work out fine. They'll come, they'll have a good time, Lisa will be happy, and then we can start in on *our* plans." I believed him, I too wanted to work for the success of the occasion and make Lisa happy.

But the day before her arrival George came to us and told us that we were not to put ourselves out in any way. When we protested that we were ready to work as hard as everyone else, he became uncomfortable, apologetic: "Everyone knows how you detest these kind of social things; and why wouldn't you—you're artists, after all."

"What about you, George?" I asked.

"Oh I," he said. "I. Everyone's given up on me long ago."

"I haven't," I said. "Teddy and I believe in you."

He kissed us both, thanked us. Then he added, "But you know, she's right."

"She? You mean Maggie who's always right?"

"She wants to help me. She already has—opening my eyes to a lot of things. To myself, principally."

Teddy and I both wanted to contradict whatever it was he had been told about himself, but he repeated, louder, "No she's right! All my life I've been self-indulgent and fooled myself. Just because I have money doesn't mean I can write or paint or whatever." He went on quickly, "I'm talking about myself, Helen, not you. Of course you're an actress and you have to continue to work at it and not let anything take you out of your way. That's why it's better for you not to be here tomorrow; so you won't be taken out of your way."

"Maggie says it's better?"

"And Lisa. They both believe in you, that you'll do something. They don't think I will, so they say I should stay here and be—sort of—you know, the master of the house, if that doesn't sound too ridiculous. But they think I have something of Father, some of his personality. Maybe because I'm kind of fat," he said humbly.

"You're not fat, George. You're big, like Father was."

"Maggie wants me to start smoking cigars. She's ordered Father's brand, Cuban or whatever. I told her I can't stand the smell let alone smoke them, but try telling Maggie anything she doesn't want to hear." He chuckled, but then went on very seriously: "And just think—Helen! Teddy! Think how happy it would have made Father to see his house and everything in it used the way he wanted it: guests having a good time, eating and so on—that's what he bought it for; that was his dream." George's eyes shone, so it appeared to be his dream now too.

At the edge of the property there was a little clapboard house—not much more than a hut—where the gardener used to stay when we had one. It had been empty for years and was full of spider webs, and raccoon and other droppings. Teddy tried to clean it up for the two of us to stay in that weekend; he succeeded to some extent—anyway, we had no choice, since all the rooms in the house were taken. Lisa and her party arrived early in the morning, and then throughout the day more and more cars drew up and businessmen and their wives and children came tumbling out in holiday mood. It was a glorious day, drenched in sunshine and blue sky, and a garden party had been arranged with a buffet table in a tent as yellow as the sun. Guests strolled around the lawns or sat on the white Victorian benches and were sprinkled by cool drops from the fountain. Some of the wives had brought parasols, and from a distance these looked like flowers bobbing around. Swings and other amusements had been hired and the voices of chirping children carried all the way to the gardener's hut where we sat. We could also hear the string band that Maggie had engaged to play summer tunes.

It was too far for us to make out any faces, but Teddy had his binoculars, which I had given him on his last birthday to help him identify birds. He adjusted the view, and we focused on Lisa. She was wearing a new dress, a floral silk that Maggie had helped her choose; she looked prettier than we had ever seen her—she had had her hair done, and her skin toned, and her face glowed with inner satisfaction. When we had gazed our fill at her, we focused on Maggie, trailing over the lawn in her gown. She darted from person to person, smiling here and smiling there, with some curt commands to waiters and other hired help. She moved so swiftly that George, whose arm she was holding, had difficulty keeping up with her. He appeared as contented as Lisa, and looked very impressive in his naval blazer and panama hat. He was trying to smoke a cigar, which was making him cough.

The party went on for a long time, till the shadows lengthened and the sunlight dimmed. The voices of the children became plaintive, and while the band went on playing, their tunes were slower now and somewhat melancholy. Teddy and I continued to sit on the wooden bench outside our hut. Some melancholy had crept into our mood as well—at least into mine, and Teddy set out to dispel it. He had plans for us, which would take us away from the house to wander he wasn't quite sure where and to do he wasn't quite sure what; but it would all be new, a fresh start for the two of us. Teddy was even thinner now than when I had first seen him chopping wood, and his face was very pale and lined. I was glad to think that he would never have to shift and starve again. There would be my money now for us both, including my share of the lease of Springlake (which George would scrupulously pay). I don't know if this occurred to Teddy—no, I'm sure it did not. He was only thinking of everything we were going to do, he and I, and he talked as he used to, breathless with enthusiasm; and at that moment I loved him as I used to, and when I kissed him, I found his lips as fresh and sweet as I remembered them.

5
A Choice of Heritage

DURING THE latter half of the last century—maybe since the end of the 1939 war—nothing became more common than what are called mixed marriages. I suppose they are caused by everyone moving more freely around the world, as refugees or emigrants or just out of restless curiosity. Anyway, the result has been at least two generations of people in whom several kinds of heritage are combined: prompting the questions "Who am I? Where do I belong?" that have been the basis of so much self-analysis, almost self-laceration. But I must admit that, although my ancestry is not only mixed but also uncertain, I have never been troubled by such doubts.

Many members of my father's totally English family have served in what used to be called the colonies—Africa or India—where they had to be very careful to keep within their national and racial boundaries. This was not the case with my father: at the time of his marriage, he had been neither to India nor to Africa. He met my mother in England, where she was a student at the London School of Economics and he was at the beginning of his career in the civil service. She was an Indian Muslim, lively, eager, intelligent and very attractive. She died when I was two, so what I know of her was largely through what my aunts, my father's sisters, told me. My father rarely spoke of her.

It is through my Indian grandmother, with whom I spent my school holidays, that I have the most vivid impression of my mother. This may be because my grandmother still lived in the house where my mother had grown up so that I'm familiar with the ambience of her early years. It was situated in the Civil Lines of Old Delhi, where in pre-Independence days British bureaucrats and rich Hindu and Muslim families had built their large villas set in large gardens. This house—with its Persian carpets spread on marble floors, pierced screens, scrolled Victorian sofas alternating with comfortable modern divans upholstered in raw silk—seemed to me a more suitable background to my mother's personality, or what I knew of it, than the comfortable middle-class English household where I lived with my father.

My grandmother, no doubt because of her royal style, was known to everyone as the Begum. Every evening she held court in her drawing room, surrounded by male admirers who competed with one another to amuse her and light the cigarettes she endlessly smoked. Her friends had all been at Oxford or Cambridge and spoke English more fluently than their own language. Some of them had wives whom they kept mostly at home; one or two had remained bachelors—for her sake, it was rumored. She was long divorced and lived alone except for her many servants, who were crammed with their families into a row of quarters at the rear of the property. They too vied with each other to be the closest and most important to her, but none of them ever captured this position from her old nurse, known as Amma. It was Amma who had learned to mix the Begum's vodka and tonic and to serve their favorite drinks to the visitors. During the hot summer months the household moved up into the mountains where there was a similar large sprawling villa and another set of admirers—though they may have been the same ones, except that here they wore flannel trousers and handknitted cardigans and came whistling down the mountainside carrying walking sticks over their shoulders like rifles.

There was one visitor who was different from the rest. His name was Muktesh, and when he was expected, she always gave notice to the others to stay away. He had not been to Oxford or Cambridge, and though his English was fluent, it sounded as if he had read rather than heard it. But his Hindi was colloquial, racy, like a language used for one's most intimate concerns. He was known to be a first-class orator and addressed mammoth rallies all over the country. He was already an important politician when I was a child, and he could never visit the Begum without a guard or two in attendance (later there was a whole posse of them). He was considerate of his escort, and Amma had to serve them tea, which was a nuisance for her. Tea was all he himself ever drank, pouring it in the saucer to cool it. He had simple habits and was also dressed simply in a cotton dhoti that showed his stout calves. His features were broad and artic-ulated like those of a Hindu sculpture; his lips were full, sensual, and his complexion was considerably darker than my grandmother's or any of her visitors'.

He was definitely not the Begum's type yet she appeared to need him. She was very much alone and had been so for years. At the time of Partition she was the only one of her family to stay behind in India while the rest of them migrated to Pakistan; including her husband, who became an import-ant army general there and also the butt of many of the jokes she shared with her friends. They had been separated since the birth of my mother, one year after their marriage. He took another wife in Pakistan, but the Begum never remarried. She preferred the company of her servants and friends to that of a husband.

And Muktesh continued to visit her. He made no attempt to be entertaining but just sat sucking up his tea out of the saucer; solid, stolid, with his thighs apart inside the folds of his dhoti. There were times when he warned her to make arrangements to go to London; and shortly after she left, it usually happened that some situation arose that would have been uncomfortable for her. It is said that Hindu-Muslim riots arise spontaneously, due to some spark that no one can foresee; but Muktesh always appeared to have foreseen it— I don't know whether this was because he was so highly placed, or that he was exceptionally percipient.

I always enjoyed my grandmother's visits to London. She stayed at the Ritz and I had tea with her there after school. Sometimes she had tickets for a theatre matinee, but she was usually bored by the interval and we left. Amma accompanied her on her London visits and splashed around in the rain in rubber sandals, the end of her sari trailing in puddles. She grumbled all the time so that the Begum became irritated with her. But actually she herself tired of London very quickly, though she had many admirers here too, including most of the Indian embassy staff. After a time she refused to leave Delhi, in spite of Muktesh's warnings. "Let them come and cut my throat, if that's what they want," she told him with her characteristic laugh, raucous from her constant smoking. And instead of coming to London, she insisted on having me sent to her in India for the whole of my school holidays.

If it had not been that I missed my father so much, I would have been happy to stay in India for ever. I felt it to be a tremendous privilege to be so close to my grandmother, especially as I knew that, except for me, she really didn't like children. I learned to light her cigarettes and to spray eau-de-toilette behind her ears. In the evenings when the friends came I helped Amma serve their drinks, and then I would sit with them, on the floor at the Begum's feet, and listen to the conversation. When she thought something unfit for me to hear, she would cover my ears with her long hands full of rings.

I felt totally at home in Delhi. I had learned to speak the Begum's refined Urdu as well as the mixture of Hindustani and Punjabi that most people use. All this came in very useful in my later career as a student and translator of Indian literature. I ought to explain that my appearance is entirely Indian, with no trace of my English connections at all. None of them ever commented on this but accepted it completely—accepted *me* completely, just as I was. And so did the Begum, though I bore no resemblance to her either, or to anyone in her family of Muslim aristocrats. Both she and my mother were slender, with narrow fine limbs, whereas I have a rather chunky build and broad hands and feet. My features are Hindu rather than Muslim—I have the same broad nose and full lips as Muktesh. My complexion too is as dark as his.

I always took it for granted that it was me whom Muktesh came to visit. It was to me that he mostly spoke, not to the Begum. When I was small, he always brought me some toy he had picked up from a street vendor, or made the figure of a man with a turban out of a handkerchief wound around his thumb to waggle at me. At least once during my stay, he would ask for me to be brought to him, and the Begum sent me accompanied by Amma, who became very haughty as if she were slumming. At that time Muktesh had the downstairs part of a two-storey whitewashed structure with bars on the windows. He had three rooms, two of them turned into offices where his personal assistant and a clerk sat with cabinets full of files and a large, very noisy typewriter. The remaining room, where he ate and slept, had the same kind of government-issue furniture standing around on the bare cement floor. The walls were whitewashed, and only the office had some pictures of gods hung up and garlanded by the personal assistant. Muktesh himself didn't believe in anything like that.

However, he did have a photograph of Mahatma Gandhi in his own room, as well as that of another Indian leader—I believe it was an early Communist who looked rather like Karl Marx. Muktesh explained to me that, though he had never met them, these two had been his political inspiration. At the age of sixteen he had joined the Quit India movement and had gone to jail. That was how he had missed out on his higher education and had had to catch up by himself; first in jail, where other political prisoners had guided him, and afterward by himself with all these books—these books, he said, indicating them crammed on the shelves and spilling over on to the floor from his table and his narrow cot: tomes of history, economics, and political science.

It was through his interest in these subjects that he first developed a friendship with my mother. Since I only knew her through the memories of other people, it has been difficult for me to grasp the dichotomy between my mother's appearance—her prettiness, her love of dress and good taste in it—and the fact that she was a serious student of economics and political science. Even after her marriage to an Englishman, the development and progress of India remained her most passionate concern. Outwardly, she became *more* Indian while living in England; she wore only saris or salwar-kameez and her Indian jewelry. She often attended functions at the Indian embassy in London, and it was there that she first met Muktesh. He was a member of a parliamentary delegation—I don't know the exact purpose of their mission, something to do with tariffs and economic reform, anyway it was a subject on which she had many ideas. Perhaps her ideas interested him, perhaps she did, and he invited her to discuss them with him when she next came to Delhi. Since she was there at least once and usually several times a year to be with the Begum, she was soon able to take him up on his invitation.

They must have had long, intense discussions—about public versus private ownership, economic reform and the expansion of social opportunities. From what I have heard of her, I imagine her doing most of the talking, eager to impart all her theories. She walks up and down with her gold bangles jingling. Getting excited, she strikes her fist into her palm, then laughs and turns around and accuses him of laughing at her. And perhaps Muktesh really does smile—his rare, sweet smile with slightly protruding teeth—but mostly he remains massively still, like a stone sculpture, and only his eyes move under his bushy brows to watch her. This is the way I imagine them together.

I must have been seventeen or eighteen when the Begum first spoke to me about my mother and Muktesh. She came out with it suddenly, one day when he had just left us—as usual with all his security personnel and the convoy of jeeps that accompanied him everywhere (there had been too many assassinations). "In those days," the Begum said, "he didn't need to have all those idiots hanging around drinking tea at our expense. He and she could just meet somewhere—in the Lodhi tombs, by the fort in Tughlakabad: God only knows where it was they went to be together." This was my first intimation of the affair—I had had no suspicion of it, but now the Begum spoke as if I had known or should have known all along:

"One day I cornered him—after all he's a sensible person, not like your poor mother . . . I told him, 'You know how we live here: how everywhere there are a thousand eyes to see, especially when it's someone like you . . .' He waved his hand the way he does when he doesn't want to hear something, like you're a fly he's waving away . . . 'Yes,' I said, 'it's fine for you, but what about her? And her husband, the poor chump? And this one—' meaning you, for you had been born by that time (a very ugly baby, by the way) . . ."

After this warning, Muktesh seemed to have made some attempt to stay away from my mother. It was hopeless, for when he didn't show up on the morning of our arrival from England, she commandeered the Begum's car and drove to his flat and made a scene there in front of his staff. So even if he had been serious about ending the relationship, he never had a chance, and they went on even more recklessly. When he gave a speech in Parliament, she was up in the public gallery, leaning forward to listen to him. She gatecrashed several important diplomatic parties, and if she had difficulty getting in somewhere, she had herself taken there by the Begum, for whom all doors always opened. Consequently, the Begum told me with amusement, a new set of rumors began to float around that it was she, the Begum, who was having an affair with Muktesh. There were all sorts of allegations, which were taken up and embellished by the gossip magazines; and not only those published in Delhi but also in Bombay and Calcutta, for he had already begun to be a national figure. His appearance in these pages was an anomaly—especially in the role of lover, at least to anyone who didn't know him.

One year, when my mother had come to India with me, my father took leave for a week or two to join us. He gave no notice of his impending arrival beyond a sudden cable announcing it. My mother took it straightaway to her mother: "Do you think he's heard something?" The Begum shrugged: "How could he not? The way you've been carrying on."

But if he had, it seemed he gave no sign of it. I have tried to give an impression of Muktesh, and now I must try to do the same for my father. If you think of the traditional Englishman—not of this but of a previous era—then you would have some idea of my father. He was tall, upright, and athletic (he had been a rowing blue), with an impassive expression but an alert and piercing look in his light blue eyes. During weekdays in London he wore a dark suit and his old school tie and always carried a rolled umbrella against the weather; in the country, where we spent most weekends, he had a baggy old tweed jacket with leather elbow patches. He smoked a pipe, which he did not take out of his mouth when he cracked one of his puns or jokes, at which he never smiled. He wanted people to think he had no sense of humor. Otherwise he did not care what anyone thought of him. He cared for his duty, for his work, for his country—for these he had, as did Muktesh, a silent deep-seated passion; as he had, of course, again like Muktesh, for my mother.

His time in Delhi was largely spent playing cards with the Begum or doing crosswords with her, finishing them even more quickly than she did. Unfortunately it was the middle of the hot season and, perspiring heavily, he suffered horribly from prickly heat. Like myself in later years, my mother loved the Delhi heat—the mangoes, the scent of fresh jasmine wound around one's hair and wrists, and sleeping on string cots up on the Begum's terrace under a velvet sky of blazing stars. My father was very interested in early Hindu architecture, like the amphitheater at Suraj Khund, but on this visit it was much too hot for him to go out there. Since this was a private visit, he did not think it proper to call on any of the senior government officials—his opposite numbers here, whom he knew quite well from their visits to London. I think he himself was relieved when the two weeks were up and he could return home. The Begum said she certainly was; as for my mother and Muktesh, they never told anyone anything, but no doubt they were glad to have these last few weeks of her stay to themselves. She and I followed my father to England in September, after the monsoon, but we were back again the following January. She could never stay away for long.

During the months in between her visits to India, my mother led a very conventional life at home. I have this information from my father's two sisters ("your boring aunts," the Begum called them). My mother seemed to have charmed them, and they gave the impression that she too had been charmed—by England, by their way of life: the family Christmases, fireworks on Guy Fawkes night, the village pageant of medieval English history. In her country garden she gathered plums and apples from her trees and bottled jams and chutneys; although in India she had, like her mother, hardly been inside a kitchen, she learned to roast, to baste, to bake, with a rattle of the gold bangles that she never took off. Both my aunts had very happy marriages and took their devotion to their husbands too much for granted to feel the need to demonstrate it. But my mother couldn't do enough to show her love for my father. When he came home from his long day at Whitehall, she would make him sit by the fire, she would light his pipe, and bring his slippers and whatever else she had heard or read that English wives did for their husbands. "No, let me," she would say, "let me," when he protested, embarrassed at having such a fuss made over him.

Yet her visits to India became more frequent, and longer. He made no objection, perfectly understood that she wanted to see her mother, was homesick for India. How could she not be? And he was grateful that, while she was with him in England, she gave no indication of her longing for that other, different place. During her absence, he wrote her long letters—which she did not open. The Begum kept them, also without opening them, so I have been the first person ever to read them.

And having read them, I can understand my mother's reluctance to do so. They express him completely, his personality shining through the small neat civil service script and his longing for her through his deadpan account of domestic trifles: how Mrs. Parrot the housekeeper and the milkman had got into a fight over some cream that had prematurely gone off; how he had tried to have a quiet dinner at his club but had been caught by a very tiresome chap who knew all about India; how he had rescued a sparrow from the jaws of next door's cat and had given it water and a worm till it was calm enough to fly away . . . Each letter said not once but several times that everything was fine, he was muddling through, and yes of course not to think of coming home till the Begum had perfectly recovered from her bout of flu.

My mother died of cholera—not in India but in England, where this disease had been wiped out so long ago that English doctors failed to identify it in time. One of my aunts took me away to her house and kept me for several months until my father was able to have me back. Although my aunts loved to talk about my father's happy marriage to my mother, they never spoke of her death and how it affected him. It was as if they didn't want to remember their brother—so calm, so anchored—as he was during that year. They were reluctant to return me to him but he insisted. He never re-married. My mother's portrait, painted by an Indian woman artist, hung in our living room in the country, an enlarged photograph in the flat in town. In the former she is pensive, with sad eyes, in the latter she is smiling. Perhaps the painter wasn't very good but, to me, the portrait conveys less of her than does the photograph. Or it may be that to smile—to be lively and alive—was more characteristic of her, of the way that people told me that she was.

Muktesh never married, which is very unusual for an Indian. He spent his days and nights—he rarely slept more than a few hours—in the service of his party, of parliament, of politics. When he said he had no time to get married, it was true. He rarely managed to get to see his old mother in Bikaner. He used to tell me how she despaired at his lack of a wife: "And when you're sick, who will look after you?" He would smile and point upward in a direction he didn't believe in but she did. He didn't get sick but he didn't get married either. Year after year, more and more desperately, she found brides for him—girls of their own caste, modest, domesticated. But he was used to my mother who argued with him about subjects of vital concern to them both. When they took long car rides together, he whiled away the time composing poetry; she worked on her PhD thesis that she didn't live to present.

Their last long car ride together was to Bikaner. He had to go to a meeting of his election committee in the district from which he was returned year after year. They traveled for a day and a night, across long stretches of desert. They got very thirsty and drank whatever was available—the glasses of over-sweet and milky tea that Muktesh was so fond of, or buttermilk churned out of fly-spotted curds. Once, when there was nothing else, they made do with stagnant water out of an old well. Neither of them ever had a thought for disease, she out of recklessness (the Begum called it stupidity), he out of his optimistic fatalism.

I have only his account of that day in Bikaner, and he was

busy till it was time to set off again the same night. All day he had left her in his mother's house, with no comment other than that she should be looked after. His mother was used to his arrival with all sorts of people and had learned to ask no questions. She was an orthodox Hindu, and for all she knew he might have brought her untouchables, beef-eaters; but from him she accepted everything and everyone. By the time he had finished his meetings and returned to the house, he found his mother, and mine, sitting comfortably together on a cot in the courtyard, eating bread and pickle. The neighbors were peering in at them, and his mother seemed proud to be entertaining this exotic visitor—her fair-complexioned face uncovered and her vivacious eyes darting around the unfamiliar surroundings, taking everything in with pleasure the way she did everywhere.

Even well into her sixties, the Begum continued to be surrounded by admirers. They came in the evenings and had their usual drinks, no longer served by Amma but by Amma's granddaughter. Otherwise everything was unchanged—including the Begum herself who still chainsmoked. At home she was always in slacks and a silk shirt and her hair was cut short and shingled; but there was something languid and feminine about her. She relaxed in a long chair with her narrow feet up and crossed at the ankles while she joked and gossiped with friends. They had two favorite targets: the crude contemporary politicians who amassed fortunes to cover their fat wives and daughters with fat jewels, and the wooden-headed army generals one of whom had long ago had the misfortune to be her husband. "What did I know?" she still lamented. "My family said his family was okay—meaning they had as much money and land as we had—and at seventeen I liked his uniform though by eighteen I couldn't stand the fool inside it."

It was only in Muktesh's presence that she was not exactly tense—that would have been impossible for her—but less relaxed. By this time he was very important indeed and his visits involved elaborate security arrangements. He himself, in handspun dhoti and rough wool waistcoat, remained unchanged. Whenever I was there, he came as often as he could, mostly very late at night, after a cabinet meeting or a state banquet. The Begum, saying she was very tired, went to bed. I knew she didn't sleep but kept reading for many hours, propped up by pillows, smoking and turning the pages of her books. She read only male authors and went through whole sets of them—ten volumes of Proust, all the later novels of Henry James, existentialist writers like Sartre and Camus whom everyone had been reading when she was young and traveling in Europe, usually with a lover.

Muktesh talked to me about the reforms he was trying to push through; he spoke of dams, monetary loans, protest groups, obstructive opposition parties and rebels within his own party. He spoke to me of his concerns in the way he must have done with my mother; but his mood was different. When he was young, he said, he could afford to have theories, high principles. Now he didn't have time for anything except politics; and he drew his hand down his face as if to wipe away his weariness. But I felt that, though his mind and days were swallowed up by business and compromise, the ideals formed in his youth were still there, the ground on which he stood. And I might as well say here that, in a country where every public figure was suspected of giving and receiving favors, his integrity was unquestioned, unspoken even. It wasn't an attribute with him, it was an essence: *his* essence.

Whenever Muktesh came on one of his official visits to

London, he took off an hour or two to be with me and my father. We usually met in an Indian restaurant, a sophisticated place with potted palms and Bombay-Victorian furniture and a mixed clientele of rich Indians and British Indophils who liked their curry hot. In later years, there were always several security people seated at a discreet distance from our table. My father was the host—he insisted, and Muktesh, though always ready to pick up bills and pay for everyone, gracefully yielded. He and my father were both generous in an unobtrusive way, and it was not the only quality they shared. My father was as English as it was possible to be and Muktesh as Indian, but when I was with them, I felt each to be the counterpart of the other. Although they had many subjects of interest to them both, there were long silences while each prepared carefully to present a point to the other. They both spoke slowly—my father habitually and Muktesh because he was expressing himself in English, which he had first learned as a teenager in jail. Muktesh ate rapidly the way Indians do, neatly scooping up food with his fingers, and he was already dabbling them in a bowl with a rose-petal floating in it, while my father was still following his Gladstonian ideal of chewing each mouthful thirty-two times. Occasionally they turned to me, in affectionate courtesy, to ask my opinion—as if I had any! I wasn't even listening to their conversation. I knew nothing of the checks and counterbalances between an elected government and a highly trained bureaucracy—one of their favorite subjects—but I loved to look from one to the other. The evening always ended early because Muktesh had to return to the embassy to prepare papers for his next day's meetings. When we got up, so did the security personnel. Several diners recognized Muktesh and greeted him, and he joined his hands to them and addressed them by name if he remembered them, which as a good politician was surprisingly often. A splendid doorman bowed as he opened the doors to the street for him. "Aren't you cold?" I asked Muktesh, for even in the London winter he wore the same cotton clothes as in India, with only a rough shawl thrown over him. He laughed at my question and drew me close to say goodbye. I could feel the warmth of his chest streaming through the thin shirt and his strong heart beating inside it.

In what was to be the last year of his life, he wanted to take me to meet his mother. But when I told the Begum of this plan, she shouted "No!" in a way I had never heard her shout before. She lit a new cigarette and I saw that her hands were shaking. She always hated to show emotion—it was what made her appear so proud and contemptuous; and it was also one of the reasons, a physical as well as emotional distancing, that she didn't like to be touched. I knew that her present emotion, the mixture of anger and fear, was a revival of the past, when my mother had returned from her visit to Bikaner—travel-stained, exhausted, and with the beginning of the sickness that would flare up on her journey back to England. I tried to reassure the Begum: "You know Muktesh doesn't travel that way any more—" for nowadays there was always a special plane and a retinue of attendants.

But it wasn't only fear of the journey that upset the Begum: "God only knows where and how she lives."

"Who lives?"

"And she must be ninety years old now, probably can't see or hear and won't care a damn who you are or why he brought you." Although this was her first reference to the possible alternative of my begetting, she cut it short, dismissed it immediately—"Well go then, if that's what he wants—but if you dare to eat or drink a thing in that place, I'll kill you." She had a way of gnashing her teeth, not with anger but with a pain that was as alive now as it had been these last twenty years. Or if there was anger, it was at herself for not being able to hide it, or at me for witnessing even the smallest crack in her stoical surface. "All right," I said, "I promise," and I kissed her face quickly before she had time to turn it away.

But my other grandmother—if that was what she was—liked to touch and to be touched. She sat very close to me and kept running her fingers over my hair, my hands, my face. Muktesh had gone off to his meetings and left me with her the way he had left my mother, without explanation. Or had he told her something about me—and if so, what had she understood that made her so happy in my presence? We were in the same house and courtyard that my mother had visited, maybe even sitting on the same string cot, now several decades older and more tattered. Many years ago, to save his mother from the usual lot of a Hindu widow, Muktesh had taken a loan to buy this little house for her. The town had grown around it, new and much taller buildings pressing in on it so that it seemed to have sunk into the ground the way she herself had done. As the Begum had guessed, she was almost blind. The iris of one eye had completely disappeared and with the other she kept peering into my face while running her fingers over it. At the same time she tried to explain something to me in her Rajasthani dialect that I couldn't understand. When at last Muktesh reappeared, with all his convoy of police and jeeps, she chattered to him in great excitement. Muktesh agreed with what she said, maybe to humor her, or maybe because it really was true. When I asked him to interpret, he hesitated but then said—"She's comparing you with all her female relatives—your nose, your chin—and your hands—" she had taken one of them into her own bird claw and was turning it over and over—"your hands," Muktesh said, "are mine." "Bless you, son, bless you, my son!" she shouted. He bent down to touch her feet, and the people watching us—neighbors had crowded every window and some were up on the walls—all let out a gasp of approval to see this son of their soil, this great national leader, bow down to his ancient mother in the traditional gesture of respect.

A university press had commissioned me to bring out a volume of modern Hindi poetry. When I asked Muktesh if he had any poems for me to translate, he smiled and shook his head: what time did he have for poetry? Yes, sometimes on his way to a rally, he might compose a little couplet to liven up a speech. That wasn't poetry, he said, it was propaganda, not worth remembering. And there was nothing else, nothing of his own? He shrugged, he smiled—perhaps he might at some time, in the heat of the moment, have scribbled something of that kind, maybe in a letter long since destroyed.

I knew that the Begum had some of his poems addressed to my mother. On my return from Bikaner, when it was time for me to return to my teaching job in London, I asked her to let me take those poems with me. At first she hesitated— I knew that it wasn't because she was reluctant to part with them, but that she didn't want me to take them away to England, where they did not belong. I had heard some of what he called his "propaganda" verses—I had seen him write them, in a car while being driven from one election meeting to another. They were all poems with a social theme, humorous, sarcastic, homely, with a sudden twist at the end that drew amused appreciation from his audience. His poems to my mother were completely different, yet if you knew him—really knew him—it was recognizably he who breathed in them. And not only he but poets dead a thousand years, for he belonged to their tradition of Sanskrit love poetry steeped in sensuality. As they did, he loved women—or rather, a woman: my mother, and with her the whole of life as he knew it, the whole of nature as he knew it, with its sights and smells of fruits and flowers. He wrote of the rumpled bedsheets from which she rose as the Sanskrit poet did of the bed of straw on which his mistress had made love; of the scent of her hair, the mango shape of her breasts. He longed to bed and to be embedded in her. His love was completely physical—to such an extent that it included the metaphysical without ever mentioning it, the way the sky is known to be above the earth even if you don't look up at it.

After his retirement, my father lived mostly in the country, and I joined him whenever I was free from my teaching assignments. It was there that I did most of my translations, and I was working on one of Muktesh's poems when the news of his assassination reached us. My father heard it on the little radio he kept in the kitchen. He came upstairs to my bedroom, which was also my study. He sat on my bed, holding his pipe though he had knocked out the ashes before coming upstairs. I turned around to look at him. At last he said, "Muktesh." He was not looking back at me but out of my bedroom window. My father's eyes were of a very light blue that seemed to reflect the mild and pleasant place where he lived. Instinctively, I put my hand on Muktesh's poem. It was too alive and present with a passion I wanted to hide from my father, who had all my life hidden his knowledge of it from me.

My next visit to India coincided with the beginning of the trial of Muktesh's assassins, and every day the newspapers carried front-page stories of it, together with their photographs. Muktesh had been shot at the moment of leaving a function to commemorate the birth date of Mahatma Gandhi. Although one man had carried out the murder, it had been planned by a group of conspirators, including two accomplices ready to do the deed if the first one failed. They were all very young men—the youngest seventeen, the eldest twenty-four—all of them religious fanatics with tousled pitch-black hair and staring pitch-black eyes. If they had been older, their views might have been less intransigent, might even have approached Muktesh's tolerance (for which they had killed him). And as I read about their lives—their impoverished youth, their impassioned studies, their wild ideas—I felt I could have been reading about the young Muktesh himself. And when I went to court to look at his assassins on trial for their lives, it could have been the young Muktesh standing there—as defiant as they, fierce and fervent in dedication to a cause.

But I knew there were other sides to him. I knew it from translating his poems, and also from his manner with me. He was as reticent about my singular appearance as the rest of my family. Yet sometimes he gazed into my face the same way my father did—I knew what for: for some trace, some echo of something lost and precious. He never found it, any more than did my father, but like him Muktesh showed no disappointment. Instead he smiled at me to show his pleasure in me, his approval, his acceptance, and his love, which was as deep in his way as my father's was in his, and the Begum's in hers.

She of course had her own manner of showing it. Ever since I was small, she insisted on going through my hair with a louse-comb. "Your mother used to come home every day from school with something," she told me to explain this practice, which she extended right into my adult years. I think she just liked to do it, it made up for the other intimate gestures that she so disdained. My hair is coarse and deeply black, quite different from my mother's, so she said, which had been silky like the Begum's own and with auburn lights in it (by this time the Begum's had turned almost red with constant dyeing). Sometimes, while wielding her louse-comb, she commented, "Who knows where you got this hair—it's certainly not ours." After a while she said, "But who knows where anything comes from and who the hell cares." Tossing the comb to Amma's granddaughter with instructions to wash it in disinfectant, she began on a story about her ex-husband's family. His mother, my great-grandmother, had for thirty years had a wonderful cook:

"A very lusty fellow from Bihar who made the most delicate rotis I've ever eaten. Which may have been the reason why my mother-in-law couldn't bear to be parted from him for a day. *May* have been—and anyway, who knows what goes on in those long hot afternoons when everyone is fast asleep."

"Did this cook have hair like mine?"

"I couldn't tell you," she said, "he always wore a cap." She made a face and then she said, "Ridiculous," dismissing the whole subject as unworthy of further discussion.

6
My Family

MY DAUGHTER Debbie is a very boastful mother. She is proud of both her children and finds it difficult to accept that one should be doing better than the other. She thinks, or pretends to think, that it is Andrew's fault he is not as successful as his sister, and that if only he tried harder, he would catch up with her. Debbie sees it as her duty to make him try harder, just as she did when he was at school. Andrew never did well at school—to others Debbie asserted it was because he was too brilliant, but at home she gave him no peace. From early morning, even before she had had her coffee and when she is never at her best, she nagged him about his poor performance. This had the effect of making him stop going to school altogether, and for a period, when he was about fifteen or sixteen, no one knew where Andrew was, or with whom. It was also the period during which his tastes were formed, among the group of older men who took him along to their studios and favorite downtown bars and uptown gallery openings. In this milieu Andrew grew up quickly—fortunately with a basis of seriousness that made him recognize his need for education.

At around twenty he entered architecture school but soon turned to other arts, several of them. He wrote the libretto for an opera and also, during a time when his best friend was a dancer, he designed and painted the scenery for a ballet. His next best friend was a young Indian film-maker who introduced him to Indian music, and together they made a documentary about a famous shehnai player. Debbie became very proud of him and her attitude to him changed completely. Now she would never appear before him in the morning the way she used to, shrew-like in curlers, but always careful to be her best, in appearance and manner. She even, when she remembered, developed a special way of speaking to him, more thoughtful and refined, with her lips slightly pursed. She soon reconciled herself to his homosexuality, confiding to her friends that it was inevitable among those of an artistic temperament. She also claimed that the frequency and strength of Andrew's passions came from her, and although I never contradicted her, I knew it was not so. In her relationships, Debbie has always managed to remain in control, of herself and of circumstances, indignation overcoming pain, and marital settlements compensating for unsatisfactory husbands. But nothing could compensate Andrew for what he suffered; and Debbie herself marveled at the all-consuming extent of his passionate relationships which obliterated everything else in his life, including whatever work he was engaged on.

His sister Veronica—fifteen years younger and from a different marriage—is the opposite. She is cool and detached in all her relations—part of the fascination that has made many people fall violently in love with her, and probably also the cause of her emotional pull with audiences. She is a film actress, at twenty-four already famous; whenever there are articles about a new generation of young stars, her name is prominent among them. She has beauty, of course, but she carries it lightly, as lightly as she moves, her long dress, which seems to be always the same, clinging to her like a length of cloth thrown carelessly over a classical statue, not to hide but to outline her figure. Her dark hair is long and free and sometimes she winds it into a knot to put it out of the way. But

I need hardly describe Veronica, her picture is often in magazines, and sometimes on billboards ten feet tall.

Although Veronica has received training from some notable acting coaches, including a famous and tyrannical eighty-year-old actress from Berlin, it was always, and still is, her brother to whom she turns for guidance. This began in her childhood, when she was six and Andrew twenty-one. Whatever he happened to be doing became her interest too—painting, poetry, even music, though she wasn't musical. Every morning he would assign a poem for her to learn, and when he came home—this might not be till next morning—she would be waiting to recite it for him; and however exhausted he might be (for God only knew where he had been all night), he would patiently listen to her recital; and then she waited, and when he said, "Very good," she let out her breath as if she had been holding it in anticipation of that moment. When she discovered her talent for acting, he encouraged and began to train her. He introduced her to classical drama, and at sixteen she was declaiming Phèdre to him while he, book in hand, modulated her like an orchestral conductor. Sometimes, to raise her pitch of passion, he accompanied her with tremendous chords struck on the piano. Or later, when she had begun to act in summer stock, he would take the text and read it with her. One of their favorites was Chekhov, especially *The Seagull*. She was Nina—and who more apt to play that youthful bird of hope aspiring to art and greatness?—while he read the young poet already doomed to failure. Only at that time there did not seem to be a breath of failure on Andrew, no diminution of his brightness. Except for the thinning of his hair, he was the same he always had been, slender and quick, with quick green eyes.

Are suicidal tendencies hereditary? I know that from the 1890s onward they were almost endemic in many assimilated

German-Jewish families, including my own. Much later, I tried it too, and so did Andrew, who cut his wrists. Debbie found him and took him to the hospital, and afterward she kept him by her at home, nurturing him more than she had been able to when he was small and she had been going through her first divorce. The idea of someone relinquishing life has remained utterly incomprehensible to her. Although both I and my husband Gerd had come to New York as refugees, Debbie acquired all the attributes of a standard American optimism. She grew up in our West Side apartment, among our books of philosophy and theology, many of them in German, our collection of classical records, our copies of Renaissance sculptures and Impressionist paintings, as though it were a suburban villa with a two-car garage and breakfast of pancakes and orange juice. She was rosy and blonde, healthy and pretty, with a meticulous taste in bobby sox and saddle shoes and boys as popular as herself, whom she cheered at their football games. Now, in middle age, Debbie is still an all-American type. She has been married three times, divorced twice, and is in the process of another divorce. She lived for a while in California—this was when she was married to a studio executive—and now has moved back to New York on the Upper East Side, across the Park from my apartment. Through all her vicissitudes, she has retained her faith in her ideal, which is success in the sense of a complete development of one's human potential. Whether it is being the most popular girl in the class, or having the best decorated house, or the most highly promoted husband, she regards falling short of it as a sin of character that has to be atoned for and corrected by psychoanalysis, psychotherapy, medication, divorce, diet, or whatever else her friends have tried out and recommended.

"I'm not an intellectual," she used to tell us. As a girl, this difference from her parents was a matter of pride to her; but now, in view of how her children have turned out, she has become defensive about it. She still looks as far from an intellectual as she did as a bobby-soxer. She has remained blonde—though her hair is more a burnished gold now and built up to give her more height, for she has always been short. She has also tended to be plump, but since menopause she has had a real weight problem, compounded by what she calls her eating disorder, as a result of which she is always nibbling something. She has not changed much from when she was a little girl in short frocks with a frill at the hem. She is still wearing a version of those frocks, though a more expensive one, from Bergdorf's or Saks designer salon. However, she has now largely disowned her teenage tastes in favor of her children's. She has become interested in modern art and dance. She has also tried to read some of the books Andrew has bought for Veronica, and she likes to scatter them around where her friends can see them. These books, with their bright jackets and photographs of the author on the back, look more accessible and attractive than those she grew up with in our apartment, or saw at the Hochs.

Debbie did not know until she was middleaged that Gerd, my husband, was not her father. Although in earlier years he and I had discussed the pros and cons of enlightening her, we kept postponing it and finally I did not tell her till after he died. It had turned out to be impossible while he was still with us and so devoted to her. He had delighted in all her plump, blonde, feminine ways, had loved to watch her ice-skate and tap-dance and whiz around on roller-blades, as graceful and vivacious as he was slow. After being a wonderful father to Debbie, he became a devoted grandfather to her children, who often stayed with us, and for long periods of time. Andrew and Gerd used to go for walks together by the river or sit in a park while Gerd told him about the planets and all the world's natural and architectural wonders. He took him to the Metropolitan museum and led him, week by week, month by month, from the Egyptians to Cézanne (which was as far as Gerd himself had got in the history of art). By the time Veronica arrived, fifteen years later, Gerd had had two of his many operations and was mostly in a wheelchair, so they sat together in what had been his study, he with a tartan blanket on his lap, and she on the carpet with her frock drawn over her knees, listening to the English children's classics he had already read first to her mother and then to Andrew. My apartment is full of photographs of Gerd with our two grandchildren.

Gerd and I had been fellow students at Freiburg, and when that was no longer possible, in New York. Indeed, we had known each other as children and had been brought to play together under the supervision of our nannies while our mothers went to their coffee parties and matinée concerts. Later we arrived about the same time in New York and joined the same course under the famous Professor Hoch. During the first year or two in New York we formed a small, rather inward-looking group with other refugee students. Although some of us came from Germany and others from France or Italy, we had more in common with each other than with the American students— if only that we were adrift from the solid land of our own background and social assumptions, and our language. None of us was entirely fluent in English, though we were determined to become so and spoke nothing else, in a variety of accents and sometimes with comical mistakes. (Gerd and I never spoke German together again, till Debbie came, and then only when we didn't want her to know something.) As children, Gerd and I had often played at weddings together, and although later we did not speak about marrying, there remained an assumption between us. But it was a point of honor among all of us to leave each other perfectly free; we were quite smug about it. I know that Gerd never availed himself of this arrangement, not even during those times when I did—and there were occasions, before Professor Hoch, when I could not resist trying out an affair with another of our refugee friends. I was adventurous at the time, afraid of missing something, ready to be stimulated by others or to take the initiative myself. But I really liked Gerd better than any of the other students.

Gerd and I were married when I was six months pregnant with Debbie. We hosted a noisy, highspirited wedding lunch in our favorite Irish pub-style restaurant with a bar and checked tablecloths, and our friends' epithalamia made jocular reference to the maternity smock I was wearing. No one except Gerd and I knew that Debbie—only we thought she was a boy, to be called David—was not Gerd's child. Professor Hoch was not present; we all stood in too much awe of him to invite him to such an intimate occasion. It was very different with Gerd, when he in due course became a professor of philosophy and attended all his students' celebrations. Hoch never hid his low opinion of his students— donkeys he called most of them, always in German, "*Esel.*" But Gerd not only loved, he esteemed his young people. I have seen him with tears in his eyes over a paper he was marking, only to have a student get something right; and it was the student he praised and admired, taking no credit at all for his own part in this achievement.

I still live in the West Side apartment that the University allowed us to keep after Gerd's retirement and even after he died. It is an enormous, cavernous place, and our furniture is also dark, standing on claw feet and embellished with carved clusters of grapes. We had bought it all second-hand, as soon as we could afford it, and in imitation of the furniture we had known in our childhood. On one of my birthdays Gerd gave me a chandelier. All through our years here we filled the place with friends and students. There were always house-guests, and people eating, either at impromptu meals or helping themselves out of our large ice-box. We also took every excuse for a party—New Year's Eve, birthdays and anniversaries, Easter and Passover, we didn't care what it was as long as people ate and drank and talked through the night. None of us was very tidy and there were books lying about, and records, used cups and glasses, and suitcases belonging to whoever happened to be staying. We often forgot to turn off the lights, so that lamps and the chandelier burned all through the day.

The Hoch family lived in an almost identical West Side apartment, and their furniture was as ponderous as ours. Only theirs was not second-hand, for though they were also émigrés, they were voluntary ones who had been able to bring their possessions with them. Professor Hoch left Germany with the first dismissal of his Jewish colleagues and in protest at everything that was happening there. In New York they continued to live in a solid bourgeois German way. Frau Professor Hoch—Hedda—ran a strict and orderly household, to the exclusion of all dust and noise. Their two sons—tall, tow-headed—were models of respect and good behavior. Students were not encouraged to visit, except once or twice a year when there was a gathering at which Hedda played Bach two-handed clavier with her son. Only the Professor's favorite students were invited; Hoch made no pretense of not having favorites. I was always included, Gerd only rarely.

The front rooms in the Hoch apartment were given over entirely to the Professor, one to his study and two to his library, which also acted as a buffer against any disturbance from the rest of the household, or from the world in general. All domestic activity, including that of his growing sons, was confined to the other rooms leading off the long corridor. Here Hedda, with the help of her German maid, not only kept her house swept and polished but also acted as her husband's secretary. Like the rest of us, she too had been a student of philosophy, *his* student, when he was a young docent at Weimar, so she was able to deal with his notes, to type and arrange them. There was no room for another study, and she had to make use either of the kitchen or the dining table, quickly clearing them as needed. It was always Hedda who answered the telephone, or who opened the door for the Professor's visitors—of course none of us came without an appointment, arranged by herself, but nevertheless she scrutinized us before leading the way past the umbrella stand to the study door; and it was she who opened the door and then stood aside to let us pass—as stern, tall, and stiff as a Turkish dragoman, and as full of the pride of office.

I entered of course with a beating heart—I was the only graduate student of our year whose thesis he was personally supervising, for he had allowed me to research into some minor aspect of his own work. This was like being allowed to splash in the shallows of his oceanic thought. Oceans and mountains—those were the images I associated with him, the only concepts large enough to contain my impressions of him. He overwhelmed me, not only mentally but by his physical presence. He was a big, heavy man, with a square stubbled skull; he had fought in the First World War and still looked more like a Prussian officer than a philosophy professor. When I sat close beside him at his massive desk, I hardly dared glance into his face. I kept my eyes lowered to the papers before us, so that all I could see of him was his waistcoat. He always wore a three-piece suit, with an oldfashioned gold watch-chain stretched across his stomach that rose and fell with his breathing. His breathing was heavy and became more so as his excitement mounted with his mounting thought; sometimes he seemed even to be panting like one who had climbed to a height never yet attained by man. I too felt my heartbeat increase with excitement as he spoke to me of his central idea (the reversal from the Western tradition of technology, or the excarnation of spirit into matter, to the Hindu concept of *Maya*, the incarnation of matter into spirit). And once, as if unable to sustain himself in those regions without some physical support—we are, after all, all of us here, still within the limits of our bodies—he put his hand on the back of my neck and said, "My little one." He said it in German— "*Meine Kleine*"—which was always for him the language of his earthly desires. He shut his eyes when he kissed but I kept mine open. It was the only time I really dared to look into his face. He was in his fifties then, with heavy jowls that were always somewhat red and raw from the close shave he gave himself with a huge open razor. He was greatly attached to this razor and took it with him on all his travels; when I began to accompany him, I too became familiar with it, and with the leather strop on which he sharpened it and the shaving brush that looked like horsehair but was actually beaver.

After my marriage and Debbie's birth, my work with Hoch continued, for I had begun to act as his English translator and had become indispensable to him. I had nowhere to leave Debbie, so I always brought her with me, slung in a carrier on my back, along with my notebooks. The Hoch boys took charge of her and loved playing with her, all three of them fair-haired and rosy-cheeked. Hedda Hoch was also fond of Debbie and gave her cookies and milk in the kitchen and stroked her blonde curls, confiding that she had always longed for a little daughter. I could never make out how much Hedda knew or suspected. She appeared in complete command of her thoughts and feelings, as she was, of course, of the whole situation. It was she who slept beside him in their double bed brought from Germany; and it was she who cooked and served his meals and cleaned his house (on Saturdays, her major cleaning day, I had to get to his study by stepping over rolled-up carpets and past Hedda and her maid wielding mops). In the summer the whole family left for their vacation in the Swiss Alps; they always stayed in the same hotel, where months before Hedda had reserved his favorite rooms.

Hedda lived on into her nineties and continued to work with me on the Hoch papers. Debbie often met her, but she remembered Hoch, who died when she was five, only as a threatening presence behind a forbidding closed door. The revelation that he was her father excited her perhaps more in its novel and scandalous aspect than the fact of her descent from one of the twentieth century's greatest philosophers. She was also thrilled suddenly to acquire two half-brothers, and as a result sought out the two Hoch boys whom she hadn't seen for maybe forty years. One was an engineer in Pittsburgh, the other a partner in a Washington law firm, both settled with their families in households as orderly as the one they had grown up in. They did not welcome Debbie's revelation, nor I suspect Debbie herself, hung around with costume jewelry and trailing her aura of adulteries and divorces— anyway, she came back disgruntled and seldom mentioned these half-brothers again except to say that they had inherited not one jot of their father's genius, which had, she insisted, passed in a pure straight line through her to her own two wonderful children.

※

Although she has inherited nothing from Hoch except his height—she is much taller than anyone else in our family—there is something about my granddaughter Veronica that is reminiscent of him. This may be her complete absorption in what she is doing—that is, in her career, her stardom—and, with it, her absorption in herself. One has the feeling with her, as before with Hoch, that nothing can really touch her; that within herself, in her own sense of dedication, she is inviolate. The word ruthlessness attached itself naturally to Hoch, and so it does to Veronica. Yet her attitude to her own success is one of apparent indifference. She seems to regard it as her natural due, something she was both born for and works for, with all the strength of her ambition. And she has ambition—she is tense with it, always has been since childhood, even before she knew what she was going to do. Hoch's ambition was to reach the loftiest heights of thought; hers is to star in what she herself sometimes characterizes as "dumb little movies": in both cases the result has been a complete and utter singlemindedness. Not that there is any resemblance between Hoch's personality and his granddaughter's. He was ponderous, and it is her business to enchant. I think of her returning to us from one of her trips—and she is often away, on location, or in Beverly Hills, where she has recently bought a house. She comes to us straight from the airport, either to my apartment or to Debbie's, wherever Andrew happens to be living at the time. Someone else has taken care of the luggage, so she arrives unencumbered—light as a butterfly in her simple frock and as if borne to us on a spring breeze (actually it was a chauffeur-driven limousine). Though protesting that she is dead tired from all that sitting on a horrible plane, she always has an amusing story to tell of something that happened to her en route, and from there other amusing stories—an encounter, maybe, with a stupid journalist—which she tells with great skill and that make us laugh. She is full of news and excitement—*her* news, *her* excitement, she doesn't expect us to have any. Aroused by what she is telling us, she can't sit still but strides up and down our living room, tall, slender, and strong: and her presence among us is wonderful—it is like having a goddess, a Diana or Ceres, descend into the middle of one's little life, irradiating it for a moment with her splendor.

Ever since his last project—a semi-fictional documentary about a dancer who had died of Aids—failed to take off for lack of funds, Andrew has started nothing new. He has had projects fail before, in his various fields of interest, and usually, after a period of depression, has been ready to start on something new. It was always a pleasure to see Andrew with a new involvement, whether in work or love—and often the two coincided. Unlike Veronica, Andrew is short like the rest of us, and although he never played any sport, he used to have a firm, compact body like an athlete; for years he retained a boyish quality, as if he had only just started out and was unmarred by experience (this air of innocence remained even after his suicide attempt). But the other day I encountered him in the long corridor of my apartment when he was coming out of the toilet and zipping himself up. He wasn't wearing a belt and his stomach, which had once been so flat, drooped over his pants; he was in slippers and was shuffling a bit and was suddenly—this seemingly perennial boy—a middleaged man.

The reason he is staying with me is because of his mother. Debbie is the same with him now as when he wasn't doing well at school and she thought she could improve him. And he reacts now as he did then, by running away: this time not into the world at large with strangers but home to my apartment, where he stays all day in the library with the door shut.

When Debbie comes, and she comes all the time, he locks it while she stands outside and shouts at him through the door. He doesn't answer and there is a terrible silence.

I must have seen more than one production of *The Seagull* over the years, but I remember it chiefly from Andrew and Veronica's readings, when she played Nina and he Konstantin the young poet. In the last scene of the last act Konstantin locks himself up in a room, and the last line of the play is "Konstantin has shot himself." Not that Andrew has a gun, or would know what to do with it if he had one. But living alone with him, I'm in constant anxiety, which I dare not share with Debbie. She has high blood pressure, and when she gets worked up, her face swells under her golden hair and a pulse beats dangerously inside her rosy rouged cheek. After shouting at Andrew through the closed door, she turns on me: "What's he doing in there?" she says, as though his locking himself away were my fault.

Andrew was the person most strongly affected by my revelation that not Gerd but Hoch was his grandfather. When I look back, I realize that it is from that time—which was also the time of his last project—that Andrew seems to have lost heart. It is as if the shadow that great men tend to cast on their descendants has caught up with Andrew at the age of forty. He has been trying to read Hoch's works; that is what he has been doing behind that closed library door. I have many editions of those works and in many languages; the English ones are mostly by myself, though I have not yet translated the last two volumes he published. They are impossibly difficult, for right till the end—even after his stroke—Hoch was penetrating into seemingly inaccessible areas of thought. Now a younger person than I will have to try and render them into English and so complete my life's work. Hoch's earlier phases have by now been absorbed into philosophical tradition and are thus accessible to those with the right training and background. But Andrew's interests have always been in the arts, never—maybe in reaction to Gerd and myself—in philosophy; and without a thorough academic grounding in both Western and Eastern thought, Hoch cannot be understood. When Andrew and I are alone, he has sometimes asked me to explain, and this is not at all difficult because, like all truly universal thought, the gist of it is simple to formulate. But to follow the steps— the long ascent—by which this peak has been reached, is not possible without many years of study and discipline. I go into the library and I stand behind Andrew where he sits hunched over Hoch's tome, which must seem like a tomb of cognition to him; he is running his hands through his sparse hair, and when I touch his shoulder, he looks up at me and his intelligent green eyes are dimmed with reading and incomprehension.

When Debbie asks me what he is doing, I say, "He's reading."

"What's he reading?" When I tell her, she snorts and says, "We've had enough of all that." Secretly I agree with her. Although it has been my whole life, I don't want it for Andrew any more than Debbie does. At least once a day she comes around to my apartment; she knocks on the study door in vain and then stands there and looks at me. She has always been jealous that Andrew should so often prefer to be with me, his grandmother, instead of with her, his mother. But now, standing outside the locked library door, we are united in our anxiety for him. I don't tell her about *The Seagull*, but my fear is so great that I now confess to her a secret Andrew and I have shared for the last two years. Ever since my heart attack, I have been on strong medication; Andrew goes regularly to the pharmacy to have the prescription refilled and to get whatever else Dr. Stein has ordered for me. When Andrew returns from the pharmacy and gives me the pills, I thank him and wait till he is out of the room. Then I open my chest of drawers and add the new phial to my little collection, hidden at the back of a drawer under some clothing I no longer wear. Sometimes I take out one little phial after the other to read the labels. Once it happened that Andrew came back to tell me something, and when I turned around, I saw him standing in the doorway and looking at me with a grave expression in his eyes. I shut the drawer and he went away without saying anything. Now, when he brings my prescription, he hands it to me with that same grave expression and walks away quickly, respecting my secret.

But now it is his secret too, and I have to tell Debbie about it. She does not reproach me—probably she will later, Debbie does not pass over one's mistakes in silence. She accompanies me to my bedroom and, opening the drawer, takes out the pills. Together she and I carry them to the bathroom and flush the contents down the toilet. While we are doing this, she talks constantly—not about what we are doing and why, but about one of her favorite dreams that has never yet been fulfilled: she would like to go on a trip with Andrew, just the two of them, mother and handsome son. It doesn't really matter where, although she would like it to be Italy, where she has already been twice with a party of her women friends. They had a good time, but none of them was very knowledgeable and the guides tended to rush them. But if she went with Andrew, he would explain everything so beautifully, the churches and the frescoes and the paintings, and they would live in a hotel in adjoining rooms, maybe with a shared balcony on which she would appear in the morning and call out to him.

Andrew has been to Italy many times, but never with her.

Last year he was there with Veronica, on one of her locations. Veronica too wants him with her as much as possible. She would like him to live with her in her house in Beverly Hills. Veronica has never changed toward her brother and refuses to see, or really does not see, that he has changed in himself. She will not accept any role unless he has first approved it; she won't even read the script until he has recommended it. Only then will she sit down, usually on the floor with the script propped in her lap, winding a strand of her long hair around her fingers. Debbie is proud of this relationship between her children—Veronica's continued dependence on him—but she is also irritated by it. "As if he's got nothing better to do than read her silly scripts," she grumbles to me (though to no one else). "That's not what he went to Princeton for, and is this brilliant genius." Last year, when he went to Italy, she protested that it was a waste of his time; and when he sent home picture postcards, she looked at them wistfully and said what a shame to be there with a film crew who spoil everything with their vulgarity.

But now Debbie herself has sent Andrew away with Veronica. This is the way it happened. Veronica had been on a publicity tour for the film she had just finished and was about to start shooting the next one, again in Italy, in Florence. On her way, she touched down in New York for a day to persuade Andrew to go with her. She called Debbie from the airport—"Is he with you?" then switched off when she heard he wasn't.

Debbie was soon with me: "She's back. She's asking for him—of course not a word for me; no 'How are you, Mummy? How have you been?' Just 'Where is he?'"

Veronica was with us sooner than we expected. Andrew was asleep, or pretended to be. When she knocked on his bedroom door, he didn't answer. Then she came to talk to me—all charm, all radiance; she perched on a footstool at my feet, her dress pulled over her knees the way she had done as a little girl. She gazed at me out of her dark blue eyes, clear under her high square forehead—Hoch's lofty brow— her hair swept back and falling away from it, so that the steady gaze of those beautiful eyes gave an impression of serene sincerity. Her voice too was full of sincerity. She asked after my health, laying her hand on mine in deep concern, then laying it on her heart in anxiety: "Are you okay—here? You're sure?" Naturally I lied, and she was glad to accept my lie. She hadn't come here to talk about my health.

She looked at her watch: "But where's Andrew? We have to go."

"Who's we?" said Debbie.

Veronica smiled into space. Then she consulted her watch again and began to tell us everything she had to do: fly to Florence, then back to L.A. for more interviews, then to London for some fittings—she made it all sound rushed, breathless. As usual, she stalked around restlessly—an anomalous presence in my living room with its furniture and rugs worn out by years of family use, and the old clock I always forget to wind, and the photographs of the children with Gerd.

Andrew appeared in the doorway, rubbing his eyes and looking somewhat bedraggled—so he hadn't been pretending, he really had been asleep. "What's the time?" he said. Veronica replied: "It's three o'clock. What are you doing sleeping in the middle of the afternoon?" He didn't respond but sat down on the sofa, yawning, and rubbed his hands through his hair.

"Naturally, he's tired with all the reading and studying he's been doing," Debbie said. When he looked at her quizzically, she went on, "Well, what else is it you're doing locked up in there with all those books?"

"Oh those books: they'd make anyone fall asleep, they're so damned erudite." He smiled, and yawned again.

I could see that he was making Debbie frantic with irritation and misery. But all she could think to say was, "You need a vacation."

"A vacation! How exciting! Is it you and I who are going?"

Debbie's lips trembled: "Yes, I could do with a change too."

But Veronica really had no time to waste: "You promised! Yes you did, when I phoned from L.A. you said you'd go with me."

"Where to? Are we going anywhere really adorable?"

"What will be really adorable is to have you with me—one real person instead of all those creeps." It was rare for the two of them to touch each other, but now she laid her hand on his shoulder: "I need you. You have to come." She sounded desperate—of course, Veronica has been trained in all the emotions, but in relation to her brother, they may often have been real.

"Andrew has to stay with Grandma," Debbie said, "I don't want her left alone."

"But Grandma's fine!" Veronica cried. "She's told me herself!"

"Oh she'll say she's fine of course," Debbie said. "She'll never admit she needs a doctor or anyone else, not if it kills her."

"But I *am* fine," I protested, looking at Andrew.

He nodded, adding, "And in case of an emergency, you always have your pills." The way he spoke, I realized he had already looked for them in their hiding place and found them missing.

Probably Debbie realized it at the same moment; or else, what was it that suddenly changed her mind? She shrugged—an uncharacteristic gesture for someone with her strong opinions and feelings. "It's a total waste of your time of course," she said, "but if she's giving you a free air ticket, you might as well go."

Andrew has seen Hoch only in published photographs. Besides the formal portrait used as a frontispiece to the collected works, there are those in the two biographies that have already been written about Hoch. These include early family photographs—for instance, his mother in 1895, as stern and stiff as Hedda and encased up to her jawline in a blouse like a breastplate; and of Hedda herself, and the two sons. The only mention of myself in these two biographies is as his translator; he never kept any of the letters I wrote to him. He was nervous about receiving them, but sometimes I couldn't help myself, I had to write them; of course he wrote no letters to me. Yet for twenty years he and I led a secret life together—never here in New York but when he went away on one of his many conferences and symposia and allowed me to follow him. Somehow I scraped up the fare by giving tutorials, or secretly doing clerical work, addressing envelopes at so much an hour. Board and lodging were free, for I shared his hotel room, where I waited for him every night to return from whatever dinner or reception he had to attend. For the sake of appearances, I would slip out at dawn and walk around in the nearest park; this was all right in the summer, but less pleasant at conferences held in Sweden during his winter break. When he left the hotel for the day's session, he gave orders at the desk for his secretary to be admitted, so I took the key and stayed in his room. He also left his breakfast tray for me with the remains of the English breakfast of bacon and eggs he had ordered, which would sustain me for most of the day. I was ready to be alone and wait all those hours since I knew that finally, however late, he would return to me. The first thing he did was to sit on the hotel bed and ease himself out of his big brown boots. This took some time because they were laced right up to the top, ending in a double knot that was difficult to untie. Next he took off his gold watch and chain and laid them on the bedside table, and after that he unbuttoned his waistcoat. It was only then that he turned to me and said, "Kiss me." Although in the morning he had given himself a close shave with his open razor, by this time his cheeks were rough again with grey stubble: rough and manly.

I cannot say that these excursions were the happiest hours of my life, but they were certainly the most ecstatic. It is impossible to describe the bliss of being with him, this stolid Prussian professor thirty years older than I, who after making love at once turned over on his side and went to sleep, snoring tremendously. But he performed as a lover as he did everything: with all the force of his being—which was, after all, that of a man who had explored and conquered vast territories, impenetrable thickets of the mind. I adored him. But also, when he was not there and I was left alone all day in his hotel room, I shed bitter tears at the humiliating nature of the affair, and its futility.

Before we left on our conference trips together, his wife would give me instructions. These were partly professional, for whereas I had translated the paper he was to present, it was she who had prepared the final typescript. After he had been diagnosed with high blood pressure, she would also instruct me about his diet and other precautions. Although she only did this when she knew our work for the day was finished, her intrusion irritated him. Ignoring his mood, she carried on in slow and meticulous detail, driving him mad, especially when she warned against the red meat and red wine for which he had such a huge appetite.

"Yes yes yes, we know all about that," he growled.

She turned to me: "I rely on you."

He sneered at her: "Wouldn't it be best to hire a nurse-maid for me?"

"We can't afford one, let alone her fare. If we could, I'd come myself to make sure you don't kill yourself."

She looked at him out of her flat, pale eyes that always seemed empty of expression to me; but not, it seemed, to him, for he looked away from her and muttered a curse in German. But I never had to remind him about her instructions; he followed them carefully, as though she were there with us.

When I became pregnant with Debbie, he offered me money for an abortion. That was the only time he ever offered me money, and when I refused, he said no more about it and we continued our work. We did not mention the subject between us again, either then or subsequently. It happened to be a stressful time, for we were working on an important paper he was about to publish. One day, a week after I told him my news, he became very impatient because I kept failing to get my translation right. This happened every time he made some further advance in his thought, since any new concept of his was impossibly difficult to grasp, and then to find English words in which to express it . . . I became desperate—because he was angry and because I was failing him. I was hampering his great work not only with my dull mind but now also with my body and its uncalled-for pregnancy. It was making me nauseous and causing pain in my breasts and other unworthy symptoms—unworthy, that is, of the work to which I was called.

He was by nature an impatient, irascible man, especially

when interrupted or obstructed in his train of thought. For me his wrath was like a storm at sea or a mountain avalanche, where I could only cower and pray—and on that day this is what I did, hiding my head in my arms. At the sound of his raging voice Hedda came bursting in, overcoming her own fear of the closed door and even without knocking. She was intent on a rescue mission—rescuing him, that is, from the storm of blood rushing into his brain (it is his high blood pressure that Debbie has inherited). She didn't ask what had caused his outburst but said, with her heavy humor, that it couldn't be all that bad, we're not all going to be hanged, are we? So why not just sit down quietly and drink the cup of good coffee that she would make and bring for him. She called him by his first name, Helmut—the name I never used; for me the most intimate address was Hoch without the Professor, and that only when we were alone together in some place away from home. He was spluttering with fury but did what she said and sat down. I was still holding my head in my hands, but neither of them took any notice of me. When I looked up, I saw them together like that, husband and wife; she was caressing his sleeve, but at the same time her eyes swept over my sheets of translation spread over the desk. She wore the usual impassive expression she reserved for my work with him; it was the one task she had to delegate, for her English never became good enough for her to displace me. She waited for him to simmer down, then said she would make that cup of good coffee for him. She didn't offer me any, and I saw it was time to leave them together.

At that time I lived in an old row house off First Avenue, in a railway flat I shared with two other refugee girls, Eva and Renate. We had two bedrooms and took turns sleeping on the couch in the living room, though this arrangement changed whenever one or other of us had a man friend staying the night. That morning, before leaving to work with Hoch, I had washed some stockings, and on my return I went straight into the bathroom to take them down; there was also some underwear belonging to the other girls, and none of it was quite dry yet, but I needed the rope. I pulled out the table in the living room and placed it under a hook in the ceiling; a previous tenant must have had an electric fan, which he took away with him when he left. I placed a chair on the table and climbed up on it. My principal worry was that table and chair would break under me while I was fastening the rope. All our furniture was old—some donated by friends, some found abandoned on the street.

There was a ring at the door—the bell went through me like an electric shock. It was only then that my heart started beating fast, as though shocked into life; before that I had been calm, cool, doing everything correctly. I stood waiting, hoping the caller would leave, yet also waiting for the bell to ring again. As I counted the seconds, it rang again, and then again. I went to the door: the visitor had started calling my name, knocking on the door till I opened it to him. It was Gerd. He was holding a bunch of flowers.

"Thank heaven," he said. "I thought you weren't home, and then what would I do with these?" He stretched them out toward me. They were cheap flowers, all any of us could afford at the time, bought on the street and wilting from the city dust while they waited to be sold.

I didn't ask him in; on the contrary, I stood blocking his way.

"Should we put them in water?" he asked. For a few seconds more, we stood facing each other, his smile uneasy but persistent.

To prevent him from going into the living room, I led the way down the passage to the bedroom at the other end. The door of the living room was open—did he turn his head to look in, and if so, how much did he see? He said nothing, but followed me; when we got to the bedroom, it was he who shut the door behind us. Although by nature a shy, reticent person—we had never yet slept together—he did not hesitate to take the initiative. He sat down on the bed and, making me sit close beside him, put his arm around me; for the first time in our relationship he was in charge.

I told him I was pregnant, and by whom. Perhaps he thought that this was the only reason for what he had seen through the open door of the living room. *If* he had seen— we were married for over fifty years, and never once did he refer to that open door. He reacted to my news with such a rush of joy that it overflowed into me. He convinced me that it was the most wonderful thing that had ever happened to me, and to him. And this was how it was between us from that moment on—through our wedding day, for which Hoch and Hedda sent a set of kitchen utensils, so sturdy that they are still in use—and then through all my years with him and Debbie, and with Hoch. For my life and work with Hoch continued, even our journeys together to conferences and the waiting for him in hotel rooms, although in his last years I was allowed to accompany him to the conferences, for he needed someone to help with his notes and, after his stroke, to help him physically too.

Usually I fulfilled my function with him without demur or question; but there were times when I felt the same as on that day when Gerd came with the flowers. Although these depressions tended to occur during the summer months— about the time the Hoch family left for their vacation in the Swiss Alps—I always thought of those days as my frozen winter days. And always, like that first time, it was Gerd who melted the ice that had formed around my heart, asking me perhaps to explain some aspect of Hoch's new ideas that I had been working on. Gerd freely admitted that he really was the donkey that Hoch took him for, and it is true I had difficulty getting some of these ideas across to him. But it was always worth it because when a glimmer of their meaning began to dawn on him, Gerd would clasp his hands and cry out, "What a man! My goodness, what a great man!" Then I realized all over again the joy and privilege of working with Hoch. And Gerd made out that he too felt privileged to be part of this situation.

7
Dancer With a Broken Leg

M Y FIRST husband was the most ambitious person I have ever known. This is strange, because when I was with him and we were both very young, we thought ourselves to be totally free of any desire for worldly advancement. We both admired Lalit Kumar—or L.K., as he was known to everyone—and wanted to be like him in living up to the noble ideals we held at that time.

I had met L.K. on a bus going from Kanpur to Delhi. It was one of those inter-state buses, piled on top with baggage and bundles and maybe a crate of chickens, some of them dying on the way; and inside it was crowded with farmers, clerks, pregnant women carrying infants, and children vomiting out of the barred open windows through which dust and pollution flowed in. L.K. seemed not very different from the other passengers; he looked poor in his cotton clothes frayed from too much washing. But he *was* different—he addressed the people on the bus like one used to making speeches. His voice was loud and dramatic like an orator's, and he must have made many witty and humorous remarks because people shook their heads and laughed. It was all in Hindi, but when he saw me—a pale foreign girl—he politely translated himself into English. It wasn't the sort of English I was used to—not American English of course, nor modern English either, but a sort of florid oldfashioned prose that he must have read in books and not spoken very much.

When we reached Delhi, L.K. took me to the flat where

he was staying. I was used to going with people I happened to meet on my way. It was how I lived in India at that time, wanting to be far away from home and other people's expectations of me, far away from my parents' quarrels and divorce proceedings. So for me India was this place to be free and to travel in. I really had no understanding of anything and didn't realize that the household to which L.K. took me was very unusual. It consisted only of a mother, Dharma, and her son, Vidia; later I learned that the father hadn't lived with them since Vidia was six months old. L.K. had more or less taken his place, at least for part of the time, whenever he was in Delhi.

Dharma was, or had been, a dancer: not of the hereditary caste that dancers at that time mostly came from—that is, one classed with semi-prostitutes—but from a prominent South Indian family. Like other young girls, she had learned dance as a social accomplishment but had continued for the love of it, for her talent, and inspired by a famous teacher under whom she studied. Her unconventional enthusiasm didn't stand in the way of a conventional marriage arranged for her with another prominent South Indian family. I had no idea what a revolutionary step it had been for Dharma to leave her husband and join a troupe of dancers. She was with them for several years, traveling around India and abroad, keeping Vidia always with her, so that he grew up in a makeshift, bohemian atmosphere. Later, during an engagement in Paris, she broke a leg, and after that could never dance again. Her family paid her a stipend to stay away from the South, and her husband, who had married again and had another family, contributed something toward Vidia's education. When L.K. took me there, they had already been for some years in Delhi, often shifting house but always staying together in a tight bond with each other.

I had grown up listening to my parents' quarrels, before, during, and after their divorce; but whereas they hated each other, Vidia and his mother quarreled in a different way. They were both intensely passionate—at least she was, and at that time I thought Vidia was too. I fell in love with him at once: he was so handsome, slender, his limbs delicate yet supple and strong, dark Indian eyes that smoldered, and sometimes blazed. We shared the same ideals; we both hated sham, pretension, money, the power and greed of materialism. I rejected this hateful world by traveling around with no responsibilities; he wanted to change it by taking on responsibilities, even if necessary entering politics to fight corruption from within.

L.K. had spent his life in politics. He had been a trade union organizer and also a freedom fighter, who had been jailed many times by the British. He was again in jail when Independence was won, and by the time his release papers came through, a new government had been formed and its prime posts filled by those lucky enough not to be in jail. He detested the members of this present regime, who were very different types from himself. He was a peasant, self-taught, while they were widely traveled aristocrats with hereditary lands and perfect English accents. He didn't express his dislike the way Vidia and I would have done. Reading some item in an English newspaper, he looked sly and ran his tongue over his lips. "Ah, here's Madam with a new hairstyle signing away another chunk of Mother India to her favorite international imperialists," he would say, about India's lady ambassador to the United Nations. "Very generous, very nice." Vidia would snatch the paper away from him, read the caption under the photograph, and then tear out the page and crush it in his fist. L.K. laughed and pinched his cheek. For L.K., Vidia had remained the little boy he had met with his mother out for a stroll at India Gate; he had given him some of the candy that he always carried in his pocket for children encountered on the way.

L.K. and Dharma were an unlikely pair—he an impoverished labor leader from a North Indian provincial town, she a South Indian dancer, or *artiste* as she called herself. Although he shared her bedroom, this may have been because it was the only one; Vidia slept in the living room on a string cot. I didn't have a sense of any physical relationship between L.K. and Dharma; he was twenty years older and maybe more of a father figure to her. He certainly had a calming influence on her, which she needed—she was very explosive, especially in her quarrels with Vidia. If L.K. was there and felt they had gone too far, he intervened; at that time, when I first met them, he had great authority with them both.

We had the upstairs flat in a two-storey house—I say "we" because it didn't take long for me to become part of the family. Although fairly new, the house looked old—cracks in the cement and dark patches left by the monsoon rains. The other houses looked the same, and there was a lot of illegal construction and makeshift shops or stalls at street level. Although built as a middle-class residential colony, it had become not unlike an old city bazaar; this was altogether convenient, for we could always run down and buy snacks freshly made on the sidewalk. Also, it was easy to get transport, for cycle rickshaws and horsedrawn carriages plied up and down, along with barrows selling peanuts and slices of coconut. With all this traffic and the cries of passing hawkers, it was very noisy during the day. It was never really quiet at night either, for even when everyone was asleep, the air was always full of sounds: dogs barking, sometimes a shriek of jackals, or the fragrant sound of a prayer meeting with its hymns floating to us from far away. Some of the smells were also fragrant, as of jasmine and Queen of the Night, intoxicating but only partly drowning out the daytime smells of petrol fumes, rotting vegetables, urine.

I became familiar with these summer nights, for when it was very hot, Vidia and I moved our cot on to the balcony overlooking the street. This balcony was just outside Dharma's bedroom, so that whatever we were doing must have been clearly audible to her. It might be thought that she would be jealous of my relationship with her son, but not at all: she was delighted. Sometimes she even called out to us: "What's going on there? Are you making me a grandmother? I'm too young!" And she laughed, though Vidia got angry and called back to her to shut up and mind her own business. Then she replied that she had no business, that she was young but not that young; and she laughed again.

Dharma was my friend—she really was, as though we were the same age. The local housewives had their own little clubs and assemblies to which Dharma, with her strange background, was not invited. But she was used to having girl friends to share secrets and snacks, the way she had done with the young dancers in her troupe. Now I was her girl friend—her "*sakhi*" she said, explaining to me the role the *sakhi* played in Indian legend and dance: the messenger, the consoler, the go-between of Lover and Beloved. There were many other aspects of the dance she explained to me: the meaning of each tiny gesture of finger and eyebrow, one saying "Come here," another "Where are you?" and then, "I miss you, I cannot bear this absence O lotus-eyed One and who made those scratches on your neck?" She had some records of a woman singer with a raucous voice, and while she listened, it was clear that the love and longing that came crackling out of the old turntable were also in Dharma's own heart.

She spoke to me about other things too, like clothes and cosmetics of which she was very fond. Her broken leg had left her with a limp, but this was skillfully hidden by her dress and the way she carried herself. She moved in a cloud of gauze veils and loose garments, glittering with sequins and jingling with rows of ornaments. She wore a lot of make-up, day and night—I never saw her without a layer of powder, circles of rouge on her cheeks, her eyes, extended with kohl, huge and alive under arched eyebrows: a dancer made up for her performance. When he was angry or impatient with her, which was often, Vidia would accuse her of making herself look like a lady from the G.B. Road (the red light district of Delhi). At first she would laugh but the next moment she was terribly angry and would shout how she was an *artiste* and that he had no respect for her art, or any art or anything beautiful.

When he and his friends got together, they talked about politics. At first he wanted me with him all the time, so he took me along to the coffee-house where they all met. They spoke in a mixture of English and Hindi, discussing both student and national politics; I didn't listen much, I was just glad to be sitting there with him. I must add here that he never, either before his friends or before his mother and L.K., made any kind of tender gesture toward me, or touched me, though I was longing to touch him. His friends were shy with me—shy and very polite—they were not used to having a girl with them, let alone a foreign one. But when they got deeper into their argument, they forgot about me—as did Vidia too. They always met in the same coffee-house, a dark place with torn plastic seats and a waiter with only one eye and a grimy uniform. And they always placed the same order, cold coffee and potato chips with tomato ketchup, the latter congealed in its bottle so that it had to be shaken and got splashed over the tablecloth. If anyone ordered anything more, they had difficulty paying for it, and I picked up the check, for I always had plenty of money.

It astonished Vidia, the way I always had money. Sometimes he came with me to the American Express office, where other young travelers stood around, waiting for their allowance from home. There were also some who did not have parents to keep them supplied; there was one rather wasted French girl, for instance, who was always asking for money—to buy air mail stamps, she said. I only had to cable my father and he would immediately respond. "Is he very rich?" Vidia asked me, and I had to admit that he was. I didn't say that my father thought it was his fault I had dropped out of college and was traveling around in this way in a far-off place, that he felt guilty for breaking up my home and so on—it was a story I had no interest in telling. After collecting my money, I often gave most of it to Vidia; he was standing for election to some student committee and needed funds to print posters and treat supporters with snacks in the college canteen.

All this was about the time of his final exams, which he was determined to pass in the first division. He studied far into the night, and in the early hours of the morning he joined me in our bed out on the balcony. Even on moonless nights, I could make out his features by the yellowish light of a street-lamp near our house. I saw his eyes and his teeth gleaming while he made love to me. When he turned around and went to sleep, I pressed myself against him, against his back. I felt such pride in him, in his beautiful body, his wonderful mind; I lay awake, drenched in my own happiness, and in his and my perspiration from the heat of a Delhi summer night.

When the exam results were posted up in the University, Vidia scorned to join the crowd of students jostling to read them. L.K. went instead, and when he came back, he stood in the doorway, with his arms raised, one of them holding his stick: "Triumph!" he announced. "Triumph and blessings have been showered on this home!" Vidia had passed in the first division and was second in the whole University. "Second," Vidia sneered at himself, but it was his way of hiding how pleased he was. Dharma of course hid nothing— she danced around the room on her lame leg and clicked her fingers to make a noise like castanets. L.K. quoted one of the nineteenth-century English poets he was so fond of— " 'Victory rattles her drum!' " and went on: "Now we shall see something—now we shall see how Youth will conquer feeble Age!" By feeble Age he meant all the old men, and a few old women, who were running the government. He had very definite plans for Vidia.

L.K.'s union supported a small opposition party who were searching for a suitable candidate to field in the next general election. L.K. was eager to introduce Vidia to them—a student leader, with a brilliant degree reflecting his brilliant mind. I glanced at Vidia when this suggestion was made, and I saw his face radiant with a totally new expression. But I had hoped that, once his exams were over, he would have a lot more time for me—we had spoken about how we would go traveling together the way I had done on my own, around India and perhaps also to other places: Tibet, Thailand, China, the world was open to us and so was my father's bank account. When I reminded Vidia of these plans of ours, he said L.K. was giving him a wonderful opportunity to work for the ideals he and I cherished—freedom, justice—right from within enemy territory. He was known as one of the best debaters in the inter-University team, and it was not difficult for him to persuade me, especially when he pressed his lips against mine and I could feel his persuasive tongue moving inside my mouth.

Dharma too was not happy with L.K.'s plan for her son. "Leave him alone," she said to L.K. "He'll do something great, don't worry, everyone says."

"Who says?"

"Everyone!"

L.K. was patient the way he always was with her, explaining about the election and what a good chance they had of winning it. At first Dharma said she didn't understand anything about it, and then she said yes yes, she understood—but what could she be expected to know, a dancer, an *artiste*? She lived in a different world.

She didn't dare provoke Vidia himself on this subject, but she talked to me about it. She sat in her bedroom before the little low table on which a mirror was fixed. She applied stuff on herself from all the little pots standing there—kohl, rouge, henna—trying out colors till she arrived at one that she liked. While she was doing this—"I hate politics," she said. "I've seen what it has done to L.K." She tried out some cosmetics on me too but had to admit they didn't suit me.

"A very simple man," she said about L.K. "Simple and poor." He was born in a village, the son of peasant farmers, and at the age of fifteen he had gone to a nearby town to earn money to send home. He had found a job in a shoe factory but was dismissed for his involvement in union politics. She thought that his first regular meals had been in jail—where he also got an education from the other political prisoners and was introduced to the English classics he loved so much. But what good did any of it do him? In the end, she said, it was others who gobbled up the government with all its plums and perks.

L.K. continued his cynical comments about the ruling elite. He read the newspaper reports of the seminars they arranged in New Delhi, in the brand-new banquet hall of a brand-new luxury hotel. He read of the appointments handed out to ministers and ambassadors—"Of course," he commented about the newly chosen ambassador to France, a relative of the Prime Minister's, "he has to have his cousin in Paris, to send his shirts there for laundering. Our poor Indian washermen, what do they know about such fine shirts?"

"Yes and look at the rag on your back—do you think that's what I want for my son?"

Dharma's own plans for Vidia changed from day to day. Sometimes she wanted him to be a bureaucrat like her father; on other days she thought he ought to devote himself to literature and perhaps become a poet. "Don't you think he looks like a poet?" she asked me. I agreed—his deep eyes, his fine brow with a lock of hair always falling across it.

L.K. pointed out: "He never writes poetry. He doesn't even read it." But then he went on to say that it was not poets of the word who were needed today but poets of the sword— to cleave the Gordian knot of contemporary politics and of caste-ridden elections. He shook his fist in the air so that his sleeve fell back and exposed his feeble arm. "Be careful," Dharma laughed. "A sword is heavy to lift!"

In spite of his vague rhetoric, L.K. was really very practical. He and Vidia often sat huddled on the balcony discussing what steps to take to secure Vidia's adoption as a candidate, while I waited for them to finish so that I could lie down with Vidia on our bed. But even after L.K. had gone, I found Vidia still sunk in thoughts of their discussion. He lay on his back with his arms folded under his head and looked up at the stars. When at last he turned to me, I thought it was the light of those stars I saw reflected in his eyes, and of his love for me. But now I think it was the prospect of the promises L.K. had made him.

L.K. did a lot of traveling in connection with his work.

Now he began to take Vidia with him to the various districts
he visited, to introduce him to local committees and local
bosses who had control of a lot of votes. While they were
away, Dharma's mood was grim; and when they returned, it
was worse. L.K. tried to soothe her, sitting beside her and
making tender noises as to a child or a pet. She pushed him
away: "Pooh, you stink! Go and bathe before you come near
me!" He had just come off an inter-state bus and was soaked
in its grime and smells and sweat. "And that one!" she cried,
pointing at Vidia who had just come off the same bus. "You're
making him the same as yourself, pulling him down to your
own low level!" L.K. slunk off obediently to the little hole
of a bathroom where a bucket of water had always to be
kept filled because of the irregular water supply. But Vidia
pulled off his filthy shirt and flung it at her feet: "Go and
wash it then!" He stood with his eyes blazing and his chest
bare like a warrior's. "Look at him," she said, her voice
suddenly soft. She tried to touch him, his smooth satin skin,
and when he pushed her hand away and turned from her,
muttering "Madwoman," she looked after him with tender
eyes and nudged me to do the same.

Whenever they needed money for their expeditions, she
gave them all she could out of her small monthly stipend.
I didn't have much sense of money, and never realized how
she deprived herself. One day, when the milkman came to
the door with his cans, she asked me to tell him that no
milk would be required today. When he began shouting,
she came flying out and shouted back at him. This was all
in Hindi, and she explained to me in English, "I'm telling
him he'll be paid, just wait, my goodness, why can't he
wait!" The milkman appealed to me—he held up several
fingers which I assumed to be the sum due to him. I had
money right there in my pocket, and I took it out and gave

it to him though she tried to stop me. He offered to give us milk, but she banged the door shut in his face and then burst into tears.

I felt sad that she hadn't confided in me, and when I asked her always to let me help her, she cried more and said, "Am I a beggar?" I assured her that money was no problem to me at all because of my father. She wiped away her tears and the black kohl they had smeared over her face. She praised my father, what a good man he was and kind. Her own father too had been very good and kind, she said; what a mistake she had made in taking the path she had chosen! But there had been no choice, she added at once. If she had stayed one day longer with Vidia's father, she would have either died of boredom or run off with a lover. Not that there hadn't been lovers—later, on tour, other dancers in the troupe, admirers in Paris and London—oh she was not always, she smiled, this wreck with a lame leg and no one but a broken-down old man like L.K. to be at her beck and call.

When they returned from their tour, L.K. stood in the doorway, his arms raised as at Vidia's exam results, and announcing "Victory!" Vidia had been adopted as the official candidate of L.K.'s splinter party. For that evening at least, Dharma shared in their triumph. Whispering to me for some cash which she would repay the day her stipend arrived—she had kept a very middle-class attitude to money—she sent out for biryani and mutton curry, which we ate Indian style with our fingers. I never learned to do this properly, but I loved watching Vidia, the skillful way he used only the tips of his fingers and brought them to his mouth without spilling a grain of rice or a drop of curry. It was part of his refinement, his fastidiousness: every action was neat and precise—as when he washed his hands or drank from a glass without ever putting it to his lips. Dharma explained, "He's a brahmin"—she spoke proudly, for though she had long since left all considerations of caste and religion behind, she still had a pride in her origins and the refinements she had passed on to her son.

He was also meticulous about his appearance. As a student, he had worn Western-style trousers and shirt, but now, as a political candidate, he had to appear in Indian dress. He saw himself in a wardrobe as refined as that of the Prime Minister, who had started a fashion in high-collared jackets and always wore a fresh rose in his buttonhole. Dharma and I too were thrilled to think of Vidia in Indian clothes, and we went with him on a shopping trip to the cloth bazaar. The merchant, his stomach flowing over his thighs, sat crosslegged on a platform, directing two assistants who clambered to the top of the high shelves to bring down finer and finer bolts of cloth for inspection. Both Vidia and Dharma were very particular, and it all took a long time. Then we were directed to an adjoining shop where a tailor sat with his sewing machine. The day before, Dharma had been to the pawnbroker with some gold bangles—this was a familiar routine for her—so she had a bundle of money tucked away in her large handbag. I told her to get back her bangles because I had just received a money draft. She objected, and we had a whispered conversation about it, while Vidia was sternly supervising the tailor crouched at his feet to measure him. Finally she gave way, but instead of redeeming her bangles, we went the same afternoon to the jewelers' market to buy a set of ruby studs for Vidia's new Indian coat. These too were carefully chosen by Vidia and Dharma, their heads close together over the jewels spread on an embroidered cloth in another shop, this one sweet-smelling with incense burning before the gilded picture of a saint.

When the clothes were ready, Vidia brought them home and modeled them for us. Dharma burst into tears of joy, and I too was moved by his beauty. But L.K. was angry; it was the first time I had seen him openly express anger instead of disguising it in sarcasm. Did Vidia not have any idea what sort of people he was representing, he said—those who did not have enough to put into their mouths, or into their children's mouths or to bring medicine for those same children when they lay shivering with fevers, or for their wives to prevent them from dying in childbirth? And while he spoke he trembled and wiped sweat from his forehead and eyes. I felt bad about his outburst, but Vidia didn't seem affected at all. He said L.K. was old now and could not be blamed for having outmoded ideas and seeing the world through Marxist eyes—black and white, bourgeois and proletariat. Then he forgot about L.K. and concentrated on me; he said that we should get married.

I was not yet eighteen at the time, but Vidia said no one would bother about my age. The magistrate was an acquaintance of L.K.'s, and as a favor he came to the flat with his clerk, who filled up the form for us to sign. They didn't seem particular about what they put down, and the only question the magistrate asked was about me—was I a boy or a girl? He was puzzled because, on account of the heat, I had cut my hair very short. I had also bought two identical white muslin kurta-pajama sets for Vidia and me; and since we both had the same kind of build, I suppose we could have been taken for twins, except that he was dark and I wasn't. There was not much ceremony to the proceedings, and that suited everyone for we were all agnostics. Dharma was the most insistent in her non-belief—maybe because she had had the most to overcome in getting there. Anyway, she had left it all behind long before she had even met L.K. with his cynical references to a God who had no idea what was going on in a world He claimed to have created but simply left to its own rotten devices.

The magistrate didn't give us any kind of speech but only read out the printed matter on the form, which said that our declaration was true, though if it wasn't, we understood that we were liable to a fine or a term of imprisonment or both. When we had signed, the clerk gathered up the form and put it in his gunny-bag, and the two of them went away without accepting the sherbet and pink sweets that Dharma offered. She was disappointed and had some hard things to say about the magistrate to whom marriage was just a fee of fifty rupees to be collected. It had been asked for in advance, and since I was the only one with ready cash, I had paid it.

L.K. was not at all put out by the lack of ceremony. He was deeply moved, and when he embraced us, there were tears in his eyes—those dry old eyes that I thought could only melt at the suffering of the poor. He made up for the magistrate by showering his own blessings on us—some in quotations from Shakespeare, but also in ideas of his own about marriage and its commitments. We were surprised by the many thoughts he had on the subject. In a society where everybody was married off at the first opportunity, he had remained single and alone, dedicated to his cause. Now it turned out that he was full of feelings both romantic and also very pure, maybe because they had not been tested by personal experience.

I was never careful about keeping count of my periods, and it was a while before I realized that I hadn't had one for some time. When I told Vidia, he understood immediately, having grown up close to his mother and a whole troupe of young women dancers. "Now we'll have to tell him," he said, for we had been debating whether or not to tell my father about our marriage. I said, "Daddy would love to be a grandfather," which was true, he was always talking about grandchildren in a longing way. "So we should make him happy," Vidia said, indifferently. But next moment he added, "Really? Really, you think he'd be pleased with us?" He himself didn't seem to have strong feelings either way.

Neither did I at first, but then my morning sickness started, and I felt miserable all day. Dharma soon made out what the matter was, and she was very angry with Vidia. "She's only a *child*," she said, and to prove it, she spanned her hands around my waist and they still went all the way around.

But L.K. was as deeply touched and delighted as he had been by our marriage. This pleased me at first, but then I found that it worked against me. L.K. and Vidia were about to start on an extended election tour, and I had been planning to go too. Now L.K. wouldn't hear of it. He said that in my condition it was impossible to travel the way they would have to—not only in the crowded buses and third-class trains I was used to, but by bullock cart and sometimes on camel back, sleeping on the floor of village huts, eating and drinking whatever was available, and always surrounded by crowds and hecklers and police with bamboo sticks. It all sounded fine to me, and anyway I couldn't bear to be separated from Vidia; but L.K. said, "No no no," and he stroked my hair, saying I was their tender flower they had to shield and protect. So they left without me.

I became more sick and miserable, and Dharma took me to a lady doctor who told me that I was farther along than I had suspected. On the way home, Dharma said, "You'll have to decide." I *had* decided, and Dharma didn't try to dissuade me. But she said, "For God's sake, don't tell L.K. He's such a sentimental old fool." She showed me how to do things like jumping down the stairs and riding on motor rickshaws that shook violently. Nothing worked, and Dharma said we would have to make arrangements. She confessed that she had several times been in the same situation, on tour abroad as well as in India, so it was nothing new to her.

She found a doctor—this one was not a lady doctor but an unshaven little man in a tenement within a city alley. The stone stairs up to his flat were littered and betel-stained, but they opened on to a wide verandah overlooking the city. There was no doctor's name on a board but a nursery class was being conducted on the verandah by a thin and harassed-looking woman. She took no notice of us other than waving us inside, as she carried on with her lesson. Dharma whispered to me that she was the doctor's wife who had started the school to keep them going after he lost his licence to practice.

We entered a small unfurnished room, and then the doctor appeared and took us into another small room; this one had a bed covered by a greyish sheet with faint bloodstains on it, and also some kidney bowls and other semi-clinical objects. The doctor spoke to me about America which he had visited thirty years ago, I don't remember whether as a student or a tourist, anyway he had met some famous doctors there and also gazed on wonders like the Niagara Falls. He didn't have an assistant but operated by himself, without anesthetic and with an instrument I didn't wish to look at. Well, I was young and Dharma believed in positive thinking. Afterward, in view of my invalid state, she took me home in a taxi, which was expensive but rattled just as much as the rickshaws we usually rode in.

By the time L.K. and Vidia came back, I had fully recovered. They were both elated by the success of their tour. L.K., quoting verses about battle and victory, shook his stick in the air and cackled in his old-man way, which was at the same time youthful, childlike almost. Vidia was silent, a half-smile on his lips and his eyes shining as though he were in love—

with his future, with himself, and (I thought) with me. Now, years later, this is one way I remember him.

That night, when we were in bed together on the balcony, he didn't tell me much about their tour but what had to be done next for his campaign. One of his student friends had gone into advertising, and he had designed some very effective posters and other printed material to be distributed to voters. They had calculated the cost and it was high, higher than the funds at the disposal of Vidia's campaign.

"Have you told him yet?"

"Told who what?"

"Your father, who else."

Then I had to inform him that there was no more baby to tell my father about. At that he rolled away from me. He lay on his back; he looked at the stars; he was silent. I sat up and peered into his face, lit up by the yellowish street lamp. Gone was his half-smile; instead his lips were drawn into a thin, thin line. And that is the other way I remember him.

He said nothing more to me but next morning confronted Dharma, and they had one of their violent quarrels. L.K. sat in the middle of it all, dipping rusks into his glass of tea while reading the paper. But finally he threw it aside and said he could not stay in a place where one was not even allowed to read the newspaper in peace, though it was all nonsense and lies that were printed there. Vidia pointed at his mother and said, "Do you know what she's done?" Dharma cried "No!" and she ran into the bedroom in fright. And then, when Vidia told him about the abortion, I too became frightened of L.K. and the way he suddenly changed. His grey hair seemed to stand on end as he snatched up his stick and pursued her into the bedroom. "Murderess!" he cried—and when I followed, I saw that he had caught hold of her hair and was beating her around the shoulders with his stick. I shouted above their shouts that it was my fault, that I had asked to have it done—but as I tried to get between them, Vidia came and dragged me into the other room. He wrapped his arms around me—not in a tender way but to restrain me, and he did not let go till the shouts from the bedroom had subsided. When I went in, I saw Dharma huddled on the bed, with her hair wild and loose, and her bruised face swollen with tears. L.K. stood in front of her, drained of anger now, his head lowered in contrition. When he tried to touch her, she shook him off fiercely. After a while he went into the bathroom and returned with a wet cloth to wipe her face. She pushed his hand away several times but at last allowed him to sit beside her and wipe away her tears. Both were silent.

The cost of the posters designed by Vidia's friend turned out to be too high; and anyway, L.K. said they were suitable for an urban electorate but not for the villagers and landless laborers that their party represented. So when Vidia lost the election, no one blamed it on the lack of those election posters. L.K., who had been through many defeats of various kinds, took this one lightly and at once began to plan for the next campaign, in five years' time. "Five years!" Vidia said with a dry laugh. But he too was not at all cast down by his failure. Unlike L.K., he didn't speak of the future but seemed silently to be turning over plans in his mind. This gave him a closed, more determined look, as if a veil of sweetness had been torn away and another person revealed underneath. I loved him not less in this new character but differently; and it seemed almost right that he too should be different toward me.

I was often alone at night now, while he was away somewhere, not returning till I was already asleep. During the day he no longer wanted me with him as before. When I asked him to take me, he said it would not be appropriate. I understood that it wasn't his former coffee-house friends he met now, and when I asked about them, he waved them away as though they were child's play he had outgrown. It seemed he was meeting other sorts of people now—"serious people," he said. I was hurt; weren't our ideas serious too, I asked, and everything we had talked about and thought we were living for? In reply, he made the same sort of dismissive gesture as he had done when speaking of his student friends. But then he kissed me and I felt all right, especially as he began to take more interest in my appearance. He said I should no longer wear my hair cut so short, or the kurta-pajama outfit I liked but a sari or salwar. I was glad to oblige him, but even so he never took me along to these new places nor to meet the new people he was seeing.

When I met him again recently in New York, he failed to recognize me. How could he, why should he? We hadn't seen one another for thirty years. But I think I would have recognized him, even if I hadn't known that the reception at the consulate was in his honor. He probably hadn't thought about me much in the intervening years, and I didn't think that much about him either. But I was always interested to hear about him and had many opportunities to do so. Although I had never returned to India, I had kept in touch with Indian organizations like the Indo-American Friendship and the Asia Societies, and after my father died and left me most of his estate, I made donations to these and other organizations and was invited to sit on some committees and to be a patron at their fund-raisers. So I often heard about Vidia, who had become an important public figure in India. He was a leader of his party, which had remained in power for several years. He had held some important portfolios and might have become the Prime Minister, if it hadn't been for the scandal in his private life. Soon after my departure, he had married the daughter of a rich industrialist and they had several children. But he had left his family to live with a woman who was herself involved in politics—she held some important post, which he had maneuvered for her. They were said to be very useful to each other.

She too was there at the reception—not as his companion of course (India wasn't that advanced yet) but in her own right as the Commissioner for Women or whatever it was she represented. I looked at her with interest, which was easy since she took no notice of me: I was just another guest at the reception in Vidia's honor. She wore a badly draped sari that kept falling down, revealing an expanse of naked fat flesh swelling out from under her blouse. But she moved her big bulk with the easy self-confidence of a successful person and was very responsive to those important enough to talk to her, often laughing out loud with two perfect rows of healthy teeth.

It took me some time to get near Vidia, who was surrounded by Indian and American officials, several Indian businessmen settled in New York, and maybe some secret service personnel. I was shy and nervous of approaching him—and when at last I did, what I had feared happened. He stared at me with the fixed smile and the questioning regard with which important people shield themselves. I had to tell him who I was. For a moment the smile left him, but was almost at once replaced by a very cordial one—the sort extended to a former acquaintance whom one has not seen for a long time and is not anxious to see again. All around us there were others eager to talk to him and more coming up, and I had to give way. I'm not sure that I was not pushed aside by one of the secret service men in big shoes.

*

It was not long after Vidia lost his first election that his new contacts arranged a kind of semi-official job for him. I was never sure what this was, but it brought him into the orbit of some powerful politicians. He began to attend official functions, and sometimes an official car and chauffeur were sent for him and were admired by the children in our alley. The chauffeur was too grand to get out to open the door, so Vidia had to clamber in by himself. All the same, as he sat in the back of the car and was driven away to a destination unknown to us, he was already beginning to look like someone from a world superior to the inhabitants of our neighborhood, including ourselves.

L.K. was mostly away at this time, and in his case too among people and places far removed from us. Weeks passed and we heard nothing from him and Dharma grumbled, "Not even a postcard to ask if we're alive or what." She was not at all her usual self during his absence—she didn't even paint herself much but sat in an old cotton sari with her feet drawn up on the chair and her elbows propped on her knees. "Anyone can send a postcard—but no, it's too much trouble for him. And next time he comes I'll tell him 'Get out—get out of my home!' I've told that many times to grander men than he: get out! And they've cried and wept, yes right here at my feet," and she pointed at them propped up on the chair, broad brown dancer's feet, one of them adorned with a toe-ring.

But sometimes she spoke admiringly of his work as a union organizer and how he went to remote places where no one had ever heard of labor laws. He sat under a tree and waited, and slowly people began to come to him and he told them how to work together against being exploited. "What does he eat when he's out there for weeks and months on end, where does he sleep? No one knows. And for what?" she always ended up. "For nothing. No one pays him one single pai for his work, it's all for others. For him—starvation and jail. Do you think that's what I want for my son? Never. First carry away my corpse and burn it."

Though Vidia's work often kept him away till late at night, when he finally came home he was as fresh as he had been when he left in the morning. He only pretended to be tired when he said, "Meetings meetings meetings." He never explained to me what these meetings had been or where or with whom. But I realized that whatever it was that was happening, it was something wonderfully hopeful for him. More than ever I loved to look at him and see his wide open, wide awake eyes sparkle in the light of the streetlamp. Sometimes he turned to me and held me hard against himself, and then I had no thought that his happiness came from anything other than myself.

He never quarreled with me the way he did with his mother. I suppose he couldn't because I didn't know enough Hindi and that was always the language in which they fought. They used what sounded like some very violent invective, and it often ended with things being thrown and broken, usually by her but sometimes by him. Once he swept all the pots of paint off her dressing table. She was so furious that she threatened to jump out the window and already had one leg over the sill when he pulled her back. We were only on the second floor, he pointed out, and all she would do was break her other leg and limp even more. As he said it, he laughed, and then she laughed too, and whatever unforgivable thing had happened between them was completely forgotten.

Although he was never really angry with me, he began to be irritated—by small things I had done or omitted to do, and he remembered them for the rest of the day, and the following day too. He often accused me of not looking after his clothes properly, for he was even more particular about his appearance than before: naturally, since he had to be seen by many important people in important places. If the washerman hadn't starched his shirts well enough, it was my fault, and I often found it easier to have new ones made. I went back to the textile merchant and to the tailor where they kept Vidia's measurements; and with the jewelers' market so conveniently close by, I also bought new little jeweled studs to fasten the new shirts with, because I knew how much he appreciated them and was always grateful.

I still hadn't told my father about our marriage, and whenever I asked Vidia if it wasn't time we did, he always said to wait. In the end I never did tell my father—in fact, he never knew that I had been through a marriage ceremony in India, and he always thought that my second marriage (of which he, rightly, disapproved) was my first. What happened to that piece of paper that Vidia and I signed under penalty of a fine or jail sentence or both? Vidia told me not to bother about it—to forget it, he said—so I don't know what strings were pulled to make it disappear. It never surfaced before or during any of my subsequent marriages. Vidia too seemed not to have been troubled by it.

L.K. reappeared on a day when I had bought a new set of clothes for Vidia. Vidia was trying them on before the little mirror attached to Dharma's dressing table; this was at floor level so that he could see only his legs and feet and was complaining at there not being a decent mirror in the house. L.K., who had entered in his usual way with his stick held aloft as though announcing some victory, burst out laughing: "You won't have need of many mirrors where you're going," and then, waving his stick at the new outfit: "Or of fine clothes." He sucked in his cheeks to keep himself from saying anything more, like someone relishing a secret.

"What, no tea?" he asked Dharma, who at once began to grumble how was she to know he was going to walk in the door after not even a postcard—but at the same time she was whispering to me to go down for the milk rusks that he liked. And it was only when he was dipping these rusks into his tea that he came out with his secret. Vidia would not have to wait five years before contesting the next election. A seat had fallen vacant due to a death or resignation or expulsion, and L.K. had persuaded his party to let Vidia stand for it.

"Now we'll show them," L.K. said. "Now they'll see something new." He extended his hand to pinch Vidia's cheek in his usual way, but Vidia moved out of reach. L.K.'s enthusiasm was not dampened. "Tell your mother how you'll drive them out from all the seats and portfolios they're keeping warm for themselves," he went on. "No more shirts washed in Paris! No more rose in the buttonhole!" He laughed out loud, but Vidia only responded with a faint smile.

L.K. wanted them to leave on a new election tour at once, but Vidia said this would not be possible as he had some affairs to attend to in Delhi. And next morning he had no time at all to discuss anything because the official car came for him again and was waiting outside. I stood on the balcony to watch him leave; as usual, he never glanced back but looked straight ahead with his thoughts already fixed on the places and people he was being driven to. So he was unaware that L.K. stood on the balcony with me and that he too was looking down at the car. Although he made no comment, there was a peculiar expression on L.K.'s face, and it was then I noticed for the first time that the car driving Vidia away carried the flag and the number plate of the ruling party.

Later that day I saw Vidia and his new girl friend (subsequently his wife). I was standing outside the American Express office together with some of the others who had also come to collect their money. The office was next to an opulent restaurant that none of us cared to patronize; we had not come to India for luxury and display. But the place was popular with a modern type of Indian businessman and their elegant girl friends. We watched with disdain as their chauffeured cars drove up and the tall doorman in splendid tunic and turban opened the brass-studded doors for them.

One sleek sky-blue limousine delivered Vidia and his girl friend. I watched them get out and walk toward the restaurant. Even if he had not been with her, I would have noticed her, she was so beautiful, spilling over with jewelry, with happiness, and with laughter at what she was telling him. He was leaning toward her, listening to her with the half-smile I knew well, indicating his acceptance of his good luck. It was the way he received things I was able to buy for him—in fact, he was wearing the same new outfit he had tried on the day before while grumbling that the mirror wasn't big enough.

I thought Vidia hadn't seen me, but he had. When he came home that evening, he at once began to reproach me for standing around on the street like a common person with hippies and bums. "What about you?" I said. "I saw you were not with a common person." He didn't blink an eyelid, but went on, "You don't understand anything."

And the next day I heard Dharma say the same words to L.K. She was sobbing as he collected the few clothes he kept in the flat. "You don't understand anything," she said. "He's my son. My *son*." L.K. didn't respond but bundled up his things. He was ready to go, while she went on pleading: "Is there a mother on earth who wouldn't want everything for her son?" He proceeded toward the door with his bundle and his stick. He stopped for a moment in front of me—perhaps he wanted to say something but didn't. He looked deeply grieved, his face pulled down in the lines of sad old age. Calmer now, Dharma was wiping her eyes. She asked him at least to take some food for his journey, but L.K. said he wouldn't need anything, he was taking a train and there would be food and tea sold at every station platform on the way. When she asked him if he had money, he waved her away majestically. Then he was gone, we heard his stick thumping down the stairs.

Now, whenever I think of him, it is not the way I saw him that last time but as I imagined him on the train that took him away from us. There he is not at all the L.K. I had first seen on the bus giving speeches to his fellow passengers. Instead, he has become like other gaunt old men I had met in third-class carriages—sitting upright, staring straight ahead with eyes that don't want to see anything more. When others, unpacking their bundles, offer him bread and pickle, he holds up his hand in refusal. At station platforms he doesn't buy anything for himself but only some candy for the children in his carriage, wailing from heat and weariness.

And the way I remember Dharma is as she was after L.K. left: sitting on the floor by her little dressing table, she talks to me about love and longing; about meeting and parting; about sacrifice, and the passing of all things good and bad. But Life goes on, she says, and we with it. She is resigned, both for herself and me. She explains that often the people who mean most to us have to be left behind because they cannot follow us along our destined path. We may be born into a high-caste Indian family or as a foreign girl, a free spirit, dedicated to travel, but for each of us Life has many stages.

She turned out to be right; I did pass through many stages. When I look back at the time with her and Vidia and L.K., it seems separate from the rest—of a different quality like a dream, or one of those dances she showed me, made up of graceful gestures executed in the air to the accompaniment of ankle bells, drum, and some sort of lute.

8

Refuge in London

ALL THE people—the lodgers—in my aunt's boarding house had a history I was too young to have known. I had been brought to England when I was two—"our little Englander," they called me. I knew no other place, and I felt that this made me, in comparison with them, rather blank. Of course I liked speaking English as naturally as the girls at my school, and in other ways too being much the same. But I wasn't, ever, quite the same, having grown up in this house of European émigrés, all of them so different from the parents of my schoolfellows and carrying a past, a country or countries—a continent—distinct from the one in which they now found themselves.

They were not always the same lodgers. There was a fairly quick turnover, for some of them prospered and moved on, others had to make different arrangements when they could no longer come up with the rent. My aunt, with whom I lived in the basement, was a kind landlady, but beyond a certain point she could not afford to be generous. Also—for my sake, she said—she had to be more strictly moral than it was perhaps in her nature to be. The way émigrés live is determined not so much by conventional morality as by the emotional refuge they find in each other. There is always some looseness in these arrangements, odd marital and extramarital situations: for instance, Dr. Levicus, who had started off in one of the rooms with his wife to whom he had been married for thirty years, replaced her with a young lady of twenty, also a refugee but nowhere near his level of refinement. My aunt was prepared to wink at such behavior; she knew how difficult life could be. But she did give notice to Miss Wundt who, having taken her room as a single lady, had different men coming out of it in the mornings and could often be heard screaming insults after them as they made their shamefaced way down the stairs.

The Kohls, however, were tolerated year after year, though they were not at all regular with the rent, or in their morals. They were not expected to be; they were artists. Kohl was a painter, and in pre-Hitler Germany had been famous. His wife Marta said she had been an actress and a dancer, though not famous in either capacity. They rented the two top rooms but lived in them more or less separately. One room was his— his studio; she also referred to hers as a studio, though she didn't do anything artistic in there. She was much younger than he, and very attractive, a tiny redhead. It was unlikely that, if he had not been famous, she would ever have married someone so much older and so undistinguished in appearance. He was short and plump, and bald except for a fringe of hair at the back; he had an unattractive mustache that she called his toilet brush. He didn't seem to care that lovers came to visit her in her room; when that happened, he shut his door and went on painting. He painted all the time, though I don't think he sold anything during those years. I'm not sure what they lived on, probably on an allowance from some relief organization. For a time she had a job in the German section of the BBC, but she soon lost it. There were too many others far more competent and also more reliable than she, who found it impossible ever to be on time for anything.

Mann was another of our lodgers. His first name was Gustav, but no one ever called him anything except Mann. I disliked him. He was loud and boastful and took up more time in the second-floor bathroom we all had to share than anyone except Marta. Another reason I disliked him was that he was one of the men who spent time with Marta in her room, forcing Kohl to shut his door. I had no such hostile feelings toward her other male visitors but was as indifferent to them as Kohl seemed to be. He too was not indifferent to Mann. Whenever they met on the stairs, he said something insulting to him, which Mann received with great good humor. "Okay okay, my friend, take it easy," he said and even soothingly tapped his shoulder, at which Kohl cried out, "Don't touch me!" and jerked away from him. Once he stumbled and rolled down several steps, and Mann laughed. Mann also used to laugh whenever he passed me. I was sixteen at the time and not attractive, and he made me feel even less so by pretending that I was. "Charming," he said, fingering the navy blue school tunic I wore and hated. I was in my last years at school—too old for it, I felt, and longing for what I thought of as the real world.

Those particular years are probably difficult for most girls, and it didn't help that they happened to be the post-war ones in England, with drab food, drab climate, and clothes not only rationed but made of a thick standard so-called "Utility" material. But that didn't really matter: I wasn't so responsive to what was going on outside as to what was going on inside me. My surroundings were only a chrysalis, I felt, waiting for me to burst out and become something else. Only what? I didn't feel that I could ever be butterfly material, and whenever Mann looked at me and said his tongue-in-cheek "Charming," it was obvious that this was also his opinion.

It was different with Kohl. I often sat for him while he drew me. Unable to afford a model, he had already drawn most of the people in the house, including my aunt. She had looked at her portrait with round eyes and her hand before her mouth in only partly amused distress: "No—really?" she said. But it really was her, not perhaps as she was meant to be—as, in more hopeful years, she had expected to be—but how she had become, after the war, after survival, after hard unaccustomed domestic work, and the habitual shortage of money that was also unexpected. It was my aunt who had brought me to England, more or less tearing me out of my mother's arms, promising her that she would soon be reunited with me. This never happened: after the age of two, I never again saw my mother, nor my father, nor any other relative. Only my aunt—her name was Elsa, but I called her La Plume (from my French lesson—"La Plume de ma Tante"). She was nearly fifty at the time; some nights I saw her asleep on her bed in the kitchen alcove—her heavy red swollen face, her greying hair bedraggled on a pillow, her mouth open and emitting the groans she must have suppressed during the day. It was this person whom she did not recognize in Kohl's drawing of her.

I was always ready to sit for my portrait. Once I was home from school, I had nowhere else to go. I didn't share many of the interests of my classmates nor was I involved in their intense relationships, which were mostly with each other. When invited to their homes, I found them smaller than mine, more cramped in every way. They lived in semi-detached or terraced houses, with a rectangular stretch of garden at the back where their fathers dug and grew vegetables on their days off from their jobs as postmen or bus conductors. Only one family lived in each house whereas ours swarmed with people, each one carrying a distinct history (the load of their ruined past). The unruly lives of our lodgers were reflected in the state of our back garden. It was wildly overgrown, for no one knew how to mow the grass, even if we had had anything to mow it with; buried within its rough tangle lay the pieces of a broken statue, which had been there ever since we moved in. Ours was one of the few tall old houses left that had not been pulled down in the reconstruction of the neighborhood in the 1930s, or bombed during the war. Its pinnacle was Kohl's studio on the top floor, and when I sat for him, I felt myself to be detached from and floating above the tiled roofs of the little English villas among which our boarding house had come to anchor.

Kohl worked through the night, painting huge canvases in oil that one only saw in glimpses, for he either covered them with a cloth or turned them face to the wall. These paintings were not interesting to me—in fact, I thought they were awful: great slashing wounds of color, completely meaningless like someone else's nightmare or the deepest depths of a subconscious mind. But when he drew me, it was always by day. He perched close to me, knee to knee, holding a pad on his lap and drawing on it in pencil or charcoal. While he was working, Kohl was always happy. He and his hand were effortlessly united in one fluid action over the paper on to which he was transferring me. He smiled, he hummed, he whispered a little to himself, and when his eyes darted toward me, that blissful smile remained. "Ah, *sweet*," he breathed, now at his drawing, now at me. I too felt blissful; no one had ever looked at me or murmured over me in such a way; and although I had of course no sentiment for him—this small paunchy middleaged man—at such moments I did feel a bond with him, not so much as between two persons as in something else coming alive between us. With so many people living in it, there was always movement in the house, noise: doors, voices, footsteps. But there at the top, we felt entirely alone and bound to each other by his art.

The one person ever to disturb us was his wife Marta—and she was not only a disturbance but a disruption, an eruption into our silence. Although they lived separately in their separate rooms, she entered his as of right, its rightful mistress. Without a glance at me, she went straight to look over his shoulder at the drawing: she stood there, taking it in. I felt the instrument in his hand stumble in its effortless motion. There was a change of mood in everything except her who stood behind him, looking, judging, one little hand on her hip which was slightly thrust forward in a challenging way. Her glinting green eyes darted from the drawing to me and took me in, not as the subject of his drawing but as an object of her appraisal. After a pause, she returned to the drawing and pointed to something with her forefinger extended. "Don't touch," he hissed, but she only brought her finger closer to show what she judged to be wrong. He pushed her hand aside roughly, which made her laugh. "You never could stand criticism," she said and walked away from him, sauntering around the room; if she found something tasty left on a plate, she ate it. He pretended to go on working, but I could feel his attention was more on her, as was mine. She took her time before leaving, and even when she was half out of the door, she turned again and told me, "Don't let him keep you sitting too long: once he starts, he doesn't know when to stop." It took a long time for Kohl to recover his concentration; sometimes he couldn't manage it at all and we had to stop for the day.

Once, when this happened, he asked me to go for a walk with him. I had noticed that he always took an afternoon walk and usually to the same place. This was a little park we had in the neighborhood—an artificial little park, with small trees and a wooden bridge built over a little stream which rippled over white stones. The place seemed dull to me—I was reading the Romantic poets for my Higher Secondary, and my taste was for wild landscapes and numinous presences. Now I saw that this park, which I despised,

represented something delightful to him. It was a spring day
the first time I accompanied him, and I had never seen anyone
so relish the smell of the first violets and their touch—he bent
down to feel them—and the sound of starlings that had
joyfully survived the winter. He made me take his arm, a
gallant gesture that embarrassed me, and we paraded up and
down the winding paths and under the trees that were not
big enough to hide the sky. He said he loved everything that
was young and fresh—here he slightly pressed my arm, tucked
under his; when a blossom floated down and landed in my
hair, he picked it out and said, "Ah *sweet*," the way he did
when drawing. We sat on a bench together, romantically
placed by the rippling stream, and there he recited poetry to
me: far from being young and fresh, the lines seemed quite
decadent—something about a poet's black mistress or a
rotting corpse. According to Kohl, this had been a favourite
poet of his in his younger days, when he had lived in Paris
and sat in the same cafés as Braque and Derain.

   After that first walk, he often asked me to go with him,
but I usually refused. It embarrassed me to be seen arm in
arm with someone older than my father or my uncle—had I
had one. He never tried to change my mind, but when I saw
him walking by himself, he looked so sad and lonely that I
went with him more often than I wanted to. It was a strange
and entirely new sensation for me to see another person happy
in my company when I myself had no such feeling at all. He
was undoubtedly happy in that pathetic little park, listening
to birds and smelling flowers, walking up and down with me,
aged sixteen, on his arm. But when we sat on the bench by
the stream and he recited Baudelaire in French, I became
wistful. I realized that the situation was, or should have been,
romantic—if only he had been other than he was, an old man
in a homburg hat with an ugly mustache.

He began to invite me on other outings, such as his Sunday afternoon visits to galleries and museums. I did go with him a few times but did not enjoy it—starting from the long tube ride where we sat side by side and I wanted people to think we were not together. Looking back now, all these years later, I see that it should have been regarded as a great privilege for me to see great paintings with an artist such as Kohl who had once been famous (and became so again). He kept me close beside him, standing in front of the paintings he had come to view—usually only two or three. He made no attempt to explain anything to me, only pointed at certain details that I wouldn't have thought extraordinary—light falling on an apple or a virgin's knee—and saying, "Ah ah ah," with the same ecstasy as when he was working. Afterwards he would treat me to a cup of coffee. At that time there were only certain standard eating places in London that he could afford: dingy rooms with unfriendly elderly waitresses, especially depressing if it was raining outside, as it often was, and we had to remain uncomfortable in our wet coats and shoes. But he seemed to enjoy these occasions, even the bad coffee, and continued to sit there after the waitress had slapped down the bill in front of him. At last I had to tell him that my aunt would be worried if I came home too late. Then he regretfully got up; and it was only at that last moment, when he was picking up the bill, that his hand brushed against mine very delicately, very shyly, and he smiled at me in the same way, delicate and shy.

The only times I really liked to be with him were in his studio when he was drawing me. All I saw out of his window was a patch of sky with some chimneys rearing up into it. When it got dark and he turned on the light, even that disappeared. There remained only the room itself, with its iron bed, often unmade, a wooden table full of drawings, and the canvases that he painted at night, piled face downward one against another on every available inch of wall. The floor was bare and had paint splashed all over it. There was a one-burner gas-ring, on which I don't think he ever cooked; all I saw him eat was a herring or a fried egg sandwich bought at a corner shop. He seemed always to be working, deeply immersed in it and immersing me with him. This was what I responded to—it was the first time I had been in the presence of an artist practicing his art, and later, when I began to write, I often thought of it, and it inspired me.

Our occupation with each other was entirely innocent, but it went on too long and perhaps too often, so that others began to take notice. My aunt, La Plume, would call up, "Don't you have any homework?" or make excuses to send me on unnecessary errands. When I came down, she would look at me in a shrewd way. Once she said, "You know, artists are not like the rest of us." When I didn't understand, or pretended not to, she went on, "They don't have the same morals." To illustrate her point, she told me some anecdote about herself and my mother, who had both been crazy about opera and hung about the stage door in the hope of meeting the artists. Here she began to smile and, forgetting about artists in general, began to speak of a particular tenor. He had taken a liking to my mother who, with her shingled hair and very short skirt showing a lot of silk stocking, looked more forward than she was. He had invited the two girls to his flat—"His wife was there, and another woman we thought may have been another wife for him, you know, a mistress." Her smile became a laugh, more pleasure than outrage, as she remembered the atmosphere, which was so different from that of their own home that they had an unspoken pact never to mention their visits to the tenor's flat. In the end, they stopped going; there were too many unexplained relationships and too many quarrels, and what had seemed exciting to them at first was now unsettling. Shortly afterward both of them became engaged to their respective suitors—a book-keeper, and a teacher (my father). Winding up her story, she said, "So you see," but I didn't see anything, especially what it might have to do with me, who had no suitor to fall back on.

Marta began to intrude on our drawing sessions more frequently and to stay longer than she used to. She perched on a stool just behind him, so that he could not see but could certainly feel her. And hear her—for she talked all the time, criticizing his drawing, the state of his cheerless room, the cold that he seemed never to notice, except that in the worst weather he wore gloves with the fingers cut off. In the end he gave up—his concentration long gone—and he threw his pencil aside and said, "But what do you want?"

She stretched her green eyes wide open at him: "Want? What could I possibly want from you, my poor Kohl?"

But once she answered, "I want to invite you to my birthday party."

He cursed her birthday and her party, and her eyes opened even wider, greener: "But don't you remember? You used to *love* my birthday! Each year a new poem for me . . . He wrote poetry," she told me. "Real poetry, with flowers, birds, and a moon in it. And I was all three: flowers, birds, and moon. Now he pretends to have forgotten."

Birthdays were always the occasion for a fuss, even for those lodgers whom no one liked very much. I suppose that, in celebrating a birthday as something special, people were trying to take the place of the family we had all lost. Usually these parties were held in our basement kitchen, which was the only room large enough—the rest of the house was divided up into individual small units for renting out. My aunt was known as a good sort and was the only person everyone got on with; she was always ready to let people come down to her kitchen and tell her their troubles as though she had none of her own. For birthday parties she covered the grease stains and knife cuts on our big table with a cloth and made the bed she slept on look as much as possible like a sofa for guests to sit on. She arranged sausage slices on bread and baked a cake with margarine and eggs someone had got on the black market. Those who wanted liquor brought their own bottles, though she didn't encourage drinking; it seemed to make people melancholy or quarrelsome and spoiled the mood of celebration.

Marta's party was not held in our kitchen but in her room at the top of the house. Since this was too small to hold many people, she had persuaded Kohl to open his studio across the landing for additional space. Although the two rooms were identical in size, their appearance was very different. While his was strictly a workplace, with nothing homelike in it, hers was all home, all coziness. There were colorful rugs, curtains, heaped cushions, lampshades with tassels, and most of the year she kept her gas-fire going day and night, careless of the shillings that it swallowed. There were no drawings or paintings—Kohl never gave her any—but a lot of photographs, mostly of herself having fun with friends, when she was much younger but also just as pretty.

On that day, her birthday, she was very excited. She rushed to meet each new arrival and, snatching her present, began at once to unwrap it, shrieking. Apart from my aunt and myself, the guests were all men. She hadn't invited any of our female lodgers, such as Miss Wundt (who was anyway under notice to quit), and these must have been skulking down in their rooms listening to the party going on above. Not all the men lived in our house. Some I didn't know, though I might have seen them on the stairs on their visits to Marta, often carrying flowers. There was one very refined person, with long hair like an artist's rolling over his collar. He wasn't an artist but had been a lawyer and now worked in a solicitor's office, not having a licence to practice in England. Another, introduced as a Russian nobleman, bowed from the waist in a stately way but was soon very drunk, so that his bows became as stiff as those of a mechanical doll. To celebrate the birthday, a great deal of liquor had been brought in by the more affluent guests who were not our lodgers; one man, for instance, though also a refugee, had done very well in the wholesale garment business.

Trying to keep up with the rest of the party, I too drank more than I should have done. When my aunt saw me refilling my glass, she shook her head and her finger at me. I pretended not to see this warning, but Mann drew attention to it: "Let the little one learn how the big people live!" he shouted. And to me he said, "You like it? Good, ah? Better than school! Just grow up and you'll see how we eat and drink and do our etceteras!"

"Tcha, keep your big mouth shut," La Plume told him, and he bent down to hug her, which she pretended not to like. He was obviously enjoying himself, making the most of the unaccustomed supply of liquor by drinking a lot of it. But he was not in the least drunk—I suppose his size allowed him to absorb it more easily than others. Of course he was loud as usual, with a lot of bad jokes, but that was his style. He appeared to dominate the party as though he were its host; and Marta treated him like one, sending him here and there to fill glasses and open bottles. If he didn't do it well or fast enough, she called him a donkey.

The guests overflowed to the landing and through the open door into Kohl's studio. Some of them were looking at his paintings, making quite free with them. They even turned around those facing the wall, the big canvases he painted at night and never showed anyone. The lawyer with the long hair waved his delicate white fingers at them and interpreted their psychological significance. But where was Kohl? No one seemed to have noticed that he was missing. I only became aware of his absence when I saw the lawyer draw attention to a drawing of myself: "Here we see delight not in a particular person but in Youth with a capital Y."

It was Marta who shouted, "What rubbish are you spouting there? . . . And where's Kohl, the idiot, leaving the place open for every donkey to come and give his opinion. Where is he? Why isn't he at my party? Go and find him," she ordered Mann, as though Kohl's absence were his fault.

Mann turned to me: "Do you know where he is?"

"How would she know?" Marta said.

"Of course she knows. She's Youth with a capital Y. She inspires him."

If I had been a little younger, I would have kicked his shins; anyway, I almost did. But Marta laughed: "Sneaking away from my party, isn't that just like him. Go and find him if you know where he is," she now ordered me. "Oh yes, and tell him where the hell is my present?"

I was glad to leave the party. It was irritating to see people wander freely round Kohl's studio making comments on his paintings. The lawyer's explanation of my drawing had been like a violation, not of myself but of Kohl's work and of my share in it, however passive. And it was not Youth, it was I—I myself—whom no one had ever cared to observe as Kohl did . . . I ran down the stairs furiously and then along the street and round the corner to the little park.

He was sitting on the bench beside the stream. On his lap was a flat packet wrapped in some paper with designs on it that he must have drawn himself: an elephant holding a sprig of lilac, a hippo in a bathtub. When I asked him if it was for Marta, he nodded gloomily. "She was asking for her present," I said. He was suddenly angry, his face and ears swelled red, and I added quickly, "It was a joke."

"No. No joke. This is her character: to take and take, if she could she would suck the marrow from a man's soul. From *my* soul . . . Who's there with her? All of them? That one with the long hair and lisping like a woman? He thinks he knows about art but all he knows is to lick her feet."

It was a lovely summer night, as light as if it were still dusk. How wonderful it was to have these long days after our gloomy winter: to sit outdoors, to enjoy a breeze even though it was still a little cool. It sent a slight shiver over the stream and flickered the remnant of light reflected in the water. During the day two swans glided there, placed by the municipality, but now they must have been asleep and instead there were two stars on the surface of the sky, still pale though later, when it got dark, they would become shining jewels, diamonds. There was fragrance from a lilac bush. I would have liked to have a lover sitting beside me instead of Kohl, so angry with thinking of Marta.

"Is it true you used to write a poem for her on her birthday?" I said.

"She remembers, ha?" His anger seemed to fade, maybe he was even smiling under that ugly mustache. "Yes, I wrote poems—not one, not only on her birthday, but a flood. A flood of poems . . . It's the only way, you see, to relieve the pressure. On the heart; the pressure on the heart."

I recognized what he said—having felt that pressure, though in an unspecified way. So far I didn't quite know what it was about, or even whether it was painful or extremely pleasant.

"Is he there—that Mann? What a beast. When he's on the stairs, there is a smell, like a beast in rut. You don't know what that means." I knew very well but didn't say so, for he was wiping his mouth, as though it had been dirtied by these words.

"Here, *you* give it to her." He thrust his packet at me. "She'll get no more presents from me and no more poems and no more nothing. All that was for a different person . . . I'll show you."

He snatched the packet back, his hands trembled in undoing the knot; but he handled it carefully to avoid tearing the paper, which he—and so far he alone—knew to be valuable. Then he folded it back, revealing the contents. It was a drawing of Marta. He looked from it to me, almost teasing: "You don't even recognize her." He held it out to me, not letting me touch it.

The lamp-posts in the park were designed to resemble toadstools, and the light they shed was not strong enough to overcome what was still left of the day. So it was by a mixture of electric and early evening light that I first saw this drawing of Marta. It was dated 1931—fifteen years younger than she was today on her birthday. Still, I would certainly have recognized her.

"Look at her," he said, though holding it up for himself rather than for me. "Look at her eyes: not the same person at all."

But they *were* the same eyes. It was a pencil drawing, but you could tell their color was green. Green, and glinting— with daring, hunger, even greed in them, or passion as greed. At that time I couldn't formulate any of this but I did recognize that green glint as typically Marta's. And her small cheeky nose; and her hair—even in the drawing one could tell it was red. He had drawn a few loose strands of it flitting against her cheek, the way he always did mine. Just the edge of her small pointed teeth was showing and a tip of tongue between them: roguish, eager, challenging, the way she still was. But her cheeks were more rounded than they were now, and her mouth had a less knowing expression, as if at that time it hadn't yet tasted as much as it had in the intervening years.

He covered the drawing again, taking care of it and its wrapping, sunk in thoughts that did not seem to include me at this moment; and when he had finished tying the string, he failed to give the packet back to me but kept it on his lap. I reminded him that we had to leave, since they would soon be locking up the park for the night.

When we got to the gate, it *had* been locked. It was not difficult for me to find a foothold and to vault over, avoiding the row of spikes on top. He remained hesitating on the other side, clutching his drawing. I showed him where the foothold was and asked him to pass the drawing to me through the bars. He didn't want to do either but had no choice. With me helping him, he managed to get over, but at the last moment the back of his pants got caught on one of the spikes. The first thing he did when we were reunited was to relieve me of the drawing; the second was to stretch backward to see the rip in his pants. It was hardly visible, I lied; anyway, it was dark by now, and if we met people on the road, they would hardly bother about his torn seat. Nevertheless, he made me walk behind to shield him; every time we passed a lamp-post he looked back at me anxiously: "Does it show?"

Near our house, we could see that the party was still in progress. Lights and voices streamed out into the street and the shadows of people were moving against the windows. But inside we found that my aunt had left the party and was banging about in the basement kitchen, grumbling to herself:

"Why don't they go home instead of turning my house into God knows what."

It was impossible for Kohl with his torn pants to return to his studio, which was full of people he didn't like. "Take them off," La Plume said, "I'll sew them for you . . . Go on, you think I haven't seen anything like what you hide in there?" But when he stepped out of them, she shook her head: "What does she do all day that she can't wash her husband's under-pants?"

I fetched a blanket for him to wrap around his legs, which were very white, unsunned. They trembled slightly, not used to being naked and ashamed of it. Looking back now, I'm glad I got the blanket and do not have to remember that great artist the way he was at that moment, trouserless in our kitchen.

When footsteps sounded on the basement stairs, he sat down quickly with his legs under the table where La Plume was sewing his pants. It was Mann who entered, to borrow more glasses for the party. "Cups will do," he said and began to collect the few we had from our shelves. "And I'm not even asking for saucers."

"Thank you very much," La Plume said, "so in the morning we can drink our coffee from the saucer like cats and dogs."

"Be a sport, Mummy," he said.

"Who's your Mummy! And where do you get that sport business, as if you'd been to Eton and Oxford?"

"Better than Eton and Oxford, I've attended the School of Life," he teased her—they were always on such easy terms.

"Yes, in the gutters of Cologne," Kohl put in—not in a teasing way.

It was only then that Mann became aware of him: "So there you are. Everyone is asking for you: where is the husband, the famous artist?" Next moment his attention shifted to the packet lying on the table: "Ah, her present that she's been asking for all day. I'll take it to her—I'll tell her you're busy down here, flirting with two ladies."

Kohl instantly placed his hand on the packet, and wild-eyed, cornered, he glared up at Mann. Mann—a big man but a coward—retreated quickly with our cups held against his chest.

"Take care you bring them back washed, you lazy devil!" La Plume shouted after him. But when he had gone, she said, "He's not a bad sort though he gets on everyone's nerves. They say he was a great idealist and gave wonderful speeches to the workers at their rallies."

"We've heard all about those wonderful speeches—from him. From no one else," Kohl sneered. "And when the police came, he ran faster than anyone. It's only here he plays the great hero."

"Ah well," sighed La Plume, "everyone lives as best they can." This was her motto. "Here—I wouldn't get very high marks for sewing, but they'll do." She handed him his trousers and he got up to step into them—just in time, for while he was still buttoning them, Marta was heard calling from the stairs.

I had noticed that, whenever Marta came into a room, the air somehow shifted. I don't know if this was due to other people's reaction to her, or to some particular power in her of which she herself was unaware. I might mention here that she had a peculiar, very sweet smell—not of perfume, more of a fruit, ripe and juicy, not quite fresh.

"So where's my present? Mann says you have my present!" Her eager eyes were already fixed on it, but when Kohl held on to it, "Give," she wheedled, "it's mine."

He shook his head in refusal, while secretly smiling again. But when she began to tug at it—"Give, give"—he shouted, "Be careful!" and let go, so that it remained in her hands.

She untied it, the tip of her tongue slightly protruding. The paper came off and the drawing was revealed. She held it and looked at it: looked at herself looking out of it, and as she did so, he watched her, the expression on his face becoming anxious, like one waiting for a verdict.

At last she said, "Not bad."

"Not bad!" he echoed indignantly.

"I mean me not you." Her eyes darted to him with the same expression as in the drawing. She held it at another angle for careful study: "Yes," was her verdict, "no wonder you fell madly in love with me."

"I with you! Who was it chased me all over town, from café to café, from studio to studio, like a madwoman, and everyone laughing at both of us?"

"Me running after him?" She turned to La Plume: "Me in love with him? Have you ever heard anything so ridiculous in all your life?"

"No, not with me. With my fame."

He spoke with dignity and pride, and then she too became proud. "Oh yes," she said, "he was famous all right, and I wasn't the only one to run after him. Naturally: a famous artist." She returned to the drawing, to his gift to her, and now she appeared to be studying not herself as before, but his work.

"So?" he asked, valuing her opinion and awaiting her compliment.

This compliment seemed to be hovering on her lips—when Mann came storming into our kitchen, followed by some other guests. As with one gesture, Kohl and Marta seized the wrapping paper to conceal the drawing—but Mann had already seen it: "So that's the present he's been hiding!"

"Don't touch!" Marta ordered, but she held it out, not only for him but high enough for others to see. They crowded forward, there were admiring cries, and Mann whistled. It was a gratifying moment for both Kohl and Marta. La Plume glowed too, and so did I; we were proud to have an artist in our house.

The lawyer spoiled it. He peered at the drawing through his rimless glasses, thrusting out his white fingers to point out beauties, the way he had done with my portrait. He may even have said something similar about Youth with a capital Y, but Marta cut him short: "You really are a donkey," and at once she wrapped up the drawing.

"You know what, children?" said La Plume. "It's long past my bedtime, and if you don't clear out, I'm going to miss my beauty sleep."

Everyone clamored for Kohl to join them. Marta too said: "Come and drink champagne with us. *He* brought it, so he's good for something." She pointed at the lawyer, who cheered up again briefly, but she had already returned to Kohl. She laid her hand on his shoulder in a familiar gesture we had never witnessed between them: "Come on—only don't give away any secrets. You're the only one who knows how old I am today."

"We all know," Mann said. "It's eighteen." No one heard him. Marta still had her hand on Kohl's shoulder: "You used to like to drink," she reminded him, "often a bit too much, both of us . . ."

"Maybe," he said; he shook her hand off. "But next morning I was up at five, working, and you lay in bed till noon, sleeping it off."

"I never had a hangover."

"No, it's true—when you got up, you were fresh and fit and ready to start making my life a misery again."

*

Marta may never have had a hangover, but there were days when she suffered a mysterious ailment about which she and La Plume whispered together. My aunt didn't want me to know about it, but when she wasn't there, Marta spoke to me as freely as she did to her. It was something very private to do with her womb—I really would have preferred not to know, these were matters I wanted to keep buried and pretend they had nothing to do with me. Marta went into unwelcome detail, though she always warned me, "For God's sake, don't tell Kohl. He can't stand women being ill."

She did however confide in Mann and the lawyer and probably everyone else too. She even told all of us that her trouble was due to an abortion brought about by herself when she was married to Kohl. "I was nineteen years old, what did I know? With a knitting needle, can you believe it? As if I'd ever knitted a thing." When we asked if she had told Kohl— "Are you crazy? He'd have run off very fast on his fat little legs. We were bohemians, for heaven's sake, not *parents*."

Although she spoke this last sentence proudly, Mann stroked her hair with his big hand and said, "My poor little one."

She jerked her head away from him: "Don't be a sentimental idiot. I wasn't going to ruin my career. I was on my way—listen, I'd already been an extra three times, the casting director at UFA was taking a tremendous interest in me, his name was Rosenbaum and he'd promised me a real part in the next production. And then of course he was fired." She made the face—one of scorn and disdain—with which she looked back on that part of their past.

She was not the only one deprived of her future. The lawyer had had his own practice in Dresden; Mann, who was a trained engineer, had been a union leader and a delegate at an international labor conference. In England they were earning their living in a humbler way, but Marta was never able to get started on anything. She said it was because her English was not good enough, but Kohl said it was because she was a lazy lump who couldn't get out of bed in the mornings. It was true that she usually slept late and had her first cup of coffee at noon.

It may have been her waiflike quality that made people want to serve her, but there was also something imperious in her personality that blurred the line between wishes and commands. During the day, I was often the only person available, and as soon as she heard me come home from school, she called down for me. She said she was too sick to get out of bed, she was starving, and though she had called and called, no one had answered. She wasn't sulky, just pathetic, so that I apologized for having been at school and my aunt on a shopping trip a tube-ride away where prices were cheaper. But there had been Kohl just across the landing—hadn't he heard her? She laughed at that: "Kohl! I could be screaming in my death agony, he'd stuff up his ears and not hear a thing." But again she was not reproachful, only amused.

He too was often waiting for me to come home from school: either he needed to finish a drawing of me or he had an idea for a new one. Of course he never summoned me the way she did; he requested, suggested, timidly ready to withdraw. It was only when he saw that she had pre-empted me and was sending me about her business that his manner changed. Once he came into her room while I was washing her stockings in the basin and she was warming her hands before the gas-fire. His face swelled red as it always did in anger: "What is she—a queen to be served and waited on? . . . You should have seen where she's come from, before I pulled her out of the mire!"

She admitted it freely—that she came out of the mire—but

as for his pulling her out: oh there were plenty of others, bigger and better, to do that.

"Then why me? Why did I have to be made the fool that married her?"

"Because you wanted it more than anyone else. You said you'd die and kill yourself without me."

"And now I'm dying with you!"

It began to happen that on the days when I was sitting with him in his room, she would call for me from hers. Then he kicked his door shut with his foot; but I could still hear her voice calling, weak and plaintive, and it made me restless. I wanted to help her; and also, I have to admit, I wanted to be more with her than with him. I was bored (God forgive me) with the long hours of sitting for him. And I was embarrassed by him, too young for his shy approaches, too unused to such respectful gallantry. I began to find excuses not to accompany him on his Sunday excursions, though I felt sorry when I saw him leave alone. Perhaps Marta felt sorry too: I heard her offer to go with him, and then his brusque, indignant refusal.

One day Kohl was waiting for me outside my school. He was standing beside someone's boy friend, a tall youth with straw-colored hair and a big adam's apple. But it was this little old man with his paunch who tucked his arm into mine and walked away with me. Next day I told everyone he was my uncle, and whenever he stood there again, people would announce that my uncle was waiting. I couldn't even tell him not to come—not only for fear of hurting his feelings (though that too) but not wanting anything significant to be read into his presence there. What could be significant? He was old, *old!* I wept into my pillow at night, ashamed and frustrated at some lack that it was ridiculous to think someone like him could fill.

On a Sunday when I had just told Kohl that I had too much homework to go with him, Marta called after me on the stairs to invite me to accompany her. I didn't dare accept there and then, with Kohl listening, but she knew how eager I was, and maybe he knew too: when we set out, I glanced up guiltily and there he was, standing at a window on the landing. It seemed she was as aware of him as I was: she put her arm around my shoulders and talked in the loud and lively way people do when they want to show others that they are having a good time.

After that first Sunday, I waited for her to invite me again, and sometimes she did and sometimes not. Outings with her were very different from those with Kohl. We were never alone, as I was with him, but Mann and the lawyer and later others joined us, and they conversed about art shows and films, and talked a lot about people they knew and seemed not to like. Although it hardly ever rained when I was with her—it inevitably did on Sundays with Kohl—they had little time for the birds and sunshine. They gathered in cafés for afternoon coffee and cake—never in the sort of depressing eating-holes which Kohl frequented but in large lavish places that doubtless imitated the luxury cafés they had once known. Their favorite was called the Old Vienna, which was not too expensive but was dense with atmosphere. There were chandeliers, carpets, red velvet banquettes, and richly looped creamy lace curtains under the red velvet drapes. Here many languages were spoken by both clients and waiters, and there were continental newspapers on poles for anyone who cared to read them. But few did—they were there to talk and laugh and pretend that everything was as it used to be. Some of the women were chic, with little hats and a lot of lipstick and costume jewelry. Yet Marta, not chic but bohemian with her red hair and long trailing skirt, drew more attention than anyone—maybe because she was enjoying herself so recklessly, surrounded by a group of friends, all male and all eager to supply and then light the cigarettes from which she flicked ash in all directions.

I was always excited after these excursions with Marta and her friends, and my aunt enjoyed hearing my descriptions of the café and its clientele, nodding in recognition of something she had once known. But Kohl frowned and told her, "You shouldn't let her go with them."

"But it's so nice for her! Poor child, what chance does she have to go anywhere?"

"She's too young," he said.

"Too young to go to a café?"

"Too young to go with people like that."

"Oh people like that," La Plume repeated dismissively in her "Everyone has to live" tone of voice.

As so often with this mild little man, he became a red fighting cock: "You don't know anything! None of you knows—what she was like, how she carried on. Every day was carnival for her—and how old was she? Sixteen, seventeen, and I, who was forty, *I*, Kohl, became her clown. She made me her carnival clown."

"Yes yes, sit down."

La Plume pressed him into a chair. She made tea for him, which he drank with his hands wrapped gratefully around the cup. It calmed him, changed the mood of his thoughts though not their subject. "What could I do? For years and years I had been alone, and poor—*poor!* And now people were coming to my studio, when I went into a café there were whispers, 'It's Kohl, the artist Kohl.' So that was meat and drink for her, other people's whispers . . . But she was always laughing at me, making a fool of me. Even her cap made a fool of me! This little striped monkey cap she wore riding on top of her hair . . . Her hair was red."

"It's still red."

"Nothing like it was!" He gulped tea, gulped heat. "I painted her, I wrote poetry for her, I slept with her, I couldn't get enough of her. I tell you, she was a flame to set people on fire." He broke off, and pleaded with me, "Come and sit for me. Come tomorrow? After school? I'll wait for you. I'll have everything ready."

That time I was glad to go. There was a stillness, a purity in his empty studio that I have never experienced in any other place; nor at any other time have I felt as serene as in the presence of this artist, drawing something out of me that I didn't know was there. But then Marta came in and stood behind him to comment on his drawing of me. He took off one of his slippers, which he always wore in the studio to save his feet, and threw it in her direction. It hit the door, which she had already shut behind her. But, as always with her intrusion, our peace was shattered.

All this was in my last two years at school—1946, 1947: after that, things began to change, and some of our lodgers left us to resume their former lives or to begin new ones elsewhere. Mann, for instance, went back to Germany—to East Germany, where he was welcomed by the remnants of his party and returned to an active life of rallies and international conferences. The lawyer started a new practice of his own, taking up cases of reparation for his fellow refugees, which made him rich and took him all over Europe. Their rooms remained empty; there were no more émigrés of the kind my aunt was used to, and she did not care for the other applicants who spoke in languages none of us understood. After some years the landlord, wanting to convert the house into flats, offered her a sum of money to quit. I was by this time living in Cambridge, having won a scholarship to the University, and only stayed with her during my vacations. She took a little flat over some shops in north-west London and led a more restful, retired life, made possible by the monthly payments of refugee reparations the lawyer arranged for her.

He also offered to arrange such payments for Marta, but she was too disorganized to locate her birth certificate or any other of the requisite papers. She also seemed indifferent about it, as though other things mattered more. Before leaving, Mann had asked her to go with him, but first she laughed at him and then said he was getting on her nerves and pushed him out. A few postcards arrived from him, optimistic in tone and with idyllic views of a cathedral and a river, which my aunt found in the waste-paper basket and put up in her kitchen.

The lawyer married a widow who had been at school with him and had survived the war in Holland. He moved into her flat in Amsterdam but was often in London on business. While we were still in the house, he had begun to bring people to Kohl's studio, and these brought other people—gallery owners, collectors, dealers—so it was often a busy scene in there. The visitors walked around the drawings on the walls, and Kohl turned over the large canvases for them to see; since he had only two chairs, Marta carried some in from her room, and then she stood leaning against the doorpost, smoking and watching. No one took any notice of her, commenting among themselves or turning respectfully to Kohl, who as usual had little to say; but if Marta tried to explain something for him, he became irritated and told her to go away.

We all attended the opening of his first show at a gallery in Jermyn Street. It was packed with fashionable people, ladies with long English legs in the shiny nylons that had begun to arrive from America; the air was rich with an aroma of perfume and face powder, also of the cigars some of the men had been smoking before being asked to put them out. Marta wore an ankle-length, low-cut dress of emerald green silk; it matched her eyes but had a stain in front that the dry-cleaner had not been able to get out. She wandered around in a rather forlorn way and no one seemed to know that she was the artist's wife. Many pictures were sold, discreet little dots appearing beside them. After this show, another was held in Paris, and after a while Kohl decided to move to Zurich. The pictures that were still left in the house were packed up under his supervision, and again Marta stood leaning in the open doorway to watch, and again if she tried to say anything, he became irritated.

When all was packed up, he came into the kitchen with a present for me. As he walked down the stairs, Marta, who seemed to be aware of his every movement, leaned over the banister and gave a street-boy whistle to attract his attention. When he looked up, she called him vile names in several languages, so that by the time he reached us, his face and ears were suffused in red. Her voice penetrated to the kitchen, where he, always shy of vulgarity, pretended not to hear. Courtly and courteous, he presented me with one of the drawings of myself—but La Plume and I didn't even have time to thank him before Marta came whirling in. Instinctively, though not aware at that time of its value, I held my drawing close for protection.

She too was carrying a drawing; it was the one he had given her on her birthday. She held it under his nose: "Here, you ridiculous animal!" She tore it across—once, twice, three times—and threw the pieces on the floor. With a terrible cry, he crouched down to gather them up, while she tried to prevent him by stamping her high-heeled shoes on his fingers. He didn't seem to notice, though when he got up, there was blood on his hands. La Plume, clasping her cheeks, shrieked at him, but he, concerned only that it should not stain the torn drawing, clutched the pieces fiercely to his breast. Marta was laughing now, as at a victory. "Children, children," my aunt said, trying in her usual way to soothe tempers; but I did not feel that those two were children, or that there was anything childlike about their quarrel.

It was only when Marta had left us that he let go of the fragments of the drawing and laid them down on the table. "Let me see your hand," La Plume said, but he impatiently wiped the blood off on his sleeve and concentrated on holding the drawing together. Although torn, it was still complete with nothing missing; he smiled down at it, first in relief, then in pure joy, and invited us to admire it with him—not Marta looking out of it with her insolent eyes but the work itself: *his*, his art.

He left the next day and I never met him again. I did see the drawing again: in spite of its damaged condition, some collector had bought it, and it was often reproduced in books of twentieth-century art and also in the book devoted to his work. Whatever we heard of Kohl himself was mostly through the lawyer, whom my aunt had engaged to recover some family property (she never got it). We learned that Kohl had rented a large studio in Zurich, in which he both lived and worked. He allowed his dealer to bring visitors but hardly seemed to notice them. He never attended any of his exhibitions, nor gave interviews to the art magazines who published articles about his work. He was always working, his only recreation an evening walk in a nearby park. He had a maid servant to cook and clean for him, a village girl fifteen or sixteen years old whom he often drew. The lawyer thought he also slept with her. Otherwise there was only his work; during his few remaining years, he grudged every moment away from it. When he died, in 1955, his obituaries gave his age as sixty-four.

Marta stayed in the house till my aunt left, and after that she took a room elsewhere. She moved often, not always voluntarily. Once or twice she landed on La Plume's doorstep, having had to vacate her room in a hurry. She never said why, but my aunt guessed that it may have been for the same reason that she herself had had to give notice to Miss Wundt.

We don't know what she lived on. Her clothes looked thin and worn; there were buttons missing from her little jacket and its fox-fur trimming was mangy. But she was always in high spirits and talked in her usual lively way. She tucked into the food my aunt prepared for her with all the gusto of someone who really needed it—but she never tried to borrow money from us. Once she asked me to take her to the cinema, not for the feature film but to see a newsreel she had been told about. When it came on, she nudged me—"Look look, that's him! Mann!" It was a shot of an international banquet, with speeches in a language I couldn't identify under giant portraits of leaders also unidentifiable. It may have been Mann—but many of the other delegates could also have been he, big and tall and cheering loudly as they raised and then drained their glasses in toasts to the speakers at the head table. She was convinced it was Mann—"The donkey," she laughed. "Can you imagine—he wanted to marry me. What a lucky escape," she congratulated herself. I had to leave, but now that the ticket had been paid for, she stayed on to see the feature film and to wait for the newsreel to come around again.

When Kohl died, it was reported in the newspapers that he had left the pictures remaining in his possession to a museum in New York and the rest of his estate to his maid servant. The lawyer told Marta that, if she could produce her marriage certificate, she would have a strong case for challenging the will. But she had no marriage certificate any more than she had a birth certificate, nor could she remember where the marriage had been registered, or when, and in fact it seemed she couldn't remember if there had been any legal procedure at all. Whenever she spoke of Kohl, it was in the same way as she did of Mann: congratulating herself on a lucky escape. She loved recalling the occasion when she had torn up his drawing—"Did you see his *face*?" she said, amused and pleased with herself. It turned out that this drawing was the only piece of work he had ever given her—just as the drawing he had given me was only one of many I sat for. What about the poems that he had written to her, I asked. She tossed her hair, which was still red but now too red, a flag waved in defiance: "Who can remember every little scrap they once had? . . . Anyway, they were all a lot of rubbish. Other men have written much better poems to me." She admitted not having kept those either; she had had to move so often, everything had just disappeared.

And then she herself disappeared, and no one knew what had happened to her. We went to ask at her last address, but the mention of her name caused the landlady to shut the door in our faces. Years, decades have passed, and in all this time there has been no trace of Marta. I have even stopped speculating about her, though when my aunt was still alive, we often did so, with conclusions that we did not like to suggest to each other. Marta may have been run over or collapsed in the street and been taken to a hospital and died there, with no one knowing who she was, whom to contact. She may have—who knows?—drowned herself in the Thames on some dark night, maybe tossing the red flag of her hair, congratulating herself on having fooled everyone by never learning to swim.

I no longer live in London. Some years ago, I had some money trouble that finally, reluctantly led me to sell Kohl's drawing. The sum I got for it was astonishing; it not only relieved me of my difficulties but gave me a sort of private income for a few years. I felt free to go where I liked, and since I had no one else close to me after La Plume, I was free in every way. I decided to go to New York. I had heard that there was a museum with one whole room dedicated to Kohl's work, and I went there the day after my arrival. Then I could not keep away.

His drawings hung on one wall, while the paintings took up the rest of the room. The drawings were mostly of Marta, though some were of me, and of a few other girls my age, one of them probably his maid servant. Although there was no resemblance between us, what we had in common was a particular evanescent stage of youth; it must have been this that elicited his little gasps of joy, his murmurs of "*Sweet,*" and these marvelous portraits. But when I saw myself on the wall of the museum, I had the same feeling I had had while sitting for him: that I was not just a type or a prototype for him, that it was not just any girl to whom he was responding, but me, myself. *I* was the person whom he had looked at so deeply and with such delight, and in a way that no one else had ever done before, or ever did again.

My decision to move to New York—and I have lived here ever since—may have been partly due, at least at first, to a desire to remain close to the museum displaying his work. But although I can't get enough of studying the drawings, I can rarely bring myself to look at the paintings. They are no longer meaningless—everyone now knows how to interpret those savage searing colors dripping off the canvas—but I still try to avoid them, even turning my back on them, unable to face what he had faced, at night and in secret, through all the years we had known him. And I still can't understand how, at the same time as he was possessed by these visions of our destruction, he was also drawing (*"Sweet, sweet"*) what is displayed on the remaining wall: girls in bloom, flowers in May.

9
Pilgrimage

A FTER MY mother died, C. sold whatever he could of her possessions, and with the proceeds he and I went to India. At that time one could still travel overland, partly by hitch-hiking, partly on a bus through Turkey and Iran, from Kabul over the Khyber Pass and into Punjab; so by the time we arrived in Delhi, we had already traversed great stretches of country different from anything we had known in England.

The hotel where C. took a room for us on arrival in Delhi was like other such places we had stayed in during our journey. It was in a narrow lane with old and crooked houses, open shops or stalls on the ground floor, stray dogs and cows snuffling among the rotting food stuffs discarded in the gutter, a broken sewer, sweet smoking sticks of incense: the usual bazaar scene except that this one also had a pig rooting up refuse. Neither of us was there for the atmosphere. I was there to be with him, and he had come to seek out a philosopher or guide he had heard about. This was at an early stage of C.'s career, before he had really worked out his own philosophy; and I might as well say at once that I wouldn't be able, even now, to explain what this was. All I know is that later many people believed in and followed him, as I did at that time.

He had of course charisma—if by that is meant a quality that would make others turn to him for whatever it was they were seeking. It may have helped that he was a very large man who towered over everyone in every room he entered.

He had huge shoulders, huge thighs, muscles like those of a construction worker. While in London, to keep himself in funds, he had taken advantage of his great strength to work as a casual laborer on building sites, or as an unlicensed porter. He had very blond hair which stood up in waves like a flame. He also had a fur of blond hair on his chest and along his arms and the back of his hands. Altogether there was something primitive, even barbaric about him: he was like a Goth, or a hunter for food in forests and mountains— not at all one's idea of a philosopher or spiritual guide.

But the philosopher whom C. had come to meet was just that: he seemed almost entirely spiritualized, non-physical. His name was Shivaji and he was already famous at that time. It was not easy for us, who knew nobody in India and were ourselves nobody, to gain access to him. He lived in a large house, in a tree-lined avenue mostly inhabited by ambassadors and cabinet ministers. The house had been taken for him by one of his followers, the wife of a rich Bombay industrialist. It was of course through this lady that C. had his first audience with Shivaji. I say "of course" because it was always through women that C. got what he needed—not that he particularly wooed them but they were always the first to respond to him. This is what happened in my case and how I came to follow him across deserts, mountains, and sacred rivers to end up with him in a small and cheap hotel room in the middle of a Delhi bazaar.

C. had been my mother Edith's lodger in the house she bought in a north-west London suburb. This was in the 1940s, during and just after the war. My mother hated being a landlady, but it was the only way she had of making a living for herself and me. We were refugees from Austria and she was lucky to have got enough money out, via Switzerland, to buy this house. She rented rooms to her fellow refugees—all like herself from well-off, cultured families, all having to start out anew in England. C. was the only male lodger and he was a very potent presence among us. He could be heard whistling while he shaved in our only bathroom, and even if he kept us waiting to use it, we easily forgave him when he emerged, still whistling, with freshly shaved cheeks raw and rosy, braces dangling, and hair waving in a blond flame.

I spent many hours sitting on the stairs waiting for him to come home. When he had earned enough money at his various laboring jobs, he studied all day in the British Museum Reading Room, preparing himself for his future career. I didn't mind waiting for him—I had nothing else to do, I was seventeen and had just failed my school leaving exam—and it was always worth it for me because, when he passed, he ruffled my hair and said something kind. He had the top room—it was an attic really—and I didn't follow him there because I knew how busy he was reading and studying and covering pages of a school copy book with his writing.

He began to take me on outings with him. We neither of us had any money, so the only entertainment we could afford was to ride on the top of a double-decker bus to the end of the line and back again. We passed miles and miles of small houses and small shops and small businesses; often it rained and everything melted away and we might as well have been under water. We passed one place that was almost like country, with a field and several trees, and once he made us get off there and sit under a tree large enough to shelter us. Here he spread his leather jacket—it was bought secondhand in a street market and had some of its leather rubbed away. He invited me to lie on it; I did everything as best I could, which I know wasn't very good. He tried not to hurt me, and since I didn't cry out, he thought he had succeeded. There was quite a lot of bleeding, so I didn't put my panties back on;

instead he dug a hole to bury them, and we made a little ceremony of it. After that we often got out at the same place to lie under the same tree. It sheltered us against any light drizzle, but if it rained more heavily, we were drenched and had to sit on the bus all the way home in our wet clothes. We didn't mind, and neither of us ever caught cold.

But when we got home, my mother Edith would be waiting for us. Edith had kept the two downstairs rooms for herself, one of them was her bedroom and the other what she called her salon. This she had furnished with what she managed to retrieve from her past life—a low divan, a Matisse rug, an Art Deco lamp, and a little smoking table with an ashtray on it; the ashtray was always full because Edith and all the friends who visited her smoked incessantly. She also brewed Turkish coffee in a tiny brass pot, and the fumes of coffee and cigarettes created a haze in which she could have thoughts and feelings other than her usual worries about money and lost status.

These thoughts and feelings revolved, as mine did, around C. At first they were mixed up with her money concerns— he was always behind with the rent and she often had to ask him for it, which was something she hated doing. When she knew he was settled reading and writing in his attic, she made her way up there. "Oh yes, the rent," he said, when she had managed to overcome her embarrassment at mentioning it. *He* wasn't embarrassed—the subject of money had no importance for him—and he would put his hand in his pocket: if he had managed to earn something that day and had not yet spent it, he handed it over. But she did not go away—she continued to stand looking at him, absorbed as he was in writing in his school book with a stub of pencil that he occasionally licked.

Later, when he and I had begun to go on our outings

together, she would be waiting for us in her salon. She sent me upstairs and invited him in for cigarettes and coffee and to talk to him about me: how young I was, how unformed, how incapable of dealing with my emotions. She talked about love in general, and about herself and her past and her affairs and her unhappy marriage to my father and her longings and so on. It was always very late when he came upstairs, and if I had fallen asleep, he woke me up. By this time I had got into the habit of spending most of the night in his attic room, and we could hear her roaming up and down the stairs outside.

Before this, Edith and I were used to being only with each other. She and my father had separated shortly after I was born, and he emigrated to Argentina about the same time that Edith managed to get a visa for herself and me to go to England. She was a cultured person and hoped I too would grow up to love literature and music. And though her hopes were mostly centered on me, she never showed disappointment when I didn't live up to her expectations. After I failed my exam, I heard her tell her friends that I was too imaginative to fit into the groove of education meant for ordinary girls.

But sometimes, when I came home from school, I would find her alone in her salon, her cheek propped on her hand. I put down my satchel—"What's happened, what's wrong?" She covered her face with her hands and said, "There's nothing left, only to die." Each time I was terrified. I didn't know the cause of her despair; I think it was often financial, there were days when she didn't know how we were going to get through the next week. Or it was emotional, something to do with a love affair, for she had one or two in those years, mostly with fellow refugees as cultured and as newly poor as she. These never worked out well, maybe because she was no longer young and also so full of anxieties; and she may have been too frantically eager—which could be seen in the way she smoked, deeply inhaling and smearing the cigarette with lipstick almost half its length as if she had been trying to swallow it. When she talked about killing herself, I became so desperate, I clung to her and made her promise, promise never to leave me. And she did and seemed comforted and lit another cigarette. Then later, when I started being with C., she several times said that there was nothing left for her, that she would kill herself. But by that time I had heard it so often, I no longer paid much attention and anyway I was too immersed in my own emotions to have room for hers; also I was no longer so terrified of being alone if she left me.

Edith loved to speak of the grand life-style—probably exaggerated in her mind—that had been hers in her family's house in Vienna. Of course it had all gone long ago and was familiar to me only from her nostalgic descriptions and her own small attempts at recreating it in her salon. But then, after long dusty traveling in buses and trucks, I found it all again in India: the carpets, the crystal, the silver Edith had described. It was the ambience created for Shivaji by his patroness Renuka, the industrialist's wife. She herself was born to such things and took it for granted that she had to provide them for him. He was the center of the house Renuka had taken for him: literally its center, for one had to pass through various ante-rooms before a final silk curtain was parted and there he was, crosslegged in the lotus pose on a Persian rug on a marble floor. The room was tall and had only ventilators set high up into the walls, so it was always dark: and on first entering, one's eyes were drawn at once to Shivaji in his starched white muslin, gleaming like a lamp perpetually lit to illumine the room, the house. I have never seen anyone embody holiness the way Shivaji did. He was a high-class brahmin with a light skin that was paper-thin; very graceful, delicate. His lips were narrow, his nostrils somewhat pinched, giving him the serious expression to be expected from one with such a serious message to deliver. But when he laughed— and he laughed often—this was entirely dispelled.

Renuka had a daughter called Priya, who hated her mother's guru. She said he was everything that was demeaning to women like her mother; that he took advantage of their higher striving and the unhappiness of their marriages (Renuka and Priya's father had been separated for years, with him making money in Bombay and she spending it on Shivaji). In her view, his message was a fraud and designed only for his personal gain. Priya had strong ideas—she was a strong person; I had never met anyone like her, though I had gone to school with clever girls who went on to college and became professional women. Priya too had gone to college, in America; she had recently graduated from Bryn Mawr, majoring in (I think) psychology. Now she had come home to India to see what she could do for her own country. She was the first modern Indian girl I had met. I was astounded by her brains and her beauty, but she took them as much for granted as the money that was always at her disposal. The one thing she and her mother had in common—about every- thing else they fought continuously—was their taste for fine saris and jewelry. Every day shopkeepers came to spread their wares in one of the verandahs that encircled the house, and mother and daughter sat side by side, each buying lavishly. There was another taste they shared, and this was one for great men. But the particular great man that each chose was as different as their preference in saris and jewels.

Nothing could be more distinct from Shivaji's delicacy than

C.'s rough-hewn personality. My mother used to sneer and call him the village blacksmith. But I know that was only to turn me against him and that secretly, deep inside herself, she too was attracted by this particular quality in him. And so was Priya, for all her refinement: "He's so real," she would say. Certainly, compared with Shivaji who seemed almost to float above the earth, C., with his big feet in big sandals, was firmly planted on it. In the beginning, Priya would ask me to tell her about C.—she had absolutely no conception of the background of a person like him.

Since the time he moved into our house as a lodger, I used to hear Edith and her friends speculate about him. They discovered that he had given several different versions of himself. Sometimes he said that he had run away from a Hungarian orphanage; then that he had been found in a forest in the Bukovina being suckled by wolves; another time these wolves were humans who hunted him down, so that in the process he himself turned into a wild beast hiding in caves. Yet everyone agreed that, far from being hunted, it was he himself who looked like the hunter. Here, over their cigarettes and Turkish coffee, they really let themselves go: they imagined him tearing meat from the sides of animals he had killed and eating it either raw or roasted over a fire he had lit by rubbing stones together. But at this point they burst out laughing and said that it was all a lot of rubbish. Most likely he came from some very modest home—his father a shoemaker, his mother cooking vast pots of kasha—in some country with fluctuating borders and several languages. I've heard him speak German, Hungarian, and Rumanian, all of them I've been told without an accent: unlike his English, which always remained heavily Teutonic.

Although all this was fascinating to Priya, what fascinated her most was his ideas. C.'s ideas: unlike myself, Priya understood completely what they were about—or rather, as she put it, what C. himself was all about. She knew, she felt it in her guts (she had these expressions) that C. was the real thing; whereas Shivaji was (again her expression) all bunk. Not the type to repress anything, she never disguised her feelings about Shivaji; but he was just as nice with her as he was with the rest of us. He had very gentle—one could almost say "gentlemanly"—manners, a sort of physical and moral delicacy typical of high-class Hindus. When Renuka took him to England—and this was one of the many things Priya held against him—he liked to outfit himself in Savile Row suits and in shoes that had to be handmade because of his slender brahmin feet. In India he wore only Indian clothes, of the most exquisite muslin with Lucknow embroidery at the shoulders and sleeves. And whereas in Europe he enjoyed lamb and wine, in India he was a pure vegetarian, eating out of silver bowls on a silver tray which Renuka herself carried in to him.

Usually he ate alone, but once a week we had what he called a feast, with all of us gathered around him. Nothing serious was ever said at these feasts; he made them playful occasions for everyone to enjoy, with laughter and teasing. He loved to tease and he didn't spare C. Shivaji himself always ate with his fingers, very skillfully and without spilling a drop; but when C. tried it, he got into a terrible mess, as Shivaji pointed out for everyone's amusement. C. also had difficulty sitting crosslegged on the floor—he was too large, his legs were like pillars, impossible to tuck under him, and about this too Shivaji teased him and made everyone laugh, C. the loudest. Only Priya scowled and said she saw no particular virtue in squatting on the floor, and though she spoke quite rudely, Shivaji made out that it was all in the same spirit of friendly fun.

For Priya, Shivaji was already "past it," as she put it: his ideas were too naive, too simplistic to appeal to the educated of her own generation. But her mother was Shivaji's ardent devotee, and also in complete charge of his practical and financial arrangements. She had given herself and her whole life over to him. She hardly spent any time in Bombay with her husband—"Of course Daddy is glad to be rid of her," Priya assured us. Later, when she got to know us better—when she got to know us very well—she also shared her grudge against her father with us and told us of his scandalous affair with a Bombay film actress who made as free with his money for her young lovers as Renuka did for Shivaji.

Priya didn't suggest that her mother and Shivaji were lovers. The word "suggest" is not right in regard to Priya, whose language was always direct, not to say blunt. I had never known anyone so uninhibited. At first this was strange to me, a contrast to the traditional modesty of the sari she so elegantly draped around herself, or the grace of her Indian gestures enhanced by the soft clinking of the gold bangles and ankle-chain she wore. But then, within this feminine exterior, she had a sharp, emancipated mind. She was voluble on every subject, including sex. She spoke frankly about her mother and Shivaji, explaining that yes of course *she* would have liked to have sex with him but he wouldn't, or maybe couldn't. Priya speculated about his sexual potency or orientation or both with such freedom that it was as if she intended to violate the purity under his spotless white muslin.

She was equally frank about her feelings for C. Of course he was at that time young, whereas Shivaji may even have been old. It was difficult to tell with him: sometimes his fine pale ivory skin seemed smooth and young, but sometimes it looked as if it had been stretched over his facial bones like parchment that was about to split. Also, whereas Shivaji sat enveloped in a hush of reverence within his palatial mansion, C. moved about the city, robustly enjoying everything around him. All our time in Delhi we lived in the same tiny rectangular room, with big patches of damp seeping through the walls on which many bugs had been squashed. The rooms in the hotel were always full, probably because they were so cheap. It was noisy with a whole lot of men in one room, drinking, laughing, and fighting. On hot nights they sat out in the street, in front of the hotel, where C. often joined them. I watched them from our window above and I could see what a good time they were all having together. Although he didn't as yet speak much of any local language—he learned a little more every day, he was a true polyglot—he managed to communicate with everyone, largely through humor and back-slapping. They were all large men, as large as he was, and with the same rough quality. He told me that most of them were Afghans, here on business—the business was clandestine, probably in opium, always a flourishing trade on this route. Some also had connections with the brothels located in the network of alleys around the hotel and were responsible for supplying them with new girls. Theirs were dangerous and highly competitive occupations, so it was no wonder that there were frequent fights, both in the hotel and in the street, including some stabbing incidents, for everyone carried a knife or dagger hidden under their long loose shirts.

To cater to the taste of these Afghan traders, several eating stalls had sprung up with open fire pits in which highly seasoned chickens and lumps of meat were roasted on spits. C. loved this food, and when I saw him surrounded by his new friends, all of them tearing their food with their hands— so different from Shivaji's refined table manners—it was impossible not to remember his stories of hunting and being hunted across forests and mountains. And although he was blond and they dark, dark-bearded, they were somehow of the same type: hunters, predators. They also introduced him to another of their great pleasures: Bombay films, for which we would queue up to get into the cheap seats. It was an experience to be down there in the stalls with our new friends, who knew and sang along with all the lyrics and cheered the hero and booed the villain and expired in ecstasy over the huge-bosomed heroine or with pity over her sufferings that made tears roll down her cheeks, plump as plums.

Priya deplored C.'s taste for these films, which she characterized as vulgar and childish. He went on enjoying them; he had even begun to learn the lyrics and to sing them with his friends. Although she so despised the films and their audience, Priya always came with us, for by this time she came with us everywhere. She sat around in our room for hours, though it was such a different atmosphere from anything she was used to. She never seemed to notice or to care about that. It didn't bother her even when a fight broke out in one of the rooms, or there was screeching and cursing on the stairs every time a hotel guest was evicted. She made no secret of the fact that she had attached herself to C. and wanted to be where he was. It was very unusual for a girl like her to be seen in these bazaar streets, but she walked in them as proudly as she did everywhere, just lifting the edge of her sari a little to prevent it from trailing in anything trodden into the ground. There was something so royal about her confidence that no one dared to call after or molest her in any way. I myself had had more trouble when I first came here—the only women seen in these streets were poor shabby housewives or prostitutes dressed to kill—but by now I was generally accepted as C.'s companion. In any case, I had nothing very remarkable about me to invite sexual interest. That may have been why my presence never inhibited Priya or affected her interest in C. If he was out when she came to the hotel, she simply stayed to wait for him. I sat on the floor while she lay on the bed; no other furniture was provided except for an earthenware jar to store drinking water. When Priya ran out of conversation with me, she picked up one of C.'s books and was soon immersed in reading it.

Although Priya's interest in C. was personal—and how could it not be?—that was only part of his appeal to her. Like everyone else, she felt the force of a great future in him, but in her case this went beyond a vague response to his personality. His ideas were in process of unfolding; and I think what interested her most was that they were so different from anything that Shivaji taught. As far as I understood this difference—and that was not very far—both wanted people to be more knowledgeable about themselves; but whereas Shivaji's self-knowledge was aimed at transcending this world, C.'s was aimed toward a better adjustment in it. If Priya were to read this last sentence—but she won't, she has long since moved away, physically and intellectually—she would be very impatient with me for my crude interpretation. For it was she who had tried to explain C.'s ideas to me in a way that he himself never did. He never spoke to me about these things; his relationship with me was on another level of his exist-ence—one that was completely and utterly satisfying to me and, I like to think, in some way for him too. For me, there has never been anything like the sweetness of our sessions under the tree; and perhaps some small drop of it has also lingered with him, through all his subsequent career and his professional and personal relationships with many, many others.

When our money ran out—and I never figured how he had made it last so long—Priya became our patroness. She had a large allowance from her father and could always ask him for more, so it was not difficult for her to supply our needs. Nor was it difficult for us to accept. By this time I had adopted C.'s attitude toward money, and anyway it was fun to go shopping with Priya for new clothes, which we badly needed since ours were falling to pieces. She dressed us up in Indian outfits—the choice was hers, she knew best of course and was bossy by nature. C. now wore the same kind of loose shirt and baggy pajama trousers as his Afghan friends, so that he took on even more of their warrior appearance. Priya was also ready to move us out of our hotel room—she had already chosen a rooftop flat for us in a much better part of the city— but C. wanted to stay where we had made friends and become used to the streets and stalls that supplied us with cooked food in little earthenware pots covered with leaves. The only inconvenience was that we had only one small room with a single bed in it, and while this had been fine for only C. and me, it was no longer so when Priya began to spend most of her time with us. She often found it difficult to leave because of the discussion of ideas she was having with C. Here I might mention that it was no part of his method to confine himself to abstract discussion. Far from holding aloof, he threw himself in, made himself—his expression—part of the equation. And with Priya, as probably with his later students, this took a physical turn: and since it was part of their work together, there was no embarrassment for anyone except me, who left them alone at such times though they always said it was all right for me to stay.

In this time I got to know the city of Delhi well, wandering around on my own in its streets and parks and tombs and temples and mosques. But as the season advanced and the heat became intense, I drifted more and more to the other house, where Shivaji was. Here it was cool and tranquil, and I was given almond sherbet to drink out of a silver vessel. I sat with Renuka, Priya's mother, on a brocade sofa while she spoke to me of her difficulties. Chief of these was her daughter Priya—she knew that daughters often rebelled against their mothers, but she could not understand why Priya's hostility extended to Shivaji, who was such a great and realized soul. How was it that instead Priya should attach herself to someone like C.—and here she had the same sort of questions as my mother Edith used to ask me: who is he, where does he come from? "And why is she with him so much?" Renuka also asked me. This question I could answer more easily: "They're discussing his ideas. Priya's the only person really able to understand them." Priya's mother said nothing, but bit her lips like one who could say a lot if she wanted to.

While Renuka kept her opinions to herself, Priya couldn't pronounce hers loud enough. "It's really quite sordid," she said of her mother and Shivaji. "It's all about money. She's afraid that if she doesn't come up with it, he'll just drop her and take up with someone else. He would too; he's the greediest person alive."

I didn't believe her. Along with his other visitors, I spent a lot of time in his presence, and I always tried to be there when he was singing. He had a light, melodious voice, and although I couldn't understand the words, I realized that they expressed feelings of love and devotion. Listening to him, all of us sat very still with only an occasional deep sigh of contentment. The one who sighed deepest was Renuka, and I think she would have liked to do more—to cry out maybe, to dance, to roll on the ground—but Shivaji was opposed to any form of ostentatious behavior. She was an imposing, regal woman, with an imperious manner, but I noticed that, when she approached him, this manner changed entirely: she became like a humble handmaiden whose one desire was to serve him. But I also saw that this deference was extremely irritating to him—he would frown and be curt with her and send her briskly about her business (which of course was his, she had no other thought or occupation). Then she would come out of his room with tears in her eyes, and complain to me afterwards about how difficult it was to serve a saint. However, whenever he had been impatient with her, he made up for it later by singling her out for praise before everyone for her selfless work, so that she glowed with pride and was able to preen herself a little.

Priya conceived the idea that C. too had to be set up, like Shivaji, as a leader with a following of his own. He could not be wasted just on me and on herself in a broken-down bazaar hotel. She wanted to take him away—not just out of the hotel or the city of Delhi but right out into a bigger world. Shivaji already had a following in Europe, but for C. Priya wanted a new world, *the* New World, America itself. The first step was to get him there: to make his travel arrangements and set him up on a suitable scale. Of course everything had to be first-class, as it was with Shivaji. Money had never presented a problem for Priya, any more than it had for C.: in his case, because he had never had any, in hers because she had always had enough. But now her father said he couldn't support two world movements, his daughter's and his wife's. He was perfectly willing to part with a certain fixed sum, the way another husband and father might have allotted pin money; and if Priya's scheme was to be financed, then she and her mother would have to share the available amount between them. Busy with his own affairs, he left them to fight the matter out between themselves.

Renuka became very worried about not having enough money for Shivaji. It was the one thing she had to offer him, and without it she felt unworthy. There was a humility in her of which Priya had no trace. Priya felt that her contribution to C. was not money but understanding, intelligence, strength of mind, resolution, ability. She was no one's handmaiden but a muse, a partner, a spouse. That was why it was so easy for her, I think, to disregard and displace me: because she knew I couldn't be any of those things to him. I didn't even have money to sponsor him. She quite liked me—indeed, I became her principal confidante: she told me how they were going to go to America and set up there and start their work. There may even have been some suggestion that I might go with them, she didn't say in what capacity, nor did she promise anything.

It was her mother who questioned me as to what I saw as my role in their future plans. What could I tell her, since I knew nothing myself? All I had ever wanted was to be with him, but I had realized from the beginning—when my mother Edith too had questioned me about what I saw as my future with C.—that he could not be confined to only one person. He belonged to the world in all its manifestations, including all its physical pleasures that he relished so much—eating, and having sex with women he liked. It may sound strange that he enjoyed it equally with Priya and myself, and even more strange that this was acceptable to both of us. For her, it was anyway secondary and, I believe, always remained so. She stayed with him for many years in America and was largely responsible for building up the practical side of his movement. There were always many women around him, and I have heard that Priya encouraged their physical involvement with him as part of their treatment.

As for me in those early years, I began to learn to do without him. It was not that I felt differently about him—not at all, any more than he did about me. It didn't seem to make that much difference to either of us that he now spent

more time with Priya than with me. We both recognized that
a new phase had started for him, one from which he could
no more draw back than I could or would hold him back.
What belonged to us was that earlier time in London, our
times under the tree. That was sealed, sealed off in all its
sweetness, for the rest of *my* life anyway. Later I heard and
read about him in newspapers and magazines, and saw photographs of him. He grew immensely fat, mountainous. I studied
the pictures closely, trying to make out the features that I had
known so well. Probably it was my imagination but I liked
to think that I could find the original C. in that mass of flesh
and fame: that what he had given me—all that youth and
love—was still there within him and that the memory of our
tree remained inviolate in him, as it did in me.

But now came the years of change, or change-over; for the
more time Priya spent with him, the more time I spent in the
house with her mother. Renuka wanted me there, since I was
the only person she could talk to, and question about C., and
about Priya, and their project together. Driven by Priya's
energy and her organizing ability, both stupendous, this was
now really taking shape. Whenever she showed up at the
house, she was like a whirlwind, making her arrangements
over the long-distance telephone and assigning tasks and
commissions to her mother's staff. She was impatient and
high-handed—doubtless like Renuka when she had first begun
to organize Shivaji's movement. But now Renuka had to stand
by and watch her daughter setting up her rival organization.
She also had to watch her bank account being drained of its
usual allowance, for Priya had instructed her father's
employees to divert these sums to the account she had set up
for her and C.'s needs. When Renuka tried to dispute or even

discuss this new arrangement, Priya would brush past her without a word, her arms full of important files.

Renuka was desperate. She needed money for the house she had bought for Shivaji and its large staff, for entertaining the crowds of visitors who came to see him; at the same time there were halls to be hired for his public appearances, and the brochures and pamphlets to be printed. All this she confided to me—whom else could she talk to? Priya wouldn't listen, and as for Shivaji himself, she would not have dared to bring these matters to his attention. Not that he wouldn't have listened, and probably very carefully, but this was her domain, the work he had assigned to her. There was nothing else he would accept from her. And here she extended her confidence to me and spoke of that other matter she could tell no one else: her relation to Shivaji, her need for him, his coldness to her that prevented her ever showing her feelings for him, not even her reverence, for when she tried to touch his feet, the way a disciple does to a master, he drew them back and clicked his tongue in annoyance.

She chose me for her confidante, I think, because of the way I tried to listen to her: with all my attention, all my understanding. These were qualities I had not shown my mother when she needed them. At that time I was too immersed in my own happiness to pay any attention to her. And if I had listened, all I would have heard were complaints—mostly about me, how I was too young, and about C., and how no one knew where he came from. Even when she spoke more generally, as she liked to do, about the experience of love and loving, I wasn't prepared to listen because I was in the middle of living that very experience and had no need of her theories about it.

As for C., he was himself young in those London years and concerned more with formulating his ideas than with their practical application. Later I believe he did help people in trouble with their psychological problems, although even then, in America, he got into difficulties when some of his patients did not react well to his methods. Or to him—for those who came to him for guidance (or whatever) had first to deal with him, with that personality of his which played such an enormous part in his work. For some, he must have been too strong, but he was probably unaware of that, the way the waves of the ocean are not conscious of sweeping you away.

The night that Edith killed herself she had come bursting into the attic where I was sleeping with C. Perhaps she just couldn't stand it any more, creeping around on the stairs and maybe listening at the door. This time she pounded on it and then pushed it open. And she saw us in the light of a streetlamp outside—both of us naked and asleep in one another's arms. It was only when she began to tug at me that we started up out of our deep sleep. "Give me back my daughter!" she shouted. C. leaped out of bed, and as he stood stark naked before her, she began to drum her fists on his chest as she had done on the door. But he was more solid than any door, and besides he had this blond fur of hair softening her blows. "Who is he anyway?" she was shouting at me. "Where does he come from? What's he doing in our house?" C. laughed in that easy hearty way he always had, and said, "But I'm your lodger." She began to plead with me: "Let him go, darling, everything will be as it was when he's gone. He's just a coarse, common person!" That made him laugh again, so that she tried to hit him again. This time he stepped aside—more to save her than himself, I think— and she caught hold of me. She held me so tightly that, when I remember that night, I can still feel myself pressed against her heart and hear its beat. But then I was concerned only with getting free, shaking her off, and when I couldn't, I cried out against her, "Leave me alone!" Instead she held me closer, and I cried, "Go away and leave us alone! Go," I cried, "go!" and with each word I struggled more fiercely to release her arms from my neck. And when I succeeded, it was I—I, not C.—who pushed her out of the door and shut that door behind her, so that I could lie down and go to sleep again with C.

Books have been written about the number of suicides that have occurred from around the beginning of the twentieth century among middle-class Jewish women. One theory has it that the cause may have been a sense—a fore-sense—of the fate in store for them in the following years. But another reason may also have been their own psyche and the tremendous importance they had learned to attach to it. The constant analysis of their own feelings and their attempt, on the one hand, to control themselves and, on the other, not to suppress but fully to release their impulses—all this involved them in a maze of conflict from which they couldn't find an exit. And when something bad happened to them, such as a failed exam or an unhappy love affair, then the only exit was suicide and that was the route often taken. Some of them even kept the means for it close by—Edith, ever since she was a young woman in Vienna in the 1920s, had carried a phial of cyanide in her handbag.

So now it was Priya's mother I listened to with the attention I had not shown my own mother. Priya only came to the house to quarrel with her mother. Besides money, she now also demanded her share of the family jewelry. This was to have come to her only on her wedding day, but she wanted it at once to take with her to America. Renuka tried to resist, but each time she was left wounded and panting with all her pulses beating (I believe she was at that time in her menopause years) and in a despair that frightened me, remembering as I did my mother's own state and the way she had ended it.

C. no longer came to the house. Perhaps it was a sort of tact that kept him away, not wanting to interfere in a quarrel of which he was the cause. Shivaji also held aloof from it— perhaps this is how men of destiny reach their goal, by letting others manage matters for them. C. now spent his time in the hotel room, reading and writing. His Afghan friends had departed—some back to Afghanistan, others to buy arms in other countries, while some were in jail for pimping or drug-dealing. C. too seemed ready to move on, and I heard him ask Priya several times how much longer she was taking with her preparations. There was a hint of impatience in his tone, though normally he was so goodnatured and relaxed. Even now, he wasn't exactly tense but more like an athlete straining toward the next race.

Then one day Priya said, "I'll settle it right now, once and for all." Looking grim, she left us to fight it out with her mother. The moment she had gone, we sank almost in relief on to the bed together. We kissed the way we used to under our tree. He was as he had always been with me, and that is the way I shall always remember him, though the later image I have of him is of a very different person. It was said that, in the process of establishing his work, he became dictatorial, even cruel toward opponents, especially toward former followers who dared to leave him. Many lawsuits were filed against him—by the relatives of young people he was said to have seduced away, or of those who had made over their properties and monies to him. He also had to fight an extradition order from Holland, where he was accused of forging a will in his own favor. But all this was in a future that I did not share with him.

Priya returned in triumph, bringing a casket that held not

only her own wedding jewelry but some of her mother's too. She spilled it on to our crumpled, sagging bed—a shimmering cornucopia of gold and precious stones that made me hold my breath at so much beauty. But for Priya there was only the satisfaction of her victory, while C.'s appreciation was almost ironic—such private wealth did not impress but amuse him, and he had no interest in its value except as a contribution to his work. That very afternoon Priya bought three tickets to New York; one-way, since there was no thought of return. For the two of them their future lay elsewhere. It was only I who felt regret: as if, unlike them, I had not yet quite finished here.

When I went to say goodbye in the other house, I found a terrible commotion. Servants and visitors ran around, some sobbing, some silent in disbelief. All the doors were wide open, right into Shivaji's sanctuary. It was empty—and for a moment this was what astonished me most, his absence, and the way it reduced the room to a dark shaft, a vacuum at the heart of the house. I was told that Shivaji was with Renuka in the hospital. She was in intensive care, having suffered a stroke after her last fight with Priya. When I arrived at the hospital, I found her with tubes and other machinery attached to her in an attempt to pump her back to life. She was unrecognizable; there was no Renuka at all, just this immobile mound. Probably that was what made Priya, after her visit, decide there was nothing she could do, so she and C. might as well depart, as planned. Since I decided to stay, she sold my ticket at the airport to a stand-by passenger.

After several weeks, Renuka recovered, at least partially, and it was a pleasure to help her slowly regain some of her faculties. She learned to move and talk again—never perfectly, her walk remained halting, her speech slurred. It was hard work but we persevered and made progress. This took all our effort so that neither of us had any thought to spare for what might be happening outside the hospital and its therapy center.

But there was no need of us—from the moment of Renuka's stroke, Shivaji had taken complete charge. He dealt with everything himself: the bank, the accountants, with the staff, most of whom had to be let go. At least once a day he came bustling into the hospital, full of good cheer and with the air of an easy-mannered, smiling, forceful little businessman. He wore rimless spectacles and a linen suit—one of those made for him abroad that, with his handmade shoes, had so upset Priya. In this outfit he was rattled from side to side in the motorcycle rickshaw he hired, having had to sell all the cars; it didn't seem to make any difference to him, he sat there with unruffled dignity. When Renuka regained the use of one hand, he made her sign a power of attorney to him; and with this he managed her affairs, so that by the time she emerged from therapy, he had settled everything. We never even had to go back to the house, which he had meanwhile sold with all its furniture and fittings. He used the proceeds to buy land and a house in the foothills of the Himalayas, and he brought us straight there from the hospital on an overnight train.

There is something wholesome about the climate in these foothills—the sharp mountain breezes with their hint of snow, the deodar trees rising so tall into the sparkling sky that they seem to be drawing a constant supply of fresh sap from it. Shivaji put us on a diet of vegetables grown on our land and cooked in a simple and delicious way he devised himself. A small colony of houses grew up around us, built by the people who had followed Shivaji to be close to him. He established a crafts center as part of our community and persuaded the lepers who used to beg on the bridge to learn to spin and weave the rugs that were then sold for good prices. It became a thriving business and Shivaji retained something of the brisk commercial air I have mentioned. Studying accounts through his rimless spectacles, he was quick and shrewd, and when buyers came from abroad, he would make us take out and press one of his linen suits. But mostly he remained the Shivaji I first knew, shimmering in white muslin as though filled with light from within. While the colony proliferated with more and more houses, he remained the center around which everything revolved. Just as we had done in Delhi, in the evenings we gathered in the central room of his house while he talked to us and sang, encouraging us to join in. The lepers from the workshop were also part of our community, and although during the day there were a lot of disputes among them, in Shivaji's room these were mostly forgotten. This hour we spent with him had the same effect on us as did their ritual bath for the pilgrims washing away their impurities in the holy river below.

Unlike C. and Priya and their movement, we never became very famous. Even so, some magazine articles were written about our work and a documentary film was made for German TV, and these brought inquiries from people wanting to help. Shivaji dictated answers to all these letters, and he was very specific about what was required: some were asked to send money, others to come to the crafts center and help with the work there. The TV crew had given him a VCR, and he often asked for tapes to be sent to him. He was particularly fond of American films—especially Westerns, and comedies of the 1930s and '40s which always made him laugh. He had me wheel in Renuka to watch these films with him, and she also laughed when he did. Although no longer walking or talking, she seemed calm and happy. We lived there for many, many years, and she must have reached the age of ninety or more. The climate had a preserving quality, assisted in her case no doubt by the constant presence of Shivaji from whom she appeared to draw light and air, like the tall trees from the sky.

One year Priya came to visit us. She had read some article about us and was curious to see what we were up to. Renuka did not recognize her; for the last many years she had assumed that I was her daughter, and she knew that she had never had more than one. Priya had retained some features of the young Priya we had known: her elegance—she was still in the finest silk saris—her intelligence, her educated accent; she was skinny now rather than slender, and wore large black-framed spectacles that took up most of her face. She summed up our activities with one glance and made her opinion of them clear. And she was right; in comparison with her world-wide operation, we were negligible. Priya had always emanated a sort of contemptuous pride—as was perhaps her right, since she was so much more clever and efficient than most other people. But now, mixed with that, there was some other expression. It was almost as if her pride and contempt had turned inward, as if she herself, her own life hadn't come up to her expectations. And this was strange, since she had been so spectacularly successful in what she had undertaken.

She had not revised her opinion of Shivaji. She was still certain that she could see through him, though I'm not sure what it was that she saw: she could hardly accuse him now of misappropriating her mother's wealth when she herself had stripped her of it. Once she said, "What's worse than being a fraud?" and laughed, with a hard bitter sound that she had when she laughed at all, which wasn't often. "To be an unsuccessful fraud," she answered herself, and then went on, "At least that one's successful . . ." She meant C., and it was the first time she had mentioned him. Now that she had started, she couldn't stop and it came out in a rush, all the bitterness I had felt in her, not only against herself but against C. too and what he had become, and what she had helped him to become.

"You wouldn't even recognize him if you saw him," she told me. This was one night when she and I were alone outside one of the houses perched on the slope of the mountain. Shivaji and Renuka were inside the main house, watching an American Western—the sound of it came drifting out, a strange contrast to the silver silence of the stars overhead and of the river below. But Priya's thoughts were as violent as the galloping horses and the double-barreled guns of the Western. They were all about C.—how his voracious bulk had to be continually stoked with food and vulgar luxuries, and how an endless supply of money was needed to satisfy his coarse cravings. He had a fleet of twenty-seven Rolls-Royces, though he was too fat to move, so that everything had to be brought to him: including of course an endless supply of women, who became younger and younger, more and more stupid—as stupid as animals, Priya said, to please his animal appetites.

After that, what we heard later came as no surprise. Priya broke away from the movement—broke it from within by joining his enemies and providing them with crucial evidence for the many cases brought against him. At first it seemed that he was to be extradited to Holland, but in the meantime a court in Texas built up a sufficient case (something to do with a fraudulent conversion of title deeds) to bring him to trial there. He was convicted and sentenced to fifteen years' imprisonment. So it was in Texas I imagined him—a place I only knew from Shivaji's VCR tapes. How to fit C. into that landscape, among those big men in big hats? Of course he himself had always been big; but his bulk was charged with brain, alive with thought that had soared right up to the dome of the British Museum Reading Room. How could so much thinking, such high ideas become gross the way Priya had described? It was impossible—just as it was impossible to think of this large and happy person as a convict in a cell.

I became restless. My thoughts took me far from this peaceful place sealed off in its capsule of pure air. Too disturbed now to join the evening sessions of song and prayer, I remained outside under the tent of mountain stars without looking up at them, waiting for the joyful sounds to finish. It was only when Shivaji put on one of his Westerns that I joined him and Renuka inside. I wanted to see all I could of that far-off place, which I assumed to be Texas. Apart from taking in the scenery, I paid no attention to what was happening on the screen; and it was only when loud gun shots woke up Renuka and made her cry out in shock that I noticed all the fighting and screaming going on. None of it disturbed me—until the day that I saw the hero taken off to jail by an evil sheriff. I sat up and watched this same hero as part of a chain gang breaking rocks under the eyes of a foul-mouthed guard armed with guns and a whip. Then I cried out louder than Renuka had done.

Shivaji turned off the tape in surprise. He asked me to wheel out Renuka and put her to bed. As she did every night, she embraced me like a child, with her arms around my neck. I waited for her to fall asleep, and then I returned to Shivaji. I asked him to give me the plane fare to America; he said he would think about it. By next day he had made his calculations: he said he could afford a ticket to New York and from New York to Texas. He had also worked out what I would need to reach my destination and to keep me there for a month. After that, he said regretfully, I would be on my own; but that if I wanted to return, he would somehow manage to send me the fare. I agreed and thanked him. Neither of us mentioned my imminent departure to Renuka—anyway, she might not have understood. I could hardly wait to leave, and on my last night when I put her to bed, I was so impatient that I didn't wait for her to fall asleep but loosened her arms from my neck, the way I had released myself from my mother on her last night.

After some misadventures—I was no longer used to traveling, and America was a new continent to me—I reached the prison in Texas. It was like entering a fortress; it *was* a fortress with armed guards at each corner watching from high towers. A succession of metal gates slid mechanically behind me, and at each gate there were more guards telephoning up to the towers before I was allowed to pass on to the next one. The passages were lit by a light so blinding and unnatural that it was a kind of darkness. But I thought only of the person I was walking toward and went cheerfully through steel and stone.

At last I was face to face with him. True, it was through a glass partition, he on one side of it and I on the other, communicating with each other by telephone; but I could see at once that he had not changed. He wore a kind of overall in a bright orange color that suited him. There was nothing at all of the person Priya had described, the mass of flesh insatiable for luxuries and young women. He was muscular and fit, like someone who spent a lot of time outdoors. I asked him about the chain gangs—it was almost my first question, and my voice must have trembled over the telephone so that he quickly assured me that these had been discontinued. Having been sentenced to hard labor, he did do a lot of road work, breaking rocks and so on, which he said gave him a healthy appetite. His cheeks were pink; for many years, he said, he had had a beard, and when this was shaved off by the prison barber, the skin underneath turned out to be soft and smooth. His hair too had been cut, but the stubble left was a grey as light as the original blond flame I remembered. Yes, many years, a lifetime, had passed, but really he was the same. His voice too was the same, and the fact that it came transmitted through a receiver made it seem as if he were whispering right into my ear, the way he used to. And he was smiling at me through the glass while the voice in my ear told me that I too had not changed. I smiled back at him, aware as I did so that I was showing the gaps left by my missing teeth; but that didn't matter to either of us, any more than that the person he was seeing through the glass had become a scrawny old woman.

However, it did matter when I tried to get a job. I had been used to doing domestic work in Shivaji's commune, serving visitors and looking after Renuka, so I thought it would be easy to find work. Wherever I saw a notice for waitresses wanted, I went in to apply but everyone laughed at me. I realized that the waitresses there were all young and pert and wore pink skirts that reached only to the tops of their thighs. But I needed to earn money very badly, having come to the end of the month Shivaji had provided for. C. was allowed visitors every fortnight, so it was necessary for me to stay in the neighborhood. I had come to an arrangement with another woman visiting her husband in prison; he was serving a life sentence, so she let me sleep in his half of their king-size bed in return for babysitting her children while she was at work. But this did not cover the rest of my expenses, and I persevered in my search for a job until at last a short-order cook hired me to clean up after him, sweeping the peelings and scrubbing the pots, that sort of work, all very easy.

With my first earnings, I bought a new frock in which to

visit C. It was quite ordinary—it had been hanging on a rack with dozens exactly like it, all marked down—but he complimented me on it, not only once but each time I went to visit him. Although we were never alone, since on his side of the glass partition was a row of prisoners communicating with visitors on my side, we felt perfectly private, our voices trickling intimately into each other's ears. He told me about his busy schedule: this included, besides his outdoor work, teaching other prisoners chess and holding seminars for them on different subjects. I would be surprised at their wide range of interests, he said. He had also learned to play basketball, and in spite of his age, was good at it, probably because of his height. So his days were full and so were mine, with my long hours of kitchen work and looking forward all day and night to these visits. But we often spoke of an even happier future and what we would do, where we would go, when his time was up. The whole world was open to us, and we considered every possibility. At the end of his sentence, even with time off for good behavior, he would be in his eighties and I in my seventies; but neither of us ever felt that our future had shrunk from the time when we had made love under our tree, or in my mother's attic room for which he was always behind with the rent.